'Damn him...! Damn him...! Damn him!'

It was several moments before Abbie could drag her gaze away from the source of her fury, and several more before she dared trust herself to ask the burning question at the forefront of her mind.

'Are you by any chance acquainted with the gentleman who is presently holding our hostess in conversation, ma'am?'

It was sufficient for her godmother to cast a second brief glance in the direction of the door. 'No. Why do you ask? Do you know him?'

'Yes, ma'am, I know him. That is none other than my grandfather's godson, the man he is determined I should marry.'

Her godmother regarded the gentleman with far more interest this time, noting the easy grace of the long-striding gait, the superb breadth of shoulder, and that tell-tale aristocratic line of his profile. 'And you, my dear? Is that your wish also?' she asked gently, and was surprised to witness an expression of hard determination take possession of delicate features.

'Believe me when I tell you that the sun would rise in the west before I'd ever agree to wed Bartholomew Cavanagh.'

Anne Ashley was born and educated in Leicester. She lived for a time in Scotland, but now makes her home in the West Country, with two cats, her two sons, and a husband who has a wonderful and very necessary sense of humour. When not pounding away at the keys of her word processor, she likes to relax in her garden, which she has opened to the public on more than one occasion in aid of the village church funds.

Recent titles by the same author:

A NOBLE MAN*
LORD EXMOUTH'S INTENTIONS*
THE RELUCTANT MARCHIONESS
TAVERN WENCH
BELOVED VIRAGO
LORD HAWKRIDGE'S SECRET

*part of the Regency mini-series
The Steepwood Scandal

BETRAYED AND BETROTHED

Anne Ashley

MILLS & BOON®

First published in Great Britain 2005
Large Print edition 2006
Harlequin Mills & Boon Limited,
Eton House, 18-24 Paradise Road, Richmond, Surrey TW9 1SR

© Anne Ashley 2005

ISBN 0 263 18899 X

Set in Times Roman 15 on 16½ pt.
42-0106-78264

Printed and bound in Great Britain
by Antony Rowe Ltd, Chippenham, Wiltshire

BETRAYED AND BETROTHED

Prologue

1812

Although engaged in securing the pack to his saddle, Major Bartholomew Cavanagh's attention was fixed on the column of soldiers leaving the camp. His expression was sombre, but as he wasn't a gentleman given to smiling much it was sometimes difficult to assess his mood. All the same, his friend, approaching unobserved, was somewhat surprised not to detect at least a flicker of animation in the ruggedly masculine face.

'Good gad, Bart!' Captain Fergusson exclaimed. 'Anyone might suppose you were about to set off on a skirmish, instead of returning to England on a spot of long-overdue leave.'

This succeeded in igniting a flicker of amusement in Bart's dark eyes, as he turned them briefly in the direction of the young officer whose cavalry uniform made him look rather conspicuous in this section of the camp. 'You want to be careful, Giles,' he warned. 'You know your lot don't appreciate one of their own fraternising with lowly infantrymen.'

Although both had earned the reputation of being level-headed, conscientious officers, whenever together the camaraderie they had enjoyed since boyhood was never far from the surface.

'Got little choice but to mix with the scaff and raff if I want to see you,' Giles returned, having taken his friend's banter in good part as always. 'Though why the deuce a horseman of your excellence chose to become a foot-soldier defeats me.'

As this singularly failed to elicit a response, Captain Fergusson knew better than to attempt to probe further. 'Received any more news about your father?' he asked, with an abrupt change of subject.

Bart shook his head. 'As you know, I've never rated my stepmother's intelligence above average. One thing I will say for Eugenie, though—she isn't prone to exaggeration. If she says my father's health is causing concern, you may be sure he isn't well. But even if this were not the case, I should still have spent this leave at home. It's high time I made my peace with my family.'

Raising his eyes, Bart once again focused his attention on the line of soldiers marching towards the range of hills in the distance. 'These past years out here in the Peninsula have certainly changed my outlook on life. Things that once were vastly important no longer seem so.' He shrugged, straining the cloth of his rifleman-green jacket. 'Experience of war affects most of us in one way or another, I suppose. Brings out the best in some; the worst in others.'

Nodding in agreement, Giles followed the direction of his friend's gaze. 'Wellesley evidently means business. I see he's sent the Provost out with the column.'

'After the casualties suffered in recent months, he cannot stand by and do nothing when men are deserting in such numbers,' Bart commented. 'There's rumoured to be around a hundred hiding out in those hills. If they can find enough to eat, they'll possibly do well enough for now. When winter sets in it'll be a different matter.'

'I hear Wellesley's prepared to be lenient, and offer free pardons to those willing to give themselves up. But he won't hesitate to hang those who don't.'

His eyes hardening, Bart's gaze slid once again to the distant hills. 'I must confess there's one out there I'd give much to see dangling from the end of a rope. Wellesley calls the common soldier the scum of the earth. And in Septimus Searle's case he couldn't be more right. A more black-hearted devil you'd be hard pressed to find. And I was unfortunate enough to have him in my company. It's a pity I shan't be here to witness him receiving his just deserts, because I'm certain he'll never give himself up voluntarily.

He wouldn't choose to be under my command again. He knows I'd make his life hell.'

Captain Fergusson betrayed surprise, for his friend had the reputation of being considerate and fair, and was well respected by the men in the ranks. 'It isn't like you to be so vindictive.'

Totally unrepentant, Bart mounted his horse. 'Searle's committed most crimes from rape to murder. My sympathies lie with his victims. But for the next few weeks I intend to put my experiences of the Peninsula, both good and bad, behind me, and enjoy more pleasurable activities, while I become reconciled with my family.'

Chapter One

1816

Only the steady ticking of the mantel-clock disturbed the silence now pervading the parlour at Foxhunter Grange. Miss Abigail Graham, resolutely staring through the window, her eyes carefully avoiding that area of garden beyond the shrubbery where she no longer ventured, was finally coming to terms with the fact that she simply could not, would not, continue with her present lifestyle.

'Well, child? Have you nothing to say?' the master of what was generally held to be a very fine country residence at last demanded, his voice noticeably harsher than it had been a short time before, when he had calmly revealed the arrangements made for her immediate future. 'Can you not find it within yourself to offer a mere word of thanks for the trouble I've taken to ensure you will be suitably entertained during my absence? Am I not to receive the smallest token of gratitude?'

'Gratitude?' Abbie echoed, finally abandoning her silent contemplation of the late spring blooms in the largest of the flower-beds, and turning to look at him.

No one could have failed to perceive the strong resemblance between them. Although thankfully having been spared the strong, hawklike nose that characterised most male and several unfortunate female members of the family down the generations, Abbie had inherited the striking Graham colouring of violet-blue eyes and silky black hair. At a glance no one could fail to appreciate too that Mother Nature had seen fit to bless her still further with an elegant carriage, and a slim, shapely figure that even the plainness of her grey gown, more suitable for a governess, could not disguise. Nor could her hair, swept severely back and arranged in a simple chignon, detract from the loveliness and perfect symmetry of features set in a flawless complexion.

'If I thought for a moment the arrangements you have undertaken to ensure that I do not remain here at the Grange during your absence stemmed from a wish to offer me the opportunity to enjoy the company of the godmother I haven't seen for almost sixteen years, I would be exceedingly grateful.' Only the pulsating vein at her temple, clearly visible beneath the fairness of her skin, betrayed the fact that Abbie was perilously close to losing her admirable self-control for the very first time, and giving way to years of pent-up frustrations in an explosion of wrath. 'But I know you too well. The only reason you desire to see me safely packed off to Bath is merely an attempt on your part to prevent a closer friendship developing between me and our new practitioner.'

Only briefly did Colonel Augustus Graham betray a flicker of unease, as he studied the surprisingly hard set to his granddaughter's features.

'You are talking nonsense, child!' he announced, as he reached for the glass of fine brandy at his elbow with a hand that for once was not perfectly steady. 'You are clearly ailing for something. Perhaps it would be wise to delay your departure for a few days, until you are more yourself.'

'Oh, no, Grandfather,' she countered. 'Ailing or no, I shall leave early tomorrow, as arranged. If the female my godmother is kindly sending to bear me company does indeed arrive as planned later today, she should feel sufficiently restored to commence the return journey first thing in the morning.'

The note of determination clearly came as a further surprise to the gentleman whose granddaughter had always been wont to show him the utmost respect. He rose at once to his feet to rest an arm along the mantel-shelf, before once again regarding her from beneath bushy, grey brows. 'Evidently you are piqued because I chose not to disclose until today the arrangements I had made with Lady Penrose for your sojourn in Bath.'

'I should like to have been consulted, certainly,' Abbie admitted, still somehow managing to maintain her admirable self-control. 'And although I'm positive it wasn't your intention, in point of fact you've served me a good turn, sir. Living with my god-mother during the next few weeks will grant me ample opportunity to take stock and decide where and, more importantly, by what means I shall support myself until I attain the age of five and twenty, and inherit the money left to me by my mother.'

'What on earth are you talking about, child?' the Colonel demanded, making no attempt whatsoever to conceal his increasing displeasure. 'Quite naturally, you will return here. The inheritance your mother left you is a mere pittance when compared to what you'll receive from me. You'll be a wealthy woman once I'm gone, with money enough to live comfortably throughout your life…providing, of course, you give me no reason to alter my will.'

It needed only that totally unnecessary and unsubtle threat to sever the rein she had maintained on her temper. 'Change it and be damned to you, sir!'

Abbie was well aware that few men, let alone a woman, would dare to speak to her grandfather in such a fashion, but she was beyond caring now. The fact that his own eyes were glinting ominously and his mouth was set in a grim straight line, evidence of his own ill humour, could not deter her from at last revealing her strong sense of ill usage, and the unhappiness she had suffered at being treated with cool indifference by the gentleman who, throughout her childhood, couldn't have been more loving or considerate towards her.

'You are not the same man who brought me here fifteen years ago, Grandfather. You couldn't have been kinder to me then, more gentle or understanding.' She thought she detected a muscle contracting along the line of his jaw before he turned briefly to glance at the portrait of his late wife, taking pride of place above the grate. 'But all that changed, did it not, the moment I dared to go against your wishes by refusing to marry that precious godson of yours?'

'The manner of your refusal was inexcusable,' he reminded her, his voice harsh, unbending.

'It was ill done of me, yes,' innate honesty obliged her to concede. 'I should have been more gracious in my refusal. But I had only just turned seventeen. And you offered me no opportunity to discuss the matter with you in private first.'

There was no response forthcoming, and Abbie, easily discerning the taut, uncompromising set of his features, realised he was in no mood to unbend towards her even now, and faced the fact there and then that, in all probability, he never would.

'I cannot alter what has happened in the past, Grandfather. And, given the opportunity, I tell you plainly, I wouldn't attempt to try. I could never bring myself to marry a man I did not both love and respect.'

This claimed his full attention, and once again Abbie found herself on the receiving end of that hard, uncompromising gaze to which she had grown all too accustomed in recent years. 'How can you say so? You were fond enough of Bart when you were a child,' he reminded her.

'Yes, perhaps I was, a little,' she acknowledged, after giving the matter a moment's thought. 'But children grow up, Grandfather. We simply wouldn't have suited.'

He dismissed this with an impatient wave of his hand. 'And how you can say you do not respect a gentleman who has served his country so courageously during the recent conflict with France, earning a commendation from the Regent himself no less, is beyond my understanding.'

'His bravery on or off the field of battle is not the issue here,' she pointed out. 'His principles, however, are a different matter entirely.'

'Principles!' he barked. 'Let me tell you, my girl, his principles are above reproach. If it hadn't been for Bart's intervention, I would have gone after you that day and administered the thrashing you so richly deserved!'

If he had expected this admission to endear her to the godson he had always so admired, Abbie wasn't slow to disabuse him. 'Then he served me an ill turn by interfering, for I would far rather have suffered a beating than the cool indifference I've been forced to endure since that day. And if you imagine for a moment,' she went on, not granting him the opportunity to respond, 'that, after attaining my majority, the reason I continued to tolerate being treated little better than a servant was because I feared finding some means by which I might support myself, you couldn't be more wrong. I did so because I hoped that one day you'd find it within you to forgive me, and we might enjoy the wonderful companionship we once shared. But I refuse to delude myself any longer.'

Abbie could see by the contemptuous curl on his thin lips that he considered her resolve no longer to be dependent upon him an empty threat, a mere passing whim, even before he snapped, 'Don't be ridiculous, child! How on earth do you suppose you could support yourself?'

Steadfastly refusing to be disheartened by the belittling tone, Abbie returned his openly scathing look with one of her own. 'At the very least I could attain a post as a housekeeper. After all, I've been running this establishment for nigh on six years. A governess is not out of the question, either. I've been given ample time to improve my mind during those numerous occasions when you've done your utmost to ignore my very existence, and have left me to my own devices, while you've been out and about enjoying the company of your friends.'

Abbie attained a modicum of satisfaction in seeing the curl fade from his lips, and a flicker of uncertainty appear in his eyes, before she transferred her gaze to the portrait above the grate. 'And there is always the possibility that I might be able to make good use of the gift I seem to have inherited from Grandmama, a gift which only you have failed to acknowledge I possess. Then, of course, I don't rule out marriage entirely. But if and when I am ever tempted to take the matrimonial plunge, it will not be to our local practitioner, even though I value his friendship highly. And it will most certainly never be to that precious godson of yours, whom I hold in utter contempt.'

The fist he brought down hard on the mantel-shelf came perilously close to sending several ornaments toppling to the floor. 'Damn it, child, why? What did Bart ever do to give you such a disgust of him?'

The disdainful curl on her lips was a masterly reproduction of the one he had perfected only a short time before. 'It is a little late to ask that of me now, Grandfather. Besides which, I am no talebearer. If you're so keen to discover just what turned me against Bartholomew Cavanagh, then ask the man himself what took place in the summerhouse six years ago on the very day he proposed marriage to me.'

Not prepared to discuss further an incident she

would far rather forget, Abbie went across to the door. 'I shall not be joining you for dinner this evening,' she announced, 'I have my packing to organise. So I shall take my leave of you now, and wish you a pleasant sojourn with your friend in Scotland.'

Abbie did not look back before she left the room, and so omitted to see the thoughtful expression coming into her grandfather's eyes a moment before he went over to take up her former stance before the window. Raising his head, he stared across the vast south lawn at the corner of the garden, where that ornamental wooden structure stood, hardly visible now behind shrubs and trees. The summerhouse, he well remembered, had once been a favourite haunt of his granddaughter's, just as it had been a favoured retreat with both his wife and his son. It was true that for some considerable time Abbie had never ventured into that area of the garden. Why had he never appreciated that fact before?

Then he shook his head, dismissing it from his mind.

The hired post-chaise, conveying Abbie and her godmother's personal maid, reached the outskirts of Bath just after noon, three days later. They had made the journey in easy stages, and in weather that had been kind to them by remaining clement; but even if this had not been the case, Abbie would still have enjoyed the experience.

It had been many years since she had travelled any great distance from her grandfather's home, set in the heart of Leicestershire's famed hunting country, and she had discovered much on the journey to capture her interest. Most of all, it had been the companionship of her godmother's personal maid that had made the journey so vastly enjoyable.

Miss Evelina Felcham was unlike any other maid Abbie had known before. All the servants at Foxhunter Grange, wary of the Colonel's uncertain temper, were wont to treat their master with the utmost respect at all times. It had quickly become clear that Felcham wasn't in the least in awe of her mistress; nor was she reticent to voice her opinions, whether or not she had been called upon to do so.

'I do hope Godmama isn't worried because we didn't arrive earlier in the day. But I do not get to travel about the country, and I didn't wish to hurry the journey,' Abbie remarked, peering interestedly through the window as the post-chaise progressed along the busy streets in the centre of the city, and, in consequence, didn't notice she was being regarded keenly.

'Lord bless you, miss! Don't you fret none over that,' Felcham advised. 'Lady Hetta don't concern herself nowadays over much at all, leastways, not as you'd notice. Grown dreadfully indolent since the master died, so she has. Might have been otherwise had she been blessed with children of her own. But it wasn't to be. Your visit will do her the world of good, I'm sure.'

Abbie withdrew her attention from the activity in the streets, as a slightly worrying thought occurred to her. 'I hope Godmama isn't offended if I don't recognise her. I doubt I shall, you know. I didn't recognise you.'

'That's not surprising, miss. You were no more than seven or eight when your parents brought you on that visit. But I would have known you anywhere,' Felcham assured her. 'You're blessed with your father's colouring, right enough, but you do bear a strong resemblance to your lovely mama.'

'Do I?' Abbie felt inordinately pleased to hear this. Over the years she had frequently studied the only likeness she possessed of her mother, a watercolour miniature set in a silver frame, and thought she could perceive a resemblance, even though she had frequently been told that she favoured the Grahams.

She sighed. 'I do not remember either of my parents at all well, Felcham,' she admitted. 'It was shortly after we paid that visit to Lord and Lady Penrose's home in Surrey that they went off to Italy.'

'Yes, miss, I well remember,' Felcham responded softly. 'Tragic, it was—both of them succumbing to the typhoid.' She favoured Abbie with yet another of those penetrating stares. 'But you've been happy enough in your grandfather's care, so I was told. The mistress always said as how your letters were always so cheerful.'

'Yes…yes, I have,' Abbie answered, quickly turning her head to stare out of the window once more, but not before she had noticed the contemplative expression take possession of her companion's sharp features this time.

Fortunately she wasn't forced to endure those dark eyes steadfastly turned in her direction for very long. Within a matter of a few minutes only, the post-chaise had pulled up outside a fashionable residence in Upper Camden Place, and she was soon afterwards being shown upstairs by an elderly housekeeper to a charming salon on the first floor.

The room's sole occupant, whose hand hovered over a box of chocolates, conveniently positioned on the table by her elbow, turned a pair of deceptively dreamy blue eyes in the direction of the door. A flicker of recognition swiftly followed, before she rose from the chair and moved with surprising agility for someone of ample proportions to clasp Abbie in a welcoming embrace.

'Here, let me look at you!' Lady Henrietta Penrose held her goddaughter at arm's length, the better to study the delicate features beneath the poke of what was undeniably a plain, unfashionable bonnet. 'Oh, yes! I would have recognised you anywhere, my dear.'

Having been starved of displays of affection for

some considerable time, Abbie felt both moved and faintly embarrassed by the warmth of the welcome she was receiving from a lady who to all intents and purposes was a complete stranger.

'It was so kind of you to have me to stay, ma'am,' she said, after docilely allowing her godmother to draw her over to a chair. 'I'm very much looking forward to exploring the city.'

'And enjoying the entertainments Bath has to offer, too, I hope,' Lady Penrose responded, while she studied the equally unfashionable attire beneath the unprepossessing head wear. 'I wouldn't dream of trying to suggest, my dear, that we can compete with the pleasures to be found in the capital, but I'm sure we'll find plenty to amuse you while you're here.'

Abbie very much suspected that her godmother certainly enjoyed the easy pace of life in this once very fashionable watering place. Already she had detected a definite aura of lazy contentment about Lady Penrose, which gave her every reason to suppose that Felcham had been brutally honest when she had divulged that her mistress had become sublimely indolent in recent years. Yet, at the same time, Abbie felt equally certain that, although her godmother might eschew unnecessary physical exertion, her brain was rarely inactive. Unless she was much mistaken, behind that tranquil façade lurked a keen mind.

'I'm certain I'll have a lovely time, ma'am. But you

mustn't put yourself out on my account. I'm quite accustomed to living a quiet life, you know?'

The feigned look of surprise failed to disguise the
resurgence of that perceptive gleam. 'Has hunting
begun to wane in popularity, then? You do surprise
me! I had foolishly supposed the Shires continued to
attract those sporting-mad young gentlemen in society.'

'They do, ma'am,' Abbie didn't hesitate to assure
her. 'Grandpapa frequently entertains at Foxhunter
Grange. More often than not we have one or two of
his wide circle of friends staying at the house.'

'Indeed? Then you are accustomed to company
and entertaining.' Once again Lady Penrose subjected
her goddaughter to a gaze that was calmly assessing
before her attention turned to the young maidservant
who had entered the room, bearing a tray of refreshments.

After dispensing tea and encouraging her goddaughter to sample the several delicacies provided,
Lady Penrose admitted that, although surprised to receive Colonel Graham's letter proposing the visit, she
had been very much looking forward to having her
goddaughter residing under her roof, and would be
very reluctant to see her leave.

The speculative gleam that instantly sprang into violet eyes immediately following this pronouncement
did not go unobserved. Consequently, the instant the
servant returned to collect the tea tray, Lady Penrose

instructed the maid to show Abbie to her bedchamber and then to inform Felcham that her mistress wished to see her without delay.

The instant her goddaughter had departed, she rose from the chair and went across to the escritoire to take out a certain letter. She had only just reminded herself of its contents when her personal maid entered.

'What's to do, Felchie?' she demanded without preamble.

If the loyal maid was surprised by the blunt enquiry, she certainly betrayed no sign of it as she quietly closed the door and moved further into the room. 'A mystery, my lady, wouldn't you say?'

Lady Penrose shook her head. 'It is quite beyond my understanding how such a lovely young woman, who is both charming and well mannered, should have attained the age of three-and-twenty and remained unmarried.'

'Perhaps she's content living with her grandfather,' Felcham suggested, but the lack of conviction with which she spoke was not lost on her mistress.

'But you didn't gain that impression.'

'No, my lady,' Felcham admitted. 'It's my belief that Miss Graham and her grandfather are not upon the best of terms at the present time. Naturally I didn't attempt to pry. But what I can tell you is that on the morning of our departure Colonel Graham left the house early, and Miss Abbie showed no inclination to await his return so that she might take her leave of him.'

'Could it be, perhaps, that she was reluctant to visit Bath, do you suppose?'

'I wouldn't have thought so, no,' Felcham assured her.

'No,' Lady Penrose agreed, 'and neither would I. She showed a deal of enthusiasm for the entertainments I have planned for her, and yet at the same time...'

She turned her attention once more to the letter. 'The Colonel writes that, if I should feel it necessary, I may undertake to purchase some new gowns for his granddaughter and forward any bills to him.' A pained expression took possession of her plump features. 'Her attire is positively dowdy, more suitable for a servant. Are all her gowns so plain and unfashionable? If so, it will not be a bill for one or two dresses he'll be receiving.'

There was a suspicion of a twitch at one corner of Felcham's mouth. She knew well enough that her mistress, although middle-aged, and sadly growing steadily more portly with every passing year, still had an eye for fashion. 'Apart from one or two evening gowns, m'lady, there wasn't much in her trunk of which you'd approve, although it has to be said that her linen is of the finest.'

'Well, that's something, I suppose,' Lady Penrose was obliged to concede, before she began to brush the Colonel's letter meditatively back and forth across one of her chins. 'All the same, a trip to the fashionable shops in Milsom Street tomorrow morning might prove beneficial.'

Surprisingly enough not only the weather, which overnight heralded the change from over a week of pleasantly dry days to rain, made very much worse by a blustery south-westerly breeze, but also her goddaughter's surprising lack of enthusiasm forced Lady Penrose to postpone her shopping spree at least for the time being. Naturally she was disappointed by Abbie's seeming indifference to the idea of replenishing her wardrobe, and not just mildly troubled too when her goddaughter declared that she had no intention of turning herself into an advertisement for the *Ladies Journal*, and that she had brought sufficient clothing for her stay in Bath.

Yet that evening, when Abbie joined her in the hall, just prior to their leaving for what Lady Penrose was hoping would be the first of many parties they would enjoy together, she could find no fault with her goddaughter's appearance. The dark-blue silk gown, though plain, was clearly the creation of an excellent seamstress. Felcham had been permitted to arrange the dusky locks in a more elaborate style for the occasion, and the string of pearls adorning the slender neck, with matching ear-drops, definitely added to the overall air of refinement that her goddaughter exuded. All in all, Lady Penrose was not displeased with the display of quiet elegance, but wasn't prepared to admit defeat quite yet in her desire to hear her goddaughter proclaimed one of the most fashionable young ladies in Bath.

'Thank heavens the rain has stopped!' she remarked with relief, as they stepped outside to the waiting carriage. 'With luck we shall be able to visit the Pump Room tomorrow. I'm eager to make you known to all my friends, though I expect there will be a good many at Agnes Fergusson's little do tonight.'

Abbie couldn't help smiling to herself. Already she had discovered that her godmother was a sociable animal, enjoying the company of the wide circle of friends she had made during the ten years she had resided in the city. As most residents made visits on foot, and no one had been willing, seemingly, to brave the elements, Lady Penrose had appeared at a loss to know how to pass the time. Abbie, on the other hand, hadn't allowed the lack of company to detract from the enjoyment of her first full day in Bath. She had grown accustomed over the years to filling her days, and had found it no difficult matter to entertain herself.

'Do not concern yourself on my account, ma'am. I do not grow bored with my own company, and am never at a loss to keep myself occupied,' Abbie didn't hesitate to assure her, and once again found herself receiving yet another of those thoughtful glances to which she had been subjected from time to time since her arrival in Bath. She couldn't help wondering what was passing through her god-mother's fertile mind, and was not left pondering for long.

'I gain the distinct impression that you're accus-tomed to being on your own a good deal. Do you not have many friends of your own?'

'I suppose I have suffered in recent years from a lack of female companionship, ma'am,' Abbie admit-ted, seeing no reason to conceal the truth. 'Most all the friends of my own age I made during the years I've lived with Grandpapa are either married now or have moved away from the area. But I'm upon good terms with the wives of Grandpapa's neighbours.'

'All of whom, I suspect, are somewhat older than yourself.'

'Yes, Godmama,' Abbie confirmed. 'But I must con-fess, in general, I prefer the company of older women.'

'Yes, I suppose you must, my dear. But then by your own admission you are accustomed to little else.' Lady Penrose was silent for a moment, before asking, 'And are there no eligible young gentlemen living in Leicestershire these days?'

Having little doubt now in which direction the con-versation was heading, Abbie couldn't forbear a fur-ther smile. Surprisingly, she didn't resent her godmother's questions in the least. In fact, she would have been amazed if the matter of her continued single state hadn't been raised at some point during her stay. She couldn't help feeling, therefore, that making her own views clear on the subject of matrimony at this early stage would avoid misunderstandings in the future.

'We certainly see very many visiting the area, ma'am, and there are one or two eligible young gentlemen living nearby, including the local practitioner, who has become a particular friend of mine. But I have yet to meet a man with whom I could happily spend the rest of my life.'

'But then you've hardly been given the opportunity to do so, have you, my dear?' Lady Penrose wasn't slow to point out, shaking her head and appearing genuinely bewildered. 'I quite fail to understand why your grandfather waited until now before permitting you to stay with me. Since you attained the age of seventeen, I have written on numerous occasions, suggesting that you visit me in Bath.'

'I must confess I didn't know that you had, ma'am,' Abbie disclosed. 'You never mentioned anything in the letters you wrote to me.'

'No, child. I considered it only right and proper to attain your grandfather's consent first before broaching the subject with you. Needless to say, I wasn't successful.'

'No, you wouldn't have been,' Abbie acknowledged, having no difficulty in appreciating the reason why. 'Your revelations come as no real surprise to me, ma'am. Grandpapa would never risk my forming an attachment.'

Lady Penrose's expression changed from puzzlement to annoyance in a matter of seconds. 'You are not suggesting, I trust, that he is selfishly determined to keep you at Foxhunter Grange in order to bear him company in his declining years?'

'Oh, no, ma'am,' Abbie assured her. 'But he remains doggedly determined I shall marry the man he has always intended I should wed. Which, now I come to think about it, makes his acceptance of your kind invitation this time most strange.'

'Oh, no, my dear. It wasn't I who wrote to the Colonel,' Lady Penrose hastily revealed, 'but he who wrote to me, asking if I would kindly have you to stay for a few weeks. His letter came as something of a surprise, I must admit. Although, needless to say,' she added, noticing her goddaughter's frown of consternation, 'I was delighted to comply with his request. He was certain, you see, that you would far rather visit Bath than accompany him to the Scottish Highlands.'

Well, he wasn't wrong there, Abbie mused, before a puzzling thought suddenly occurred to her. Why, though, she wondered, had her grandfather gone to such trouble? If his intention had been merely to try to prevent a deeper friendship developing between her and the young doctor, then why hadn't he simply dragged her off to Scotland with him? No, something else had prompted his actions, she felt sure. But what?

The carriage drawing to a halt outside a fashionable dwelling on the outskirts of the city granted Abbie insufficient time to dwell on the conundrum, and she successfully thrust it to the back of her mind as she accompanied her godmother inside the house. Their hostess, stationed at the entrance to a large, tastefully decorated drawing-room, greeted her with real warmth, putting her instantly at her ease.

'Your friend is a charming woman,' Abbie remarked, as they moved away to allow some new arrivals to greet the hostess. 'She puts me in mind of one of Grandpapa's neighbours.'

'Yes, Agnes Fergusson is a dear soul. We've been friends for years. But you mustn't be offended if she makes a point throughout the evening of introducing you to eligible young men,' Lady Penrose warned. 'She enjoys playing the matchmaker. Understandable enough when you consider she successfully married off her five daughters without any trouble whatsoever.'

'I shan't be offended,' Abbie assured her, as they managed to find themselves two vacant chairs by the wall. 'But I hope she isn't upset when I prove to be her first failure.'

She gazed about the crowded room with interest, thereby missing the lines of concern momentarily creasing her godmother's forehead. 'Clearly your friend is a popular hostess, ma'am. If you consider this merely a small party, I should dearly like to know what—'

Curious to know what on earth could have induced her goddaughter to break off mid-sentence and her delicate features to freeze in an expression of stunned disbelief, Lady Penrose turned her head to discover a tall gentleman, accompanied by a woman of middle age and a girl of about seventeen, greeting her friend Agnes Fergusson.

She then turned back to her goddaughter, and was astonished to discover her delicate cheeks now drained of every vestige of colour. 'Why, my dear! Whatever is the matter? You've grown quite dreadfully pale.'

There was an ominous click as slender fingers tightened about a delicately painted chicken-skin fan. 'Damn him…! Damn him…! Damn him!'

Chapter Two

Only her godmother's voice, distinctly betraying concern, checked the progress of what amazingly might have become an all-consuming anger, and stopped Abbie from storming from the room. Even so, it was several moments before she could drag her gaze away from the source of her fury, and several more before she dared trust herself to ask the burning question at the forefront of her mind.

'Are you by any chance acquainted with the gentleman who is presently holding our hostess in conversation, ma'am?'

It was sufficient for Lady Penrose to cast a second brief glance only in the direction of the door. 'No, why do you ask? Do you know him?'

The response had been so prompt that Abbie didn't doubt the truth of the denial, and the suspicion that Lady Penrose might have been party to Colonel

Augustus Graham's devious stratagems swiftly began to dwindle.

'Yes, ma'am, I know him,' she admitted, after watching the object of her displeasure steer his two female companions across the room towards a sandy-haired gentleman who, only moments before, had hailed him cheerfully. 'That is none other than my grandfather's godson, the man he is determined I should marry.'

Lady Penrose regarded the gentleman with far more interest this time, noting the easy grace of the long-striding gait, the superb breadth of shoulder, and that telltale aristocratic line of his profile. 'And you, my dear…? Is that your wish also?' she asked gently, and was surprised to witness an expression of hard determination take possession of Abbie's delicate features.

'Believe me when I tell you that the sun would rise in the west before I'd ever agree to wed Bartholomew Cavanagh.'

A moment's silence, then, 'Oh, I see.'

The murmured response drew a catlike smile to Abbie's lips. 'Yes, and I too begin to see just why my grandfather went to so much trouble to ensure that I would be safely ensconced in Bath at this time. He must have known Cavanagh would be here, and was therefore confident that we would run into each other at some point.'

That deceptively dreamy haze had disappeared

completely from Lady Penrose's eyes. 'I sincerely
trust you do not suspect that I am in your grandfather's confidence, and knew his intention from the
first?'

Abbie's smile turned to one of warmth. 'No,
ma'am, I do not think it,' she assured her. 'But I'm
certain you must appreciate that it does make my remaining here a little awkward. I'm not so foolish as
to suppose I can succeed in avoiding him entirely.'

'And you would, understandably, prefer to leave,'
Lady Penrose responded, without attempting to argue
the point, and was about to attract the attention of a
passing footman in order to arrange for her carriage
to be brought round to the door, when she felt the
touch of a gently restraining hand on her arm.

In the years to come Abbie was to look back and
appreciate fully that the decision made in that fraction of a second was to determine the course of her
life. Naturally, at the time, she was blissfully unaware of the fact. All she was conscious of was a
sense of shame. Her godmother had misunderstood,
had surmised quite wrongly that she merely wished
to leave the party, when in fact Abbie's real desire
was to flee the city. Suddenly, though, she knew she
could not, would not, run away like a frightened child
from either the party or the city. She wouldn't allow
her grandfather's obsession dictate the way she lived
her life one moment longer!

'No, ma'am,' she countered, 'I do not wish to leave.

I flatly refuse to allow Mr Cavanagh's presence to influence my behaviour in the least. I fully intend to enjoy all the pleasures Bath has to offer during my stay with you.'

'That's the spirit, child!' Lady Penrose positively beamed with approval before her expression once again grew thoughtful. 'Do you suppose your grandfather informed his godson of your proposed stay in Bath, and the reason for his presence in the city is to seek you out?'

Until that moment Abbie hadn't considered this as a possibility. 'I honestly couldn't say. But I strongly suspect that Grandfather must have known Bart intended visiting this place, and that was precisely why he made contact with you. I haven't set eyes upon Bart in six years, ma'am, not since the last time he visited Foxhunter Grange, just prior to his joining the army. We've never corresponded either, not a word, but he does write to Grandfather from time to time.'

Discovering this, Lady Penrose grew more pensive, and for a full minute stared in silence at the subject under discussion, her gaze once again revealing that behind the mantle of lazy good humour lurked a keenly perceptive mind, before voicing the opinion that his actions were hardly those of a gentleman whose interests were engaged. 'His years in the army, quite naturally, would necessitate long periods of separation. But there was nothing to prevent him writing to you. You might well discover he's experienced a change of heart, and that you are worrying for no purpose.'

Abbie's spontaneous shout of laughter induced several of those nearby to glance interestedly in her direction. 'Oh, I never supposed for a moment that that delicate organ was ever involved, my dear ma'am. No, he merely agreed to marry me to please Grandpapa.'

Lady Penrose looked far from convinced. 'Well, you might be right. But I must confess that to my mind he doesn't bear the appearance of a gentleman who would be easily coerced into actions of which he didn't approve. And who, by the by, are the two females in his party?'

Abbie had been wondering about this herself. 'I've never set eyes upon either of them before, so I cannot be certain. But I suspect the girl, who does bear a resemblance to Bart, at least in colouring, might well be his half-sister, and the older female his stepmother.'

'If you are right, then I should imagine he's here as their escort, and not for the purpose of seeking you out. Furthermore, the gentleman who is at present engaging the party in conversation is Agnes Fergusson's son, Giles. He too was in the army, and injured at Waterloo, which has left the poor boy with a sad limp. Evidently they are friends. So it is not unreasonable to suppose that Mr Cavanagh is here at Giles's invitation.'

Abbie was given no time to dwell on this very real possibility, for the musicians hired for the evening struck up a chord to announce the commencement of dancing, and a young gentleman suddenly appeared before her, requesting her as his partner.

It was on the tip of her tongue to utter a polite refusal, but when it became clear that the young man was none other than a son of another of her godmother's closest friends Abbie, not wishing to cause offence, thought better of it, even though she knew that by joining the set she was in the gravest danger of drawing attention to herself by crossing a certain tall gentleman's field of vision.

The prediction turned out to be all too accurate. The steps of the dance took her and her partner past the spot where Bartholomew Cavanagh and his party remained in conversation with Giles Fergusson, and all at once Abbie sensed she was being regarded with keen interest. She succeeded in concentrating on the steps of the dance and her partner for a further full half-minute before curiosity overcame common sense, and she turned her head to discover a pair of intelligent dark eyes, set in a ruggedly attractive face, firmly fixed in her direction.

Prompted by some imp of mischief, she chose to acknowledge him by the merest nod of her head, the result of which sent dark, masculine brows rising sharply in combined recognition and surprise, a definite indication that he hadn't expected to discover her in Bath.

Consequently she was not unduly astonished, when the set had drawn to a close, and her partner had returned her to her godmother's side, to discover Bart making his way purposefully across the room towards her. Nor was she unduly taken aback when he at last stood before her and the first words she had heard him utter in six long years was his surprise at discovering her here.

'Yes, I must admit to having been—er—somewhat astonished to see you enter the room, Mr Cavanagh,' she divulged, before introducing him to her godmother who, if the mischievous glint in her eyes was any indication, had derived no little amusement out of the gross understatement.

How Abbie wished she too could experience just a modicum of the same! The truth of the matter was, though, she very much resented having to acknowledge a person whom she had held in utter contempt for half a decade and more, and could only hope she could somehow manage to conceal the fact for the time good manners forced her to converse with him.

'The Colonel didn't mention you'd be in this part of the world when he wrote to me a few weeks ago, Abbie,' he openly admitted, turning back to her, his dark eyes narrowing slightly as he detected the slight stiffening in her perfectly proportioned slender frame at his free use of her given name.

'He failed to mention you would be, come to that, Mr Cavanagh,' she returned with icy politeness.

'No?' Those expressive dark brows rose again. 'How very odd! I feel sure I informed him I would be unable to join him in Scotland as I would be escorting my sister here this spring.' He studied her in silence for a moment, his gaze penetrating, as though striving to read her inmost thoughts. 'Would you be so kind as to allow me to make you known to my sister and stepmother, Miss Graham? They have heard me speak of you often in the past, and would dearly like to make your acquaintance.'

As she considered it would have been exceedingly churlish to refuse, she acquiesced, and within a short space of time was very glad she had, for Miss Kitty Cavanagh proved to be a very likeable and vivacious seventeen-year-old girl, whose unaffected manner Abbie found refreshingly candid, even if some of her remarks were a little disconcerting.

'I suppose, Miss Graham, at your age you must have enjoyed lots and lots of Seasons,' Kitty commented, after Abbie, graciously offering her chair to Mrs Cavanagh, came to stand beside her.

'Which is tantamount to suggesting that you consider Miss Graham at her last prayers, you outrageous little baggage!' her brother scolded, thereby earning himself a speaking glance from eyes of as dark a hue as his own. 'When will you learn to put a guard on that unruly tongue of yours?'

He turned to Abbie who, not in the least offended, was doing her utmost not to laugh. 'You must allow me to apologise on my tactless sister's behalf. One of her many faults, I'm afraid, is a tendency to speak without thinking.'

'I wasn't meaning to be rude,' his sister assured him defensively. 'I think Miss Graham is very pretty, don't you?'

Abbie hardly knew where to look. She could feel the heat stealing into her cheeks, and suspected the tall man beside her was deriving no little enjoyment out of her embarrassment.

'Exceedingly,' he agreed, with a suspicion of a twitch at one corner of his shapely mouth. 'But then I have always considered her so.' He smiled in earnest as deep blue eyes favoured him with a look of mingled suspicion and astonishment. 'Her manners too, as I recall, were always above reproach. Which, I fear, is more than I shall ever be able to say about yours.'

Pulling herself together with an effort, Abbie decided that it was time to intervene before Miss Kitty Cavanagh's feathers were totally ruffled by her elder brother's strictures. Evidently the siblings had more in common than their colouring. Even so, she didn't suppose for a moment that either would find it in the least flattering to be informed that there was a certain similarity in their characters too.

'I have never been privileged to enjoy a Season in

town, Miss Cavanagh. Indeed, this is the first time I've ever travelled any real distance from my grandfather's home in a very long time.'

Receiving no response, Abbie gazed from brother to sister, unsure which of them seemed more surprised by the admission. She thought she also detected what might well have been a hint of concern in Bart's expression before he asked bluntly, 'Was that entirely through choice, Miss Graham?'

Although having already decided that he too did not boggle at plain speaking, Abbie was somewhat taken aback by the directness of the question, and unsure just how to answer.

The truth of the matter was, of course, that her grandfather had never encouraged her to travel far from home, nor indeed socialise to any great extent, simply because he had feared she just might cross the path of a gentleman whom she would desire to marry. But she could hardly reveal to Bart that his godfather had done everything humanly possible to shield her from the attentions of eligible bachelors in the belief that one day she would fulfil his fondest hope. The last thing in the world she wanted was for Bart to misunderstand, to suppose that she had been happy to comply with her grandfather's wishes. Worse still, she would hate for him to think that she regretted her decision not to become engaged six years before, and had remained single in the hope he might repeat his offer of marriage.

'I have been content enough, sir.' Uncertain whether he believed her, she added, 'And as I've never evinced the least desire to relinquish my single state, a Season in town would have been a needless expense. However, no longer being in my first flush of youth, as it were, I think it highly unlikely I'd be considered a suitable choice for any young bachelor set on matrimony, and so experienced no reluctance whatsoever in visiting Bath.'

'If you suppose that, my girl,' Bart countered bluntly, 'you must be all about in your head!'

It wasn't so much the irritation easily discernible in the deep voice that surprised Abbie as the look of annoyance she couldn't fail to perceive before he turned away to converse with Lady Penrose. Seemingly, Kitty noticed it too, for she stared thoughtfully at her brother's broad back for several moments before her dark eyes, brightened by a speculative gleam, once again turned in Abbie's direction. Her lips parted, but whatever remark she had been about to utter was held in check, and she merely continued to regard Abbie in a considering way.

Fortunately Abbie was not forced to endure having both her features and figure scrutinised for any slight flaw for very long. Mrs Cavanagh, evidently feeling that it was time to circulate, attracted her daughter's attention, and soon afterwards they slipped quietly away to mingle with the other guests. Which, thankfully, induced their escort to accompany them, and left Abbie free to enjoy the remainder of what turned out to be, surprisingly enough, a most pleasurable evening.

The following morning, as she bore her godmother company for the first meal of the day, Abbie was once again plagued not so much by misgivings over her stay in Bath as a resurgence of resentment towards her grandsire over the devious methods he had adopted to attain his ends.

At least, though, she mused, she couldn't lay any blame squarely on Bartholomew Cavanagh's broad shoulders. She might not hold him in the highest esteem, and she could never envisage her opinion of him changing to any significant degree, but she was forced to own that he was no dissembler. There wasn't the remotest doubt in her mind that he had been as much surprised by her presence at the Fergussons' party as she had been by his. Furthermore, to do him justice, apart from that one occasion when he had taken the trouble to come across to speak with her, and make her known to his female relations, he had paid her no attention whatsoever, not even once asking her to dance.

Lady Penrose, reaching for a third buttered roll, cast her silent companion a furtive glance. Although she would have been the first to acknowledge that she didn't know her goddaughter at all well, she wouldn't have supposed for a moment that she was a young woman prone to fits of the sullens. Yet this morning Abbie certainly seemed slightly subdued, and there was definitely a marked degree of dissatisfaction in her expression. What could be troubling her? she wondered. Surely she wasn't worrying unnecessarily over Mr Cavanagh's presence in Bath? There was only one way to find out for certain.

Striking dark blue eyes met hers across the table a moment after she had voiced her query. 'And really, my dear, I do not feel you need concern yourself unduly,' Lady Penrose went on, striving to reassure. 'You are three-and-twenty, after all. No one can force you to form an alliance with a gentleman, if you have no wish to do so.'

'True. But my grandfather retains the hope that he can. We didn't part upon the best of terms,' Abbie at last revealed, an unmistakable note of regret in her voice. 'Also, he could not have made it clearer to me that, if I married against his wishes, he would disinherit me.'

Lady Penrose sat quietly digesting what she had learned, experiencing a swell of varying emotions. Colonel Graham, a gentleman she had met on two occasions only in the past, was swiftly figuring in her thoughts as a cold-hearted brute who betrayed scant concern for the feelings of others, least of all his granddaughter's. Alongside this ever-swelling animosity, and a strong determination to thwart the Colonel, was a sense of shame and deep regret for never having taken the trouble to visit the daughter of the woman who had once been her closest friend. It was true that she had not wished to interfere in Abbie's upbringing, and had believed that her god-daughter had been happy living with her grandfather. Sadly, she was fast coming to the conclusion that this had not been the case, and was determined to make amends for her neglect in the past in any way she could.

But first there was much she needed to discover, not least of which was why her goddaughter was so set against marrying Bartholomew Cavanagh, for she was forced silently to own that he had left her with a very favourable impression after their first meeting.

'And are you prepared to allow your grandfather's threat to influence you in any way?' she asked gently.

'Certainly not!' The conviction in Abbie's voice was unequivocal, as was the determined set to the softly rounded chin. 'If ever I do marry, it will be to a man of my own choosing.'

Secretly impressed by this display of fortitude, Lady Penrose didn't hesitate to voice the desire to help in any way she could, but was a little surprised by the prompt acceptance of the offer.

'You see, ma'am, I had already decided, before I left Foxhunter Grange, that it would be a mistake to return to live with Grandfather,' Abbie went on to confess. 'If I thought for a moment he might relent…might accept that I have no desire to marry his godson…' She shook her head. 'His arranging for me to visit you at a time when he knew Bart would be here is proof enough that he is as determined as ever.'

Lady Penrose reached across the table. 'Have you been so very unhappy, my child?'

Abbie stared down at the plump fingers covering her hand. 'I haven't been wholly content in recent years, no,' she admitted with total honesty, and was surprised to hear her godmother give vent to a very unladylike snort.

'I'm beginning to take that grandfather of yours in strong dislike.'

'Oh, no. You mustn't do that, ma'am,' Abbie countered, surprising herself somewhat by so quickly coming to his defence. 'Believe me when I tell you that he couldn't have been kinder to me when first I went to live with him.'

Her expression grew markedly softer as her mind's eye conjured up images from the past. 'He went out of his way to spend a deal of time with me, even though he went to the expense of engaging a governess to educate and take care of me. He taught me to ride, to fish, and even took the trouble to teach me how to handle a pistol. I spent many, many happy hours in his company. It was only after I refused to marry Bart that his attitude towards me changed, and he grew remote. And to a certain extent I can understand his behaviour, and make allowances,' she went on to admit, betraying a depth of tolerance and understanding in her nature that Lady Penrose could not help but admire. 'You see, Bart possesses many characteristics Grandpapa most respects in a man. The fact that he's a bruising rider and chose to join our brave men out in the Peninsula would have been enough for the Colonel to place him on a pedestal. But his admiration was won long before Bart joined the army. In his eyes Bart can do no wrong.'

'But you, my dear, evidently do not hold him in such high regard?' Lady Penrose prompted, and saw at once a shuttered look take possession of her goddaughter's features before Abbie rose to her feet and went to stand by the window.

'No, ma'am I do not,' she admitted, her voice cold and uncompromising, a clear indication to Lady Penrose that to probe further in an attempt to uncover what lay at the root of the dislike would be a grave mistake at this juncture, but even so she could not resist asking.

'Was there ever anything official between you, or an understanding that you would one day wed?'

'Not as far as I was concerned,' Abbie answered, after a lengthy silence, 'although it wouldn't surprise me to discover that Grandpapa had considered the possibility from when we were children.'

'Have you always held Mr Cavanagh in dislike, child?' Lady Penrose asked, after a further lengthy silence.

'Dislike?' Abbie echoed, frowning slightly as she gave the matter some thought. 'No, I cannot say that I ever disliked him. To be honest, though, I did resent his presence. Grandfather always paid me far less attention whenever Bart was staying with us. And, of course, the seven years' difference in our ages meant that we had little in common. So, as you can imagine, the suggestion that we should marry came as…as something of a shock.'

'Yes, I can appreciate that it must have done,' Lady Penrose murmured, while thinking, But that most definitely wasn't the reason why you refused him.

Intrigued though she was, she once again succeeded in curbing her curiosity for the time being, and merely said, 'That, however, is all in the past, and it is your future that must concern us.'

'Yes, yes,' Abbie readily agreed, the shadow of an unpleasant memory fading from her mind. 'And you could be of immeasurable help by assisting me to acquire a position as a governess or companion, whereby I'll be able to support myself until I attain the age of five-and-twenty and come into the inheritance left to me by my mother.'

In stunned silence Lady Penrose watched her goddaughter return to the table. 'You must be all about in your head, child, if you imagine I'd contemplate ever doing such a thing,' she managed at last. 'I appreciate why you've no desire to return to your grandfather's house. Very understandable, if I may say so. But the solution to your problem is before you! You will remain here with me.'

'Oh, but—'

'Save your breath, child,' Lady Penrose interrupted, thereby revealing a surprisingly stubborn side to her nature. 'I refuse to be deprived of this golden opportunity to salve my conscience and make amends for my shocking neglect over the years. No, no,' she added, when Abbie attempted to protest again. 'My mind is made up. And what pleasure I shall derive too in making you the toast of Bath!'

Although she experienced no desire whatsoever to turn herself into a fashion plate, Abbie made no attempt to swim against the tide of her godmother's enthusiasm when, later that morning, they visited the premises of the female who was generally considered Bath's foremost modiste.

Believing there would be far less competition, Madame Dupont, alias Molly Blunt, had chosen Bath in preference to London to set herself up in business. Her judgement had not proved faulty, and she had swiftly earned a reputation for fine workmanship and attention to detail.

Lady Penrose had been one of her first customers, and had remained loyal. Consequently Madame was only too happy to set aside current orders to oblige such a valued client; and doubly so when she set eyes on the perfect figure and wonderful colouring of the young woman whom she was being asked to dress in style, even going so far as to offer a walking dress with matching accessories, which had been ordered by a customer who had been annoyingly slow in settling her bills.

The outfit proved to be almost a perfect fit, and by the time Abbie and her godmother had pored over fashion plates and selected materials for new gowns, the slight adjustments had been completed by one of Madame's employees, and Abbie was able to leave the shop dressed, for the first time in her life, in the height of fashion.

'One can always rely on Molly's judgement,' Lady Penrose remarked, after informing her coachman to return to Upper Camden Place, as she intended to continue to the Pump Room on foot. 'That outfit is most becoming. And the colour's so right for you!'

Although she had always paid more attention to neatness than style, Abbie was secretly pleased with her new attire, but could not resist commenting on the shocking price.

'Don't give it another thought, child,' Lady Penrose adjured her. 'I most certainly shan't. And I'll derive a deal of satisfaction in forwarding the bills to your grandfather. My one regret is that I shan't be there to see his expression when he is obliged to dig deep into his pockets not for just one or two dresses, but for a whole new wardrobe of clothes. Serves the old curmudgeon right!'

Abbie, unable to suppress a gurgle of laughter at this wicked sentiment, entered the famous Pump Room in her godmother's wake. Several pairs of eyes, betraying either admiration or envy, or a mixture of both, were turned in her direction, including a pair of alert brown ones, which Lady Penrose at least had noticed had been firmly fixed in her goddaughter's direction on several occasions throughout the previous evening.

Abbie, however, remained as ignorant of Bart's presence as she had been over his watchfulness at the party, until she took her first sip of the famous waters, and a deep masculine rumble swiftly followed her shuddering grimace.

'I would have expected you to have had more sense than to sample the wretched stuff, my girl,' he told her bluntly, his dark eyes warmed by amusement.

'Why, Mr Cavanagh, you turn up in the most unlikely places!' she returned, hoping she had sounded more composed than she was in fact feeling at his unexpected appearance. 'I would have thought a good gallop across the Downs would have been more to your taste than hobnobbing here in what I'm reliably informed is a veritable hotbed of gossip.'

'You're right. I would much prefer to be anywhere but in this insipid place,' he freely acknowledged. 'But needs must when the devil drives.'

She took a moment to study him closely, and could detect no fault with his appearance. Clearly his apparel had been chosen for comfort rather than style. Although undoubtedly some would consider his neckcloth too plainly arranged, his waistcoat downright unimaginative and his coat too loosely fitting to display a pair of fine shoulders to advantage, no one could fail to appreciate that he was a wealthy country gentleman whose healthy tan and muscular physique betrayed a predilection for outdoor pursuits.

So what on earth had induced him to visit Bath, where sedate strolls, polite conversation and quiet dinner parties were the preferred pastimes? Surely a sporting-mad gentleman, who thought nothing of riding at a neck-or-nothing pace, would find little to amuse him in Bath's genteel society?

'I wouldn't imagine your health has prompted your visit to this city, sir,' she remarked, drawing his attention away from the blue ribbon tied in a coquettish bow beneath her chin. 'So I cannot help wondering what particular devil has been the driving force bringing you here?'

His expression, which had betrayed mild approval, changed in an instant as he cast an exasperated glance at some spot over his right shoulder. 'My pestilential young sister is the demon that prompted my actions, ma'am. My father saw fit to burden me with shared guardianship with Eugenie, who is far too indulgent where her daughter is concerned.'

'Oh, dear,' Abbie responded unsteadily, finding the

mere thought that Bartholomew Cavanagh found his sister something of a trial wickedly satisfying. 'She is somewhat troublesome on occasions then, sir?'

'Not if she knows what's good for her,' he returned, with a certain grim satisfaction.

'My, my! How fearsome you sound!' She peered up at him through what he considered extraordinary long black lashes. 'I'm very glad you're not my brother.'

'Believe me, Miss Graham, you couldn't possibly be more pleased than I that I am not,' he purred silkily, a spontaneous smile instantly softening the harsh contours of his face, and bringing a rush of colour to her own.

Fortunately she was spared the necessity of formulating some response by the unexpected arrival of his particular demon, who appeared before them with the information that Giles Fergusson had arrived with his mother, and was wishful for a quiet word.

Bart might not have been best pleased to have what Abbie considered had degenerated into a rather embarrassing tête-à-tête brought to an abrupt end, but she most definitely was and bestowed a dazzling smile upon her unwitting rescuer.

'I'm so glad to see you here this morning,' Kitty announced by way of a greeting. 'You see, I'm in desperate need of help, and could think of no one else to turn to, and have been racking my brains to think of some way of seeing you in private.'

Although the crowded Pump Room was hardly the ideal place to achieve this objective, Abbie, intrigued, obliged her young companion by moving over to one of the windows, where fewer persons were congregating.

'And how may I be of service to you, Miss Cavanagh?' she prompted, when Kitty regarded her much as she had done the previous night: assessingly, with head on one side.

'Oh, might we not be friends? I do so hate unnecessary formality, don't you? May I not address you by your given name?' Kitty asked, looking so ridiculously young and hopeful that Abbie found herself automatically complying with the request. 'Oh, I'm so glad,' Kitty went on in a rush. 'I really wouldn't feel at all comfortable asking for your help otherwise.'

Abbie began to experience misgivings. 'I should dearly like for you to look upon me as a friend,' she reiterated. 'But if something is genuinely troubling you, wouldn't it be better to confide in your mother or brother?'

'Good heavens, no!' Kitty looked appalled at the mere thought. 'Mama defers to Bart's judgement in most everything. And as he's the very one causing me so much bother, I can hardly approach him, now can I?'

Abbie was forced to agree with this, but steadfastly refused to concede more until she knew the precise nature of the problem besetting this engaging young woman, and just why Kitty might suppose that she could be of assistance. She was not left in ignorance for long.

'I want you to help me find Bart a wife.'

Abbie received this intelligence in stunned silence, certain that she must surely have misheard. 'I… beg…your…pardon?'

Something in her tone must have alerted Kitty to the very real possibility that she was on the point of losing a worthy ally, for her expression changed dramatically from eager anticipation to that of a half-starved waif pleading for a crust.

'You will help me, won't you?'

'Assuredly not!' Abbie answered, completely unmoved by the look of helpless appeal. 'I would never serve one of my sex such a bad turn by bringing her to the notice of your brother!'

It was out before she realised what she was saying and, more importantly, what she was revealing. Sadly, it was already too late, for Kitty, after a moment's stunned silence, was already asking that all-important question.

'No, of course I don't dislike him.' Even to her own ears the assurance sounded highly unconvincing, so Abbie felt obliged to add, 'But we're hardly what one might term close friends.'

'But you've known each other for years,' Kitty pointed out. 'And I know Bart thinks highly of you.'

Although the disclosure came as something of a shock, Abbie recovered in an instant. 'Be that as it may, I feel certain he wouldn't welcome interference from me, most especially in such a delicate matter. Besides, your brother is more than capable of making his own choice of a suitable wife.'

'He already has,' Kitty astounded her by divulging. 'At least, he's well and truly smitten. I can tell.'

'In that case, Kitty, I do not perfectly understand why you should feel the need of my help,' Abbie responded, unable to suppress a frown of disapproval over her companion's indelicate choice of language.

'Because I want to make sure he comes up to scratch. We are here only until the middle of July. It might be some time before Bart can see her again, and anything might happen in the meantime. She might meet someone else.'

Abbie's frowned again at this. 'Are you sure the girl's feelings are engaged? Who, by the way, is the unfortunate…I mean, who is the young lady who has found favour with your brother?'

For several seconds Kitty appeared to find the toes of her shoes of immense interest, before she raised her head to stare rather sheepishly in the direction of the door. Then her eyes widened in excitement, as though she had been assailed by a brilliant idea.

'Why, she has just this moment walked in. And look, Bart is approaching her!'

Abbie turned her head in time to see Kitty's brother bow with lazy grace over a dainty hand. 'Was I not introduced to that young woman at the party last night?'

'Very possibly, as she was there,' Kitty confirmed. 'Her name is Caroline Whitham. She's with her brother Stephen. She's terribly shy. I wager she's blushing to the roots of her hair at this very moment, poor thing.'

She turned back to discover Abbie still studying the object of Bart's attentions. 'Oh, you will assist me, won't you? We cannot talk here, but if you could meet me in Sydney Gardens this afternoon, I'm sure we could come up with some schemes to bring them together as much as possible. I'm certain Miss Whitham mentioned that she too walks in the gardens most every afternoon, weather permitting, so it would be a simple matter to approach her if we should hit upon some idea.'

She received no response and, undeterred, added, 'You cannot know what it's like to have a brother like Bart who always thinks he knows best. I love him dearly, but he can be so overbearing on occasions, forever correcting and scolding and telling one what one may or may not do. But if Bart were to marry, all my troubles would be over. He'd be far too busy looking after his wife to pay much attention to me.'

With an arresting look in her eyes, Abbie turned to stare sightlessly out of the window. If Bart were to marry all my troubles would be over, she echoed silently.

Chapter Three

'**W**hitham's sister is a pretty little thing,' Giles Fergusson commented as his friend rejoined him.

Nodding in agreement, Bart watched the young officer who had served under him out in the Peninsula escorting his sibling to that area where glasses of the famous waters were being dispensed. 'Young Whitham is to be envied. His sister's behaviour, from what I've observed, is above reproach. Which,' he added, his brow darkening, as he transferred his gaze to a certain spot by the windows, 'is more than I'll ever be able to say about my own.'

Following the direction of his friend's disapproving gaze, Giles smiled indulgently. 'To some extent she reminds me of my youngest sister. Kitty's merely high-spirited. She'll calm down in a year or two.'

This assurance did little to console Bart. 'Perhaps. But she's more than capable of wreaking a deal of havoc before then.' His brow lifted slightly. 'Although I've absolutely no objection to her forming a friendship in that quarter.'

Once again Giles glanced across the room, only this time to study Kitty's companion. 'Ah, yes! I recall you mentioning last night that you're acquainted with Miss Graham. I spoke with her briefly myself at the party. Struck me as a very sensible young woman, as well as being immensely pleasing on the eye. If her reason for visiting Bath is to form a suitable alliance, I cannot envisage there'll be much difficulty.'

Receiving no response, Giles returned his attention to his friend to discover dark brows drawn together in a severer frown than before. 'Evidently you don't agree.'

'Oh, no, it isn't that,' Bart assured him. 'I'm not altogether sure, though, just why she's retained her single state for so long.'

'Perhaps the thought of marriage doesn't appeal to her.'

If possible, Bart's frown grew more pronounced. 'The thought of marrying me certainly did not.'

Giles was astonished, and made no attempt to conceal the fact. 'Good gad! I thought I knew most everything about you, old fellow, but I never knew you'd been tempted into parson's mousetrap.'

'My godfather suggested the match. Thank the Lord Abbie had the good sense to refuse! We were both far too young.'

'And now?' Giles prompted when Bart seemed about to relapse into a thoughtful silence.

'Now…? Well, let us just say I've sown my wild oats. I feel ready to settle down.'

Giles pursed his lips together in a silent whistle. 'Well, well, well! Sits the wind in that quarter, eh?'

Bart chose not to comment and merely watched his sister's progress as she came across the room towards them, with what he considered to be a wickedly satisfied expression on her face. He was instantly on his guard.

'What mischief are you brewing, brat?' he demanded, when at last she reached his side. 'I know that look of old.'

She favoured him with an angry scowl, equal to his own, before transferring her attention to his far more personable companion, a gentleman whom she had adored since childhood. 'I cannot imagine why Bart should always suppose I'm plotting mischief. Anyone would imagine I was still seven years old.'

'I wish you were, I'd know how to deal with you,' was her brother's muttered response, the result of which earned him a further darkling look.

'I wager Giles was never so beastly to his sisters as you are to me.'

Bart wisely refrained from teasing her further, and merely suggested that, as he had one or two letters he wished to write before nuncheon, they find her mother and return to the house. Kitty's obliging him

without demur surprised him somewhat, for she was
a sociable little creature who, in general, much preferred to be in company than sit quietly indoors occupying herself. The uneasy feeling that she was
being accommodating for a very good reason crossed
his mind.

'You appear in remarkably good spirits today,
Kitty,' he said, when she began humming a popular
tune as they set off on foot in the direction of the
house that he had rented for the duration of their
stay.

'I'm enjoying myself here,' she admitted. 'I know
I wished for a Season in London and was upset when
you flatly refused to countenance such a venture in
your usual highhanded fashion. But I've decided that
Bath isn't so dull, after all. I'm beginning to get to
know some very interesting people.'

'Yes, I noticed you speaking with Miss Graham,
Kitty,' her mother put in. 'A very charming young
woman, I thought. I wonder…do you think it's too
late to send her and Lady Penrose invitations to our
party next week, Bart?' she added. 'You wouldn't object, I trust?'

'I cannot imagine why you might suppose I'd not
approve, Eugenie,' he returned, hoping he hadn't
sounded impatient, but very much fearing from her
suddenly crestfallen expression that he had.

Falling back a pace in order to allow mother and
daughter to walk together, he took himself silently to

task over his unnecessary brusqueness. It couldn't be denied, though, that he found himself becoming increasingly irritated by his stepmother's insistence on seeking his approval over the most trivial matters. All the same, he was forced to acknowledge that perhaps his own behaviour over the years had been much to blame for this.

He had been close to his own mother, touchingly so, and her death, when he had been eleven years old, had been a bitter blow from which it had taken him considerable time to recover. His relationship with his father had been reasonably good too until his sire, without warning, had upped and married the local vicar's eldest daughter.

Kitty's arrival the following year hadn't improved the situation one iota. Instead of one interloper with whom he must share his father's affections, there had been two. Consequently he hadn't hesitated to seek the attention he had so selfishly desired by spending many of his school holidays with his godfather, a gentleman who had been only too happy to indulge him in his preference for outdoor pursuits.

Undeniably he had grown into a self-seeking young man who had cared for naught but the pursuit of his own pleasures. After leaving Cambridge, he had spent much of his time in London, enjoying the many pleasures the capital had to offer. With hindsight he now realised he may well have continued down that ruinous path, where gambling, drinking and womanising occupied much of his time, if a sudden whim, fostered by his godfather, to join his many friends fighting out in the Peninsula, had not overtaken him.

His years in the army had, he believed, improved his nature. He would never attempt to suggest that he hadn't now a flaw in his character. Far from it, in fact! But at least he'd learned to consider the feelings of others and not attempt to shirk his responsibilities.

He focused his gaze once again on the elder female walking just a few feet ahead. It was far too late now for him to forge a closer relationship with his stepmother, though God only knew the poor woman had done everything within her power over the years to create a bond between them by showing a depth of understanding towards him which he ill deserved. Nor had he any intention of becoming a hypocrite by attempting to display a deep affection that he had never felt towards her. But it wouldn't hurt to acknowledge that she had maintained high standards in the running of the household that was now legally his, and ensure she knew that he no longer selfishly resented her presence under his roof.

'I'm very much looking forward to our party next week, Eugenie,' he assured her, as they arrived at their rented accommodation. 'Apart from those few guests I've insisted upon inviting, I'm happy to leave all the arrangements to you. You're an excellent hostess, and I've every confidence the evening will be a resounding success.'

Leaving his stepmother glowing quite pink with pleasure at the unexpected praise, and his half-sister looking a mite surprised too, he parted company with them in the hall, taking himself into the library, with every intention of responding to the letters he'd received earlier in the day. He had made excellent inroads into his correspondence, when he was interrupted in his task by the unexpected arrival of his sister.

For once in her life she betrayed slight diffidence as she approached the desk. 'I'm sorry to disturb you, Bart, only I was wondering whether I might ask a favour of you?'

As he had never observed the least shyness in her character before, he was immediately on his guard. 'You can always ask, Kitty.'

'Well, I was just wondering, if you're not otherwise engaged, that is, whether you would accompany me out for a walk after nuncheon?'

Had she not seemed reluctant to meet his gaze, as she repositioned, quite unnecessarily in his opinion, the bottles in the standish, he might not have considered the request in any way out of the ordinary. 'Why this sudden desire for my company, minx? Why not take the air with your mother?'

'Oh, Bart! You know Mama is no great walker. Besides, she prefers to rest in the afternoons. It is such a nice day, I thought we might visit Sydney Gardens. I've been told by several people that it's very pretty there, and I don't want to take my maid. She daw-dles so.'

'Very well,' he relented, albeit against his better judgement. 'Providing you leave me in peace for the time being, I'll escort you.'

His prompt acquiescence earned him a sisterly peck on one cheek and a brief, spontaneous hug. His eyes narrowed as he watched her skip from the room, looking very well pleased with herself. Yes, she was definitely up to something, he decided, already re-gretting pandering to her whims.

Abbie herself was of a similar mind when she en-tered the popular gardens midway through the after-noon. Before the suggestion had been made, she had never once considered that Bart's marrying might be the solution to all her own problems. She couldn't deny she still felt extremely angry over her grandfa-ther's devious schemes in getting her safely estab-lished in Bath at a time when he was aware his godson would be there. She couldn't deny either that she remained deeply hurt over the Colonel's attitude towards her in recent years. Even so, that didn't alter the fact that she still loved him dearly, still treasured those wonderful memories of their early years to-gether, when he couldn't possibly have done more to make her happy, after the loss of her parents.

She glanced at the young parlourmaid who had been willing to accompany her out on such a fine afternoon. Given the choice, she was forced to own she would far rather return to Foxhunter Grange than remain in Bath, where she felt sure that, once the charm of novelty had begun to wane, the city's petty restrictions where young, unmarried females were concerned would soon begin to irk her unbearably, and she would then crave those extra freedoms to be had by living in the country.

Yet, was she prepared to abandon her principles and interfere in someone else's life in an attempt to attain her own ends? Misgivings once again began to assail her. She might not know Bart very well, but even so she felt certain he wouldn't appreciate anyone meddling in his personal concerns. Furthermore, would she ever be able to reconcile it with her conscience if she was to aid Kitty in her determination to see her brother safely wedded? Was she really capable of condemning some poor, unfortunate girl to a life tied to that dissolute rake?

'Why, what a delightful surprise running in to you again, Miss Graham!'

Startled out of her guilty musings by that familiar, deep voice, Abbie stopped dead in her tracks. Had she observed Bart and his sister approaching, she wouldn't have hesitated to take immediate action in order to avoid the encounter. As it was, she had little choice but to appear pleased to see them. Which was no difficult task where Kitty was concerned, even though she had almost made up her mind not to become involved in the girl's matchmaking stratagems.

'Indeed, it is a surprise, sir,' she was able to say with total sincerity, for she hadn't expected Kitty to be escorted by her brother. 'Of course I've been aware of your penchant for outdoor activities for some considerable time, but I hadn't realised that strolling in pleasure gardens numbered among them.'

A distinctly challenging gleam brightened his eyes. 'Ahh, but, Miss Graham, you must remember that you do not know me very well…at least, not yet. But that can easily be remedied. I left Eugenie in the process of sending you and your godmother belated invitations to our party next week. I hope you'll delight us all by accepting.'

'Oh, do say you'll come!' Kitty put in, when Abbie hesitated, unwilling to commit herself. 'I'm sure you'll enjoy it enormously.'

'I'm certain I should too,' Abbie agreed. 'But I simply cannot accept without first consulting Lady Penrose. She may have made prior arrangements.'

'Naturally you cannot obligate yourself now, Miss Graham,' Bart readily concurred, before his precocious sister could attempt to force the issue. 'But at least you can delight us both by remaining with us to enjoy these gardens on such a pleasant afternoon.'

Abbie glanced at the young maid who had accompanied her out, wondering whether she could possibly make her presence the excuse to decline the invitation by insisting the servant return to the house in order to fulfil her other duties.

Bart, however, proved too perceptive, reading her thoughts with uncanny accuracy. 'Be assured my sister and I shall see you safely returned to Lady Penrose, so you no longer require the services of the maid.'

The challenging look was back in his eyes, daring her to argue the point, but she refused to give him the impression that his presence in any way disturbed her. Polite indifference was the attitude she must always strive to adopt whenever her and Bartholomew Cavanagh's paths crossed in the days and weeks ahead. Besides which, his presence today might turn out to be a blessing in disguise. At least Kitty would be unlikely to broach the subject of her plans for his future within his hearing, thereby granting Abbie a little more time to decide whether she wished to become involved or not.

As things turned out, she swiftly discovered she had grossly underestimated her young friend's resourcefulness, for no sooner had she dismissed the maid, and fallen into step beside them, than Kitty instantly raised the topic of things they might do to keep themselves entertained during their stay in Bath.

'I think it would be a splendid notion to organise a picnic, don't you?' she asked, appearing the picture of innocence as she glanced up at her brother. 'We could ask some of our friends. You'd come, wouldn't you, Abbie?'

Her tongue suddenly decided to attach itself to the roof of her mouth as two pairs of brown eyes fixed themselves in her direction: one pair flashing a look of entreaty; the other glinting with unholy amusement. 'Well, I…I…do not think that I…'

'Perhaps Miss Graham feels she has too many years in her dish to indulge in such pastimes, Kitty,' her brother suggested, much to Abbie's intense annoyance. She favoured him with a dagger look, the result of which had him straining to control his mirth. 'It has been my experience that, in general, when females reach a certain age,' he added, lips twitching, 'they tend to spurn outdoor activities, preferring instead the more genteel occupations, such as needlecraft, reading and preserve making, nothing too strenuous.'

'She isn't that old, for heaven's sake!' Kitty exclaimed in all seriousness.

'Indeed, no,' Abbie put in, before Bart could utter any ribald response to his sister's backhanded compliment. 'And a picnic will make a pleasant change from all the cap-making occupying so much of my time of late.'

Unlike her brother, whose shoulders were once again shaking in silent, appreciative laughter, Kitty looked appalled. 'You haven't taken to wearing caps already, have you, Abbie?'

'Only after nuncheon, dear, when I feel the need to rest for an hour or so.'

'She's but jesting, Kitty,' Bart assured her, deciding to bring the badinage to an end. 'Although it might be wise, if you are seriously contemplating eating alfresco, to organise the outing for one morning, if you were also thinking of including your mother and Lady Penrose in the party, that is. Which I think you must do. Miss Graham might not be a schoolroom miss, but she still requires a chaperon.'

Astonished that a person of such dubious morals would consider the proprieties, Abbie shot a glance in his direction, half suspecting him of mockery. Something in her expression must have betrayed her scepticism, for his eyes narrowed and grew increasingly probing. All at once the disgraceful episode that she had witnessed taking place in her grandfather's summerhouse sprang into her mind's eye with embarrassing clarity. Powerless to prevent the sudden surge of heat rising from beneath the neckline of her gown, she could only hope that her heightened colour might be attributed to the combined effects of exercise and the warmth of the day.

His sister, at least, seemed oblivious to her increasing discomfiture. Stopping dead in her tracks, Kitty uttered a shriek of delight. 'Why, only look, Bart!' she cried, unwittingly drawing his thoughtful atten-

tion away from Abbie. 'I do believe that is none other
than Mr Whitham and his sister, sitting over there.
How fortunate that we should have chanced upon
them again today! I'll run on ahead and invite them
to join the picnic, should I?'

Without waiting for a response, she sped away,
leaving Abbie experiencing both a twinge of resentment and a pang of envy. Naturally she could not
quite like being left alone, if only for a short time, in
the sole company of a gentleman whom she didn't
hold in the highest esteem, while at the same time she
couldn't help but admire Kitty's innate ability to dis-
simulate. The girl belonged on the Drury Lane stage!
No one would have supposed for a moment that she
hadn't been genuinely surprised to come upon the
Whithams. Yet, how could this possibly be so, when
only that very morning she had assured Abbie the siblings would be in the gardens later in the day?

'Do not feel obliged to involve yourself in my in-
corrigible sister's schemes if you truly do not wish
to do so, Miss Graham.'

Startled, Abbie scanned the rugged profile, wondering if he had guessed his sister's intent. 'I'm sorry,
sir. I do not perfectly understand what you mean.'

'The picnic, Miss Graham. Do not feel obliged to
join the outing if it is not to your taste.'

Unwittingly he had offered her the golden opportunity to decline if she chose. Yet, perversely, she experienced no desire to do so. To date she had done

nothing to aid and abet his sister, so no blame could be laid at her door should he uncover Kitty's underlying purpose. Furthermore, a visit to a local beauty spot would be most pleasant. Why should she deny herself the treat? She had enjoyed precious few diversions in recent years.

'I cannot imagine why you might suppose I do not wish to join the excursion, Mr Cavanagh. I think it a splendid notion.'

The element of doubt that continued to linger in his eyes for several moments was vanquished by a smile of such warmth that the harsh lines of his features were instantly softened. 'I cannot tell you how relieved I am to hear you say so, Miss Graham. It will require the combined efforts of two sober-minded persons of advanced years, such as ourselves, to ensure the occasion doesn't deteriorate into a sad romp.'

Against all the odds Abbie found herself enjoying his surprisingly teasing manner. 'In that case, sir, I'd best play the part to the full and don one of my fetching caps.'

'Don't you dare!' he hissed for her ears only, as they approached the bench where Kitty, looking very well pleased with herself, sat beside the shy young female whom she was seemingly intent on calling sister in the not too distant future.

It was swiftly borne in upon Abbie that this goal was not beyond Kitty's reach, for no sooner had a few pleasantries been exchanged than the Whithams declared their delight in joining the proposed picnic, and the excursion was arranged to take place two days hence, at a place to be decided upon later.

'Would you mind very much, Bart, if Caroline and her brother escorted me back to the house?' Kitty asked. 'It's on their way, so I shan't be putting them out. It would grant us the opportunity to consider where would be an ideal place to enjoy the picnic. After all, they reside in Bath and so ought to know all the best spots.'

As the Whithams appeared only too happy to oblige, Bart raised no objection. Abbie, on the other hand, was less enthusiastic at having only Kitty's brother to escort her home, though she somehow managed to conceal the fact very well when she and Bart parted company with the others at the entrance to the gardens.

Amazingly enough, however, by the time they had arrived at Upper Camden Place, she had begun to revise her opinion of her escort. Although she abhorred his manners and morals, and doubted she could ever be brought to overlook these defects, she was forced to own that he was an intelligent man, well read and knowledgeable on a wide range of subjects, and had proved to be surprisingly good company.

'Would you care to step inside for some refreshments, Mr Cavanagh?' she enquired, after debating for several moments whether to issue the invitation, and then deciding that common courtesy dictated she must after he had put himself to the trouble of escorting her safely home.

As she couldn't imagine that sipping tea in an elegant drawing-room was his preferred way of spending an afternoon, she confidently expected him to utter a polite refusal. Consequently she was surprised when he accepted with alacrity, declaring that it would grant him the opportunity to invite Lady Penrose to his forthcoming party in person.

This, as things turned out, he was obliged to postpone, for they entered the drawing-room to discover Lady Penrose, for once appearing distinctly ruffled, in earnest conversation with her head groom.

'Oh, my dear, thank heavens you're back!' Lady Penrose declared, sounding genuinely relieved. 'The most dreadful thing has—' She broke off when she observed the tall figure standing behind Abbie in the doorway. 'Oh, and you have brought Mr Cavanagh with you. How very nice!'

'What has occurred to overset you, ma'am?' Abbie didn't hesitate to ask the instant her godmother had exchanged a further polite greeting with her unexpected visitor.

'Oh, it is too provoking!' she declared, relapsing once again into a perturbed state. 'The stable-lad has suffered an injury! Jenkins, here, has just this moment informed me. And it really is most inconvenient! Why must he break his leg now, of all times!'

'I cannot imagine he did so on purpose, ma'am,'

Abbie pointed out gently, before turning her attention to the groom. 'Has the doctor been summoned?'

'Aye, miss,' Jenkins responded. 'Not that there were any need. T'other lad did a proper job. Doctor said as how he couldn't 'ave sct it better 'imself.'

'Oh, do explain things properly, Jenkins,' Lady Penrose ordered, after seeing Abbie frown in puzzlement, 'otherwise my goddaughter will not understand the dilemma.'

'Well, it were this way, miss,' he began, when three pairs of eyes had turned in his direction. 'I sends young Jem out earlier to the blacksmith's to get one on the 'orses shod. While he were waiting he wandered out into the street. Now he swears he were pushed. But I reckon that's all nonsense, m'self—reckon he thought to save 'imself a right ticking off.' He tutted. 'Jem be a right dozy nodcock! It's my belief he weren't looking where he were going, and walks straight out in front of a carriage.

'Now the blacksmith, and the lad that were wi' him at the time, seemingly looking for work, goes out to see what all the to-do's about. They carries young Jem back into smithy, and the lad sets the leg there and then, no trouble. Then the blacksmith brings Jem back 'ere in his cart, while this 'ere lad takes care o' mistress's horse. So when I 'ears the lad's looking for work, I comes up 'ere to see the mistress.'

He paused to cast an imploring glance in Mr Cavanagh's direction, as though expecting one of his own sex more likely to sympathise. 'I can't manage by m'self, not with all the extra duties. And all I can say is this 'ere lad seems to know what's what. But it ain't my place to take men on, 'specially not strangers.'

'So you can understand my predicament,' Lady Penrose announced the instant her groom fell silent, but Abbie, at a complete loss, didn't hesitate to shake her head.

'My dear, I know nothing whatsoever about engaging grooms,' her godmother explained. 'My dear husband always saw to that sort of thing. I only ever concerned myself with household staff. It is true what Jenkins says, though. We do need to engage someone. Jenkins cannot be expected to drive me about and take care of you when you go out for your rides.'

'Oh, but, ma'am, there's no need to concern yourself about me,' Abbie assured her. 'I didn't come to Bath expecting to ride too often, if at all.'

'Oh, but you must, my dear!' Lady Penrose countered swiftly. 'As soon as I knew you were coming to stay, I asked Jenkins to arrange for the hire of a suitable mount for you. And your new riding habit will be delivered within a very few days, so you will be able to go out whenever you choose. I've long since known of your fondness for riding, and I do not wish you to give up any of your favourite pastimes on my account, especially as you are considering taking up residence with me permanently.'

Abbie could almost feel those dark brown orbs boring into her back, but steadfastly refused to look at the gentleman standing directly behind her, until he said,

'Ma'am, if I may be of service?' Bart transferred his gaze to Lady Penrose. 'Unlike yourself, I'm accustomed to hiring outdoor workers, although I think Miss Graham ought to be present during the interview. It is, after all, primarily for her benefit that you require the services of a groom.'

'Oh, Mr Cavanagh, that is most kind!' Lady Penrose declared, clearly delighted by the offer of assistance. 'If you would care to conduct the interview in the downstairs parlour, I shall arrange for refreshments to be brought here in readiness for your return.'

Although not altogether unhappy about having Bart there to offer support, Abbie might have wished no mention had been made of the possibility of her taking up permanent residence in Bath. She felt sure he must have experienced a degree of puzzlement, not to say shock.

Yet, surprisingly enough, he made no attempt to allude to the matter when they had attained the privacy of the downstairs parlour. He merely took up a stance before the window to stare out into the street, declaring as he did so that he was deriving far more enjoyment out of his first sojourn in Bath than he might have supposed.

Abbie wasn't permitted to speculate for long on

whether there had been some underlying meaning in the admission, for she detected the sound of a heavy tread in the passageway, and a moment later a tall figure was filling the open doorway.

In height and build there was little to choose between the stranger and the man who immediately abandoned his position by the window to come to stand beside her. There, however, all similarities ended. The new arrival was much younger than Bart, no more than two-and-twenty, Abbie guessed. A crop of bright blond hair tumbled untidily over a bronzed forehead, beneath which a pair of clear blue eyes, betraying a marked degree of diffidence, stared solemnly into the room.

'Well, don't just stand there like a stock, lad! Come in and close the door!'

Bart's brusque command had the desired effect. Accustomed to taking orders, the young man immediately responded to the voice of authority, and came forward, turning his misshapen hat nervously in his work-roughened hands.

'Now, I understand you're looking for work?'

'Aye, sir, that's reet.'

'By your accent I deduce you're not from around these parts,' Bart said, remarking on something that had instantly occurred to Abbie too.

'Born and bred in Yorkshire, not far from Kexby, sir.'

'Kexby...?' Abbie echoed. 'What a coincidence!

There's a relative of mine living near there…Sir Montague Graham.'

'Why, bless you, miss!' A boyish grin tugged at the stranger's mouth. 'That do be strange! I were born on the Graham estate. My pa were a labourer there up until he died a few year back.'

'And were you employed by Sir Montague?' she asked.

'No, miss. Since I were eight year old I've worked for Mr Remington, a close neighbour.'

'And why have you chosen to leave Remington's employ, and find work in this neck of the woods?' Bart asked, thinking it strange. In his experience country people rarely strayed far from their roots, unless it was to find work in the local towns and cities.

'Well, it be this way, sir…Mr Remington's been ill for some time. He ain't got no children. When he dies his property will be sold. Mr Remington's always been good to me, sir, very fair, and he told me straight he couldn't guarantee I'd be given work when the new owner arrives.'

'That's understandable enough,' Bart remarked, before belatedly enquiring the young man's name.

'Arkwright, sir. Josh Arkwright.'

'So, what brought you down to the West Country, Josh?' Abigail enquired, having already decided that she liked him, and would be happy to have him for her personal groom.

'Mr Remington had a favourite brood mare. He

wanted to be sure she'd go to a good home. So he ask me to bring her down to an old friend of 'is who lives a few miles south of 'ere.'

'Who is…?' Bart put in.

'A Mr Diggory, sir. My master wrote asking Mr Diggory if he could offer me work at his place, but Mr Diggory couldn't, sir. Said as times were 'ard, and he couldn't afford to take on more men. Said I might try my luck in the larger towns 'ere abouts—Bath or Bristol, if I didn't 'ave no hankering to return to Yorkshire.'

'And is there any reason in particular why you don't wish to return?' Bart was not slow to enquire.

Josh shrugged. 'There's nowt there for me now, sir. All my family's dead, excepting a sister who's married to a mill worker and lives in Halifax. And for all I know, Mr Remington might have passed on by now. He gave me a quarter's wages in advance, sir, and money enough to get back should I 'ave a mind, but…' he shrugged '…don't see that there's much point iffen I can find work 'ere.'

'You do realise the position is only temporary, until the stable-lad is up and about again,' Bart wasn't slow to point out.

'Aye, sir, I knows that reet enough. But at least it'll give me a chance to look about for something more settled, if I do decide to stay down here.'

Bart acknowledged this with a nod before asking Josh if he had retained the letter his former employer

had written to Mr Diggory, and received an immediate shake of the head in response. Abbie, however,
was not unduly concerned that he had no references,
for she had already made up her mind to offer employment, and instructed him to return to the stables,
and take up his duties immediately.

'I hope you don't come to regret that altruistic gesture, my girl,' Bart warned the instant Josh, appearing far more cheerful, had departed.

'Why should I? He's explained just why he's in
need of work. He seemed open and honest. Besides
which, I rather liked him. I think he deserves a
chance.'

Bart smiled grimly. 'One can sometimes come to
regret charitable acts. One should never judge at face
value. People are not always quite what they seem.'

'Believe me, Mr Cavanagh, I'm not as naïve as
you seem to suppose. I'm fully aware that genial outward trappings can conceal someone capable of the
most despicable acts,' she responded softly, and then
turned to leave, but not before she had glimpsed a
speculative gleam in those dark brown eyes of his.

Chapter Four

It was with decidedly mixed feelings that Abbie surveyed the unblemished June sky the instant she awoke on the morning of the proposed picnic. On the one hand, she was looking forward to her first venture out of the city to explore the surrounding countryside on what promised to be a perfect late spring day; on the other, she would far rather not have been destined to spend several hours within close proximity to someone whom she had been happy to stigmatise as nothing more than a callous philanderer; someone who, moreover, had begun to infiltrate her thoughts of late rather more than was comfortable.

She couldn't deny that she'd been grateful for Bart's support during the interview with Josh. Furthermore, she considered the fact that he had made no attempt to influence her decision to any significant degree very much to his credit. But was that reason enough to begin to question her former opinion of him, to begin to wonder whether she had been too severe in her judgement of his character? She knew the base behaviour of which he was capable. Dear Lord! Hadn't she witnessed it with her own eyes?

The arrival of her godmother's personal maid, and not the young servant girl who usually waited upon her each morning, succeeded in gaining her immediate attention, and she demanded to know if ought were amiss.

'Absolutely nothing, miss,' Felcham assured her. 'It was just that I thought I'd see to you myself, as I've already dealt with the mistress.'

'Good heavens!' Abbie found it impossible to conceal her astonishment. 'Do you mean to tell me God-mama is up and about already?'

'Yes, and downstairs at this very moment breaking her fast. She's as excited as a child, Miss Abbie. You're a wonderful influence on her, to be sure! Since your arrival here, more often than not, she's been up betimes to join you at breakfast. And I've noticed she's more inclined to walk these days rather than order the carriage. And today she's off on a picnic, of all things!'

'Yes, I was surprised myself when she accepted Mr Cavanagh's invitation,' Abbie admitted, recalling the speculative gleam in her godmother's eyes when she had learned of the proposed outing. 'She accepted the invitation to his party too.'

'Well, between you and me, miss,' Felcham said,

depositing the pitcher on the washstand, 'her ladyship has a soft spot for the strong-willed type. And
that Mr Cavanagh doesn't strike me as a gentleman
who'd stand any nonsense—knows what's what, I'd
say.'

'He's certainly nobody's fool,' honesty obliged
Abbie to concede. 'And, of course, he just happened
to be about at a time when Godmama felt in need of
a little masculine support.'

Felcham tutted. 'Don't know why Jenkins
couldn't have sorted the business out himself, instead of coming to the house, troubling her ladyship.
He'd know well enough that the mistress wouldn't
object to him having someone else to help out until
young Jem is up and about again. Though, I have to
say,' she added, collecting the new muslin dress and
burgundy-striped spencer from the wardrobe, and
laying them carefully upon the bed, 'that it's a pity
Josh isn't to stay on permanent. He seems a nice
young fellow to me, polite and hard working. And
with a deal more in his garret than both Jenkins and
Jem put together.'

'I shall reserve judgement until I've witnessed him
tooling Godmama's carriage. Which, I believe, Jenkins has instructed him to do today,' Abbie responded, as she began her toilette.

Felcham, being vastly more experienced, was a
good deal quicker than the young housemaid who
usually helped Abbie to dress and to arrange her hair.

Consequently Abbie was soon making her way downstairs to discover her godmother happily perusing the newspaper.

'Good morning, dear. Looking forward to the outing today, I trust?' Lady Penrose said by way of a greeting, and without raising her eyes from the printed sheets. 'Great heavens! The man must have grown weak in the attic even to contemplate taking such a strumpet to wife!'

Having by now grown accustomed to Lady Penrose's quaint habit of thinking aloud, this sudden pronouncement in no way astonished Abbie. 'Perusing the gossip columns again, Godmama?' she quizzed her. 'What juicy morsel has captured your interest, I wonder?'

'Lord Soames, the crass fool, has only gone and proposed marriage to the Dowager Lady Fitzpatrick! She's half his age, and the most flighty baggage who ever drew breath.'

The knife Abbie had been holding fell from her fingers to land on her plate with a clatter, instantly drawing her godmother's attention. 'Why, my dear! You're looking very pale. Are you not feeling quite the thing?'

Regaining her composure with an effort, Abbie managed a semblance of a smile. 'I'm fine.' She saw at once that her godmother wasn't convinced, and couldn't say that she was altogether surprised. She was no expert at dissembling, and there had been pre-

cious little conviction in her voice. 'It just so happens
that I'm acquainted with the lady,' she thought it prudent to admit. 'The Fitzpatricks are Grandpapa's
nearest neighbours.'

'Why, yes, of course! I'd forgotten the family estate is in Leicestershire. You would know then that
the late Sir Oswald Fitzpatrick hasn't been in his
grave much above a year.' Lady Penrose shrugged.
'Still, it's in keeping with the rest of her behaviour,
I suppose. Ever a flighty piece, she was. Married Oswald Fitzpatrick, a man old enough to be her father,
when she'd just turned eighteen. His son by his first
marriage was only a year younger than Sophia.
Clearly she favours husbands in their dotage and lovers much younger than herself. She's had scores of
admirers over the years, if what the gossips say is
true.'

Abbie had only listened with half an ear, as images
she would far rather forget began flashing before her
mind's eye, memories of a day that had effectively
changed her life: that ill-fated afternoon visit to the
summerhouse, followed a mere few hours later by the
unexpected proposal of marriage. Even now, after all
this time, she well remembered the humiliation and
disgust she'd felt when Bart had proposed, or, rather,
wholly supported his godfather's desire for a union
between them; recalled too the way she had recoiled
when he had come forward, hands outstretched to
grasp hers; how she had fled the room in a state of

near hysteria, declaring that Bartholomew Cavanagh was the very last man in the world she would marry.

'Oh, do forgive me, my dear.' Lady Penrose's abject apology blessedly drew Abbie back to the present. 'I shouldn't be discussing such matters in front of you,' she added, mistakenly supposing that embarrassment had been responsible for the bright crimson hue now suffusing Abbie's high cheekbones.

'I'm not a child, ma'am,' Abbie reminded her, having managed to suppress the surge of anger that never failed to assail her whenever she thought back to that fateful day. 'Believe me, Sophia Fitzpatrick's reputation comes as no great surprise to me.'

'Given that she used to be a close neighbour of yours, I don't suppose it does,' Lady Penrose commented. 'She's had a score of lovers over the years. Not that I blame the gentlemen, of course. There's no denying Sophia Fitzpatrick is attractively packaged. It would be a rare man indeed who would refuse what was so enticingly offered.'

Abbie failed to suppress a contemptuous smile. 'There is much in what you say, ma'am. That is perhaps why it is best that I never marry. I should never willingly accept a husband in my arms who reeked of another female's perfume.'

Lady Penrose moved her hand in a dismissive gesture. 'I do not think you need harbour any fears, my dear. I wouldn't attempt to suggest there are not those who actively seek their pleasures elsewhere after they are married. But many gentlemen remain faithful to their wives, and sensibly sow their wild oats before contemplating matrimony.'

Although Lady Penrose noticed a sudden, arresting look in violet eyes, she received no response, and decided to change the subject by revealing that Giles Fergusson and his mother were to join the picnic. 'So it looks as if it will turn out to be a very jolly outing, don't you agree?' she said, but was no more successful in attaining a response than she had been moments before.

Having experienced grave doubts about spending several hours in the company of her grandfather's godson, it was perhaps unfortunate that Abbie had been forcibly reminded about one of Bart's less commendable traits, the result of which had ultimately resulted in the unfortunate estrangement between her and her grandfather. Although she suspected Bart himself was completely ignorant of this fact, this in no way lessened his guilt in her eyes.

Hence, it was as much as she could do to acknowledge his greeting when, later that morning, she emerged from the house in time to see him draw a smart racing curricle to a halt directly in front Lady Penrose's waiting carriage.

She experienced no similar reluctance in greeting his companion, who jumped nimbly to the ground, looking every inch the excited child.

'Giles will be along with his mother directly,' Kitty informed Lady Penrose, who had emerged from the house in Abbie's wake. 'It was very good of you to offer her a seat in your carriage, ma'am. Mrs Whitham was persuaded to come, and Mama is travelling with her. I don't think we could have brought anyone else along, with all the food baskets in our carriage.'

'It's likely to be cramped in ours too,' Abbie wasn't slow to reveal. 'Godmama saw fit to bring along extra provisions.'

'A picnic isn't a picnic without champagne, and a variety of delicacies to tempt every palate' Lady Penrose announced. 'I'm certain we'll all manage to squeeze in somehow.'

Kitty cast Abbie a surprised glance. 'But surely you don't propose to make the journey in a closed carriage? Giles is driving himself in his phaeton. It will be much more fun travelling in the open air.'

Abbie was much struck by the suggestion, until Kitty added that she would bear Mr Fergusson company and Abbie was welcome to take her seat in her brother's carriage.'

'Perhaps Miss Graham would prefer not to spend time in my sole company,' a smooth voice from above drawled, and Abbie raised her head to see Bart regarding her steadily, his gaze both accusing and challenging at one and the same time.

'I don't know why you might suppose that, Bart,'

his sister responded, before Abbie had a chance even to begin to think of some reason to refuse. 'You've known each other for years and years. Quite ancient bosom friends, in fact!'

In face of this piece of gross impertinence, it was as much as Abbie could do to gape in astonished outrage as Kitty hurried away to greet Giles and his mother, who had just arrived.

'How old does she imagine I am?' she managed at last to utter in a falsetto voice, the result of which had Bart striving to preserve his countenance.

Even though the poke of the charming bonnet hid most of her face from view, he had little difficulty in imagining those lovely features slightly marred by an indignant frown. 'May I apologise on my thoughtless sister's behalf. What I believe she meant to convey was that she understood us to be friends of long standing. But are we, do you think?'

This drew her attention, as he had suspected it might, and it was no difficult matter for him to detect the wariness in her expression, before he glanced over his shoulder in time to see Kitty taking Mrs Fergusson's place in Giles's phaeton. 'It would appear my sister has had her way. Not that I'm unduly surprised. Giles is far too indulgent.'

He turned his attention back to the vision, strikingly attired today in white and burgundy, now standing alone on the pavement. 'Are you willing to be equally generous in spirit and indulge me by bearing me company on the journey?'

There was only a moment's hesitation on her part before she proceeded to clamber up beside him, though she blatantly ignored the hand he held out to assist her.

Smiling to himself, Bart glanced once again over his shoulder to ensure that Mrs Fergusson was safely ensconced in Lady Penrose's carriage, and then gave his horses the office to start, leading the small cavalcade along the street.

'Tell me, Miss Graham,' he remarked, after they had driven along in silence for perhaps five minutes, 'is it out of consideration for me that you sit in stony silence? If so, your thoughtfulness is entirely misplaced. I'm capable of handling a team and conversing at one and the same time.' He waited in vain for a response before adding, 'Or is it that you are attempting to formulate some uncontroversial answer to the question I asked a short time ago?'

If the truth were known, Abbie had been endeavouring, without much success, to ignore the contact with the muscular thigh that persisted in brushing against her skirts. She didn't even attempt, however, to ignore his last comment. 'I'm sorry, Mr Cavanagh, I cannot recall your asking any question.'

As she appeared genuinely puzzled, Bart was inclined to believe her. 'Then allow me to refresh your memory—I asked if you considered us friends?'

Although she didn't precisely stiffen, he sensed the withdrawal behind that barrier she had mentally erected between them since the very start of their renewed acquaintance in Bath. She was definitely wary of him, though why this should be was a complete mystery. As far as he could recall, he had never done or said anything to her detriment. In his youth he might not actively have sought her company, something that he found himself wishing to do increasingly of late. But was that reason enough for these frequent displays of aloofness on her part? Why was she so determined to keep him at a distance? Was it the male sex in general she mistrusted, or just him?

'I cannot in truth say that I've ever considered you a friend, sir, merely an acquaintance.'

The answer came as no real surprise, and served to increase his determination to break down that barrier she seemed intent on maintaining between them. 'But would you not agree that we have been acquainted long enough to dispense with the unnecessary formality you have chosen to adopt since our first meeting? After all, Abbie, you don't appear to object to my sister, who has known you a short time only, making free with your given name.'

He had successfully spiked her guns over this matter. Moreover, he knew by the slight smile suddenly appearing round that delectable mouth that she had already silently acknowledged this fact. True, it might be just a small victory, but at least it was a step in the right direction. All the same, he sensed that it was too soon yet to attempt building a closer relationship between them; sensed too that he must attempt to win her trust, otherwise that almost tangible barrier would undoubtedly widen and she would become increasingly remote.

Consequently he sensibly refrained from plying her with questions, even though he was determined to discover just what it was about him that she didn't quite like, didn't quite trust. Instead, he maintained a flow of conversation, touching upon nothing that might cause her unease.

By the time they had met up with the Whithams and his stepmother at the prearranged location, and were heading out of the city, his companion was at least voicing an opinion on the various topics he raised. More rewarding still was that, by the time they arrived at the place where the picnic was to be held, Bart truly believed he was making excellent progress towards a better understanding between them, for although he wouldn't have dreamt of suggesting that they were upon friendly terms precisely, at least much of her former reserve had thawed.

Nevertheless, once the rugs had been spread on the ground, and the food baskets had been removed from the carriages, she didn't hesitate to seek the company of her godmother.

'Well, I must say this is most pleasant,' Lady Penrose remarked, contentedly sipping her way through a second glass of champagne, while nibbling a savoury tart. 'I'm so very glad I came—a perfect day. One cannot help but feel at peace with oneself in such a glorious setting.'

Abbie, gazing across the grassy-covered slope, strewn with an array of wildflowers, to where the sparkling water of a gurgling stream meandered its way across the landscape, might have wholeheartedly agreed, had she not felt slightly uneasy about the real purpose behind the outing.

Turning her head slightly, she transferred her gaze to the object of her thoughts, sitting among the younger members of the party.

From the moment they had been introduced, Abbie had been favourably impressed by the Whitham family, and with Miss Caroline Whitham in particular, whom she considered a charming young woman, if a trifle shy. But whether she would make a suitable wife for Bartholomew Cavanagh was highly doubtful. In her opinion they would make a mismatched pair. Bart was the strong, domineering type who, she clearly remembered from years before, liked his own way in all things. Poor little Caroline would soon find her spirits crushed.

But it had nothing whatsoever to do with her, Abbie reminded herself. If Bart chose to marry the kind of female who would always defer to him, and Caroline was happy to play the submissive little wife, then so be it! Such an arrangement certainly wouldn't do for her. She had spent the last six years attempting to live companionably with an overbearing, irascible gentleman. Bart and her grandfather had been fashioned in the same mould. The best way of dealing with such persons was to stand up to them, she decided before her gaze slid to another member of the group.

Although she would have been the first to admit she didn't know Giles Fergusson at all well, she had been favourably impressed thus far. He could by no stretch of the imagination be considered remotely handsome, but an abundance of charm and a natural, unaffected manner, which couldn't fail to please, more than compensated for his lack of good looks. Moreover, he was the type of person who, she very much suspected, would always consider the feelings of others before his own, an admirable trait that she could never recall Bart revealing years before.

Unconsciously her gaze had shifted, and she realised with a start that a pair of almond-shaped eyes, amusement clearly visible in their dark brown depths, were staring directly back at her from beneath raised brows.

For one embarrassing moment, as he suddenly rose to his feet, she thought he was about to come over and demand to know why he had become the object of her interest. Mercifully he did not; he merely strolled up the grassy bank in the direction of the carriages, and went directly to his own light travelling carriage, extracting a small barrel from inside, and what appeared to be four pewter tankards. With the exception of Josh, who appeared more interested in examining Bart's fine bays, the various grooms were soon gathered about him, gratefully sampling the ale.

'How very thoughtful of Mr Cavanagh!' Lady Penrose announced, after following the direction of Abbie's gaze. 'Not many would be so considerate to their employees as to ensure that they too enjoyed the day.'

'No, they would not,' honesty obliged Abbie to concede. She was forced silently to acknowledge too that she might not have been totally accurate in her assessment of Bart's character. Just because she had never witnessed any acts of thoughtfulness on his part years ago did not necessarily mean he was devoid of the finer feelings. The truth of the matter was she well remembered the boy; she had yet to know the man.

Kitty caused a diversion when she suddenly jumped to her feet, and suggested a game of battledore and shuttlecock. The younger Whithams were eager to challenge her and her brother, and soon the game was underway.

While watching the energetic game, Abbie was content to sit with her godmother until Lady Penrose, at last succumbing to the warmth of the day, and the effects of the champagne, began happily dozing.

Picking up her sketch pad, which she had had the

forethought to bring with her, and a spare rug, Abbie repositioned herself several yards away, and began to scan the picturesque setting beyond the babbling stream. The outing had turned out to be far more enjoyable than she could have imagined, and she intended to capture on paper just one view that would always remind her of her first venture into the Somerset countryside.

'May I join you, Miss Graham? Mrs Whittham and my mother too are now happily lying in the arms of Morpheus.'

'Of course, Mr Fergusson.' She watched him lower himself awkwardly. 'I have yet to hear you complain, but I believe the injury you sustained at Waterloo continues to cause discomfort.'

He didn't attempt to deny it. 'Compared with many, I came through relatively unscathed. But, yes, Miss Graham, I still suffer, some days more than others. After the battle I was patched up pretty well. At least I didn't lose my leg, but the army surgeon failed to notice the piece of shattered bone embedded in my knee. I had it successfully removed earlier this year by a top London surgeon, who assured me that eventually I would be able to walk again without the aid of a stick. Although,' he added, smiling, 'it will be a while yet before I'm prepared to indulge in anything so energetic as that.'

She followed the direction of his gaze, her eyes automatically focusing on the tallest member of the quartet. 'Your friend Mr Cavanagh appears to have been one of the more fortunate ones who came through the conflict without suffering severe injury.'

'As you probably know, he was obliged to leave the army in '14, when his father died, and so wasn't at Waterloo. But you are wrong, Miss Graham. Bart sustained several injuries during the Peninsular Campaign. A French cavalryman wielding a sabre nearly cost him an arm, when he went to the aid of a wounded senior officer. His bravery earned him his Majority. And deservedly so!'

Evidently he thought much of his friend, and Abbie didn't suppose for a moment that Giles Fergusson's respect was easily won. 'I recall years ago that Bart never betrayed any nerves on the hunting field. It surprised me somewhat when he didn't choose a cavalry regiment when he decided to join the army. There's no denying he's a fine horseman.'

Giles's smile was crooked. 'His decision to become an infantryman surprised a good many people, Miss Graham, myself included,' he freely admitted. 'The truth of the matter is, I suspect, though you will never persuade him to admit as much, that Bart didn't go out to the Peninsula to exhibit his prowess in the saddle, but to fight for his country.'

For the second time in the space of half an hour Abbie was forced silently to acknowledge that she didn't know Bartholomew Cavanagh, the man. Once again she found her gaze automatically lingering in his direction, until she realised that Giles's grey eyes were regarding her keenly, and swiftly returned her thoughts to the present. 'Now, of course, you both must find life vastly different—quite tame, in fact, from what you endured during these past years.'

'Well, mine certainly is. I have few responsibilities, at least at the present time. It will be a different matter when I inherit my uncle's property. Bart, on the other hand, now manages a place far larger than the one I'm destined to own one day.' There was a suspicion of a boyish grin about his mouth as he added, 'And I think he finds his sister something of a handful on occasions.'

'There's naught amiss with Kitty,' Abbie said, coming to the girl's defence without a second thought. 'She's young and full of life, that is all. She'll calm down in a year or two.'

'Precisely what I've told him myself, Miss Graham, and I should know, having had vastly more experience of younger sisters.'

Abbie watched as he transferred his attention to the four taking part in the game, and noticed his gaze growing increasingly tender as he continued to study one player in particular, clad in a pretty primrose-coloured gown. She pursed her lips together in a silent whistle when something she had never considered before sprang into her mind. Interesting, she mused. Yes, most interesting.

She was denied the opportunity to ponder long on

her startling discovery, for the game ended and Kitty came across, happily taking Giles's place when he moved away to talk to Bart.

'Exhausted, Kitty?' Abbie enquired, as the girl lay down on the rug beside her.

'Yes. But very well pleased. We won.' She appeared smugly satisfied. 'I like to win.'

Stretching out her hand, Abbie reached for the sketch pad and box of pencils, and began to draw the animated little face, swiftly capturing the mischievous glint in sparkling brown eyes, and the playful smile pulling at the perfect bow of Kitty's mouth. 'No, don't move!' she ordered, when her subject made to sit up straight. 'You say you like to win, Kitty,' she added, quickly capturing the outline of the soft, feminine jaw, 'but I think you should be prepared to lose on occasions. I might be wrong, but I suspect you're doomed to disappointment if you suppose your brother might propose marriage to Miss Whitham.'

Abbie wasn't certain what had prompted her to say what she had. Yet, all at once she knew it was true. She had noticed Bart talking with Caroline earlier. Obviously he liked the girl, but his eyes had lacked that certain look that Abbie had glimpsed in Giles Fergusson's when he had been gazing at the subject of her sketch only minutes before.

'Oh, but he admires her,' Kitty argued, her expression suddenly guarded. 'He's always saying how charmingly she behaves.'

'That's possibly quite true. Whether or not he admires her enough to propose marriage is an entirely different matter, however,' Abbie pointed out. 'Furthermore, do you think they're suited? Your brother, as you know, has something of a strong, autocratic streak in his nature. What is more, he isn't afraid to speak his mind. Miss Whitham, I rather fancy, is the type of female who would quickly wilt beneath too many harshly spoken words.'

Kitty appeared to consider this for all of ten seconds, before suddenly jumping to her feet. 'Oh, were you still sketching me? I'm sorry, Abbie, but I cannot sit still for long. Besides, it looks as if they're ready for another game. You can take my place. I'll bear Giles company for a while, and watch.'

Having been given little choice in the matter, Abbie abandoned her drawing for the time being, and followed Kitty across the grass. Stephen Whitham suggested a change of partners, an idea that seemed to appeal to everyone except Bart, who frowned slightly when Caroline shyly joined him.

As Caroline quickly proved to be the weakest player by far, Abbie thought she understood the reason behind Bart's slightly disgruntled look. She and her partner very quickly took a commanding lead, the game ending with Abbie gently tapping the shuttlecock just over the rope, a deft little shot that had Bart flying through the air in an attempt to retrieve it, and ending flat on his face on the ground.

Abbie dissolved into chuckles, laughing so much she ended with a painful stitch in her side, and was forced to take refuge on her rug once again.

'You little baggage!' Bart muttered, dropping down beside her, and ineffectually attempting to remove the grass stains from his tight-fitting breeches.

She knew at once he wasn't really angry, and was forced silently to own that he was a good sport. 'Never in my wildest dreams did I ever imagine I would see you scrabbling about in the dirt!' she announced, still unable to control her mirth. 'I wouldn't have missed it for the world!'

For answer he cast her a look of exasperation, before lying flat on his back and closing his eyes. Abbie automatically reached for her sketch pad again, and for a while continued to work on the drawing she had begun of Kitty, until the girl herself called across, asking if she would care to join the others in a walk down to the stream. Abbie declined, preferring to continue with her sketching. She half expected Bart might go, but when he didn't offer to move, and continued to lie beside her, head resting in his hands, she couldn't resist doing a wicked caricature of him, emphasising the long, hawklike nose, the cleft in his strong chin, and mischievously adding a mulish look to the powerful jaw.

The scratching of pencil on paper eventually induced him to open one eye in time to see her adding the finishing touches to beetle-black brows.

His own instantly drew together as he eased himself up into a sitting position, the better to view the finished result. 'So that's how you see me, is it?' The scowl grew more pronounced. 'Not a very flattering likeness, if I may say so. I resemble nothing so much as a buffle-headed pugilist whose nose has been broken on several occasions.'

'It's a caricature, Bart,' she assured him, holding the pad at arm's length. 'Even if I do say so myself, I've definitely captured that stubborn set to the chin.'

Reaching out, he easily wrested the pad from her, and in so doing flicked over the page to the likeness of his sister. The expression of exasperation faded from his features and was replaced by one of dawning wonder. 'This is really good, Abbie… Excellent, in fact! You've captured exactly that look she has when she's plotting mischief.'

The thought evidently disturbed him, for he frowned again. 'What were you discussing at the time?'

She had never made a convincing liar, so didn't attempt to deceive him. 'Er—you, I believe.'

'Were you, by gad!' He was on his feet in an instant. 'I'd best make sure she's behaving herself.' He began to stride away in the direction of the stream, but turned back to add, 'I'd like to see that again when you've finished it.'

It had sounded as if he genuinely meant it, and Abbie was immensely touched by the compliment, possibly because it was so unexpected. Unfortunately she was unable to do very much more to the sketch, because the older members of the party, suitably refreshed after their repose, were keen to return to their homes.

Abbie helped to pack up the picnic baskets and fold up the rugs, so that by the time the others had returned from their walk, most everything had been carried back to the coaches.

'Can I not persuade you to bear me company on the return journey?' Bart asked, when Abbie was on the point of joining Mrs Fergusson and Lady Penrose in the carriage.

She took a moment only to consider. 'Why, yes! I rather think I'd prefer to travel in the open air.'

He bent a look of mock reproach upon her, as he helped her into his curricle. 'You certainly know how to deflate a man's ego, Miss Abigail Graham. I was hoping that it was the prospect of enjoying my company that might persuade you.'

Yet again she knew well enough that he was teasing her, and was about to respond in kind, when she realised she had left her sketch pad behind. She wasted no time in hurrying back to collect it, but even so the other carriages had moved off and were already out of sight by the time she had resumed her seat beside him.

'Don't concern yourself. It won't take many minutes to catch them up,' Bart assured her, easily interpreting the slightly troubled look. 'There's no need for you to feel the least nervous in my company, Abbie. I do not make a practice of seducing innocent damsels.'

For a moment he felt certain she had stiffened, but then decided he must have been mistaken, and that she had merely settled herself more comfortably, after placing the sketch pad beneath the seat.

In the event that she was genuinely uneasy at being left alone with him, he wasted no time in setting off to catch up with the rest of the party, and they were soon bowling along at a sensible pace, conducive to the conditions of the road.

Consequently, when it happened it took them both completely unawares. One moment they had both been enjoying the splendid views in the unfamiliar landscape; the next the carriage had come to rest in a ditch at a very peculiar angle. Hat askew, Abbie found herself sitting in a hedge, while Bart endeavoured to soothe his frightened horses.

He swiftly had them quietened sufficiently enough to turn his attention to the main object of his concern. 'Are you all right, girl?'

Anxiety had added a harsh edge to his voice, but thankfully she appeared not to notice, as she accepted his helping hand to rise, and his aid in freeing her skirts from the clutches of a particularly troublesome bramble.

'Yes, I think so…ouch!'

Before she knew what was happening, Bart had lifted her quite off her feet and, ignoring her demands to be put down at once, carried her out of the ditch, eventually settling her on the grassy bank, where he proceeded to examine the injured limb.

'Really, there's no need to fuss so,' she assured him, endeavouring to brush down her skirts, and receiving a smart slap on the wrist for her pains.

Once he had satisfied himself that the injury was nothing more serious than a slight sprain, he raised himself off his haunches, while suggesting she straighten her bonnet as it made her appear a simpleton. The resulting fulminating glance he received was sufficient to assure him that she was none the worse for her ordeal.

'With any luck, one of the others will return to see where we've got to before too long. In the meantime you sit there and rest that ankle, while I unhitch the team.'

Although he received a further speaking glance, brimful of resentment this time, she made no demur and Bart was able to turn his attention to his horses once more. He had just accomplished the task when what he had predicted happily turned out to be true. A phaeton came bowling round the bend towards them. More satisfying still was the sight of his own trusty head groom bearing his friend company.

'Hackman, here, thought you must be in a spot of bother when you didn't catch up,' Giles disclosed, as he brought his team to a halt. He spotted the wheel lying in the road almost at once. 'Not to worry. I noticed a smithy in the village where we waited for you. It's no more than a mile or so up the road. I'll go back and get help.'

'Be good enough to take Miss Graham with you, Giles, and see her safely restored to Lady Penrose,' Bart said, helping Abbie, who thankfully appeared hardly to limp at all, up into the carriage. 'There's no need for the others to linger, but I'd be grateful if you remained, just in case the wheel can't be repaired today.'

'Are you sure you'll be all right?'

The anxious note in Abbie's voice was not lost on him. Nor could he mistake the reluctance to leave in her expression. Bart didn't doubt for a moment that she would have stayed if she thought she could have been of some help. Being an immensely sensible young woman, however, she had accepted she would have been more of a hindrance than anything else.

'Don't concern yourself, Miss Graham. Any man who can face a French column ain't going to trouble himself over a simple accident like this,' Giles assured her, before giving his horses the office to start.

'Aye. But was it?' Hackman muttered, having overheard the remark. 'I checked the carriages myself this morning, just as I always do afore we set out on a journey. And it were as sound as a nut, I'd stake my life on it.'

Bart regarded the older man in silence. Hackman had worked for the Cavanagh family all his life. There was no man he would trust more, and he would certainly never doubt his word.

'Lynch pins can work loose, Hackman.'

'Aye, sir, that they can, 'specially if they're helped.'

'Are you suggesting someone deliberately tampered with the curricle?'

'Ain't saying that at all, sir,' Hackman eventually answered, after he'd satisfied himself that neither of the bays had suffered harm. 'All I'm saying is I checked the carriage over myself, as I wouldn't trust that useless, rat-eyed Dodd to do it.'

Bart smiled wryly at this. 'You really don't care for your new underling, do you, Hack?'

'Ain't a case o' liking or not, sir,' Hackman answered, running a hand through his grizzled hair. 'I knows well enough you gave the lad a job on account of thinking so well of his father. But Amos Dodd was a mite different from his son… If the work-shy young slug is his son, which I doubt. He's got no love for beasts, sir, not like that young groom o' Lady Penrose's. Now, he's another sort altogether! Knows a thing or two about 'orses, he do. Had a good long look at this turnout o' yourn back along at the picnic.'

Eyes narrowing, Bart glanced at his wheel lying in the road. 'Did he now?' he murmured.

Chapter Five

The following day Kitty and her mother paid a visit to Lady Penrose's house. Abbie felt a complete and utter fraud receiving them in the drawing-room, reclining on the *chaise longue*, rug over her knees, like some feeble invalid, when she had sustained nothing more serious than a twisted ankle. And a slight twist at that! Yet she couldn't deny that after years of being ordered by a brusque, ex-army Colonel not to make a fuss over a few aches and pains whenever she'd taken a tumble from a horse, Lady Penrose's cosseting had come as a pleasant change, though Abbie had drawn the line at having the doctor summoned over such a trifling injury.

During the visit Kitty disclosed that her brother had returned to the house well before dinner the previous evening, and that he had surprisingly left the city again earlier that morning, after receiving an unexpected express from their nearest neighbour, Lord

Warren. What might have induced him to return to their country home in Gloucestershire, she had no way of knowing. Bart, seemingly, had chosen not to confide in her, though the twinkle in her dark eyes strongly suggested that she fully intended to enjoy this period of unexpected freedom from her sibling's strict control.

Initially, Abbie too felt a sense of relief, knowing that she could go about the city without running the risk of crossing Bart's path. Yet, surprisingly enough, the period of contentment was short-lived. Before too many days had passed, instead of experiencing pleasure each time she saw Kitty and her mother without their tall escort, she suffered an acute stab of disappointment, with the result that it became increasingly difficult to dismiss the possibility that she just might have grown to like the immoral, infuriating creature. She did not, however, permit this disturbing likelihood to detract from the pleasure she continued to attain from residing in Bath, especially not when she took to riding about the city with her blond-haired groom every day.

At first Josh would always remain deferentially those few feet behind, speaking only when spoken to, and then only briefly. This state of affairs thankfully didn't last for long. Within a few days they would ride along companionably together, unless Abbie happened to speak to an acquaintance, in which case the groom would keep a discreet distance.

Josh's cheerful outlook and unfailing politeness was in stark contrast to the demeanour of the dour, middle-aged groom whose company she had been obliged to suffer whenever she had wished to explore the countryside surrounding her grandfather's home. The more she was with Josh the more she grew to like him, and inevitably the concern she felt over his future increased too.

But what could she do? She wasn't in a position to offer him a permanent situation; and it was hardly fair to expect her godmother to go to the expense of paying for the services of a groom she didn't require, once her own servant was fully recovered. Nor was it right to expect Josh to remain with her for the next few weeks if the opportunity arose for him to acquire a situation elsewhere. On the other hand, though, she very much resented the mere thought of having to lose his services before it became absolutely necessary.

After a deal of soul searching, she decided to broach the subject, when they rode out together on the day before the Cavanaghs' party was due to take place, by suggesting to Josh that it might be wise to begin looking about for another post.

His expression was all at once a mixture of surprise and disappointment. 'But why, Miss Abbie? Have I displeased you in some way? If I've been too forward, like, I'm reet sorry. Thing is, I've never been a lady's personal groom afore.'

If anything, this frank admission made Abbie feel more disgruntled than before. She doubted she would ever find another groom to suit her half so well. 'No, Josh, that isn't it at all,' she assured him. 'If I could keep you, I would. Sadly I cannot. As you know, at present I'm a guest in my godmother's home, but my future is uncertain. There's just the faintest chance I might return to live with my grandfather. But he wouldn't require your services. He has staff enough. And Lady Penrose will not retain you once her own stable-lad has recovered.'

'Aye, I know that, miss.' He gave her one of those boyish grins that made him appear much younger than his twenty-two years. 'You were straight with me from the first. But until Jem's up and about you'll want me, won't you?'

'Not if, in the meantime, you can find yourself something more permanent. What I'm trying to say, Josh, is if you do happen to hear of something you think will suit, don't stay with me through some misguided sense of loyalty, and let the opportunity slip through your fingers.'

A thought occurred to her. 'Perhaps I can be of help too. I've become acquainted with several persons here in Bath, I shall ask on your behalf if they know of anyone requiring the services of a groom. Mr Fergusson and Mr Whitham have lived in the city for some time and their acquaintance is large. There's also the possibility that Mr Cavanagh might be able to help.'

'Now, there's a man, if you don't mind my saying, miss, that I wouldn't mind working for. Knows a thing or two about horses, does Mr Cavanagh. I had a look at those bays of his, and I can tell you I ain't seen no finer.'

Honesty forced Abbie to agree with this. 'Yes, he's certainly a good judge of horseflesh.'

'I remember both the bays and his carriage horses whinnying when he came over to give us grooms a drop of ale at the picnic. My old pa use to say that if creatures takes to a man, then there ain't a deal wrong wi' 'im.'

Abbie couldn't help smiling at this quaint philosophy, even though she would never dream of adopting it herself. And with good reason where Mr Bartholomew Cavanagh was concerned! His treatment of horses might well be above reproach. He might well possess the ability to win their trust and affection with little difficulty. Even so, members of her own sex would do well to remain a deal more cautious in their dealings with him.

She chose, however, to keep these reflections to herself, especially as they had just arrived back at Upper Camden Place. After handing the reins to Josh, she went directly into the house, and was at once informed that her presence was required in the upstairs drawing-room as soon as possible.

Delaying only for the time it took to change out of
her habit, Abbie went along to the drawing-room to
discover none other than the gentleman who had in-
filtrated her thoughts far too frequently of late seated
beside his sister on the sofa. He rose at once to his
feet, one dark brow arching at the smile of delighted
surprise Abbie singularly failed to suppress.

'What a relief it is to see you, sir,' she announced,
striving to ignore the tingling sensation in her fingers
as he held them briefly in his own. 'Kitty was only
saying yesterday, when we met in the Pump Room,
that she very much feared you wouldn't return in
time for the party.'

The arch of one masculine brow grew more pronounced. 'Hoped I wouldn't be returning in time, I
think you mean.'

'No, such thing, sir!' Lady Penrose countered, noting with satisfaction the becoming colour in her goddaughter's cheeks as Abbie joined her on the sofa.
She smiled to herself before revealing, 'I do believe
you have been greatly missed.'

Masculine eyes strayed momentarily to the young
woman seated beside her. 'Indeed, ma'am? By
whom?'

'By me, for one,' Lady Penrose admitted. 'I was denied the opportunity to thank you for arranging that
delightful picnic. It was most enjoyable!'

'A pity it didn't pass without mishap.' He turned his

attention fully on Abbie. 'I trust you're suffering no lasting effects from the injury.'

'No, sir, I am not,' she assured him. 'Far too much was made of a trifling ailment.'

'If that is so, ma'am, then you cannot possibly refuse to stand up with me at the party tomorrow night.'

Abbie didn't miss the triumphant gleam in his dark eyes, clearly betraying his delight at her foolishly walking into his well-baited trap. Aid, however, came from an unexpected quarter.

'But you never dance, Bart,' Kitty reminded him. 'Or rarely so.'

'True,' he acknowledged. 'But I've decided our party will be one of those rare occasions when I exert myself to waltz.'

'In that case, sir,' Abbie announced, not without experiencing a degree of smug satisfaction, 'I'm afraid I must decline. I do not waltz.'

'Why ever not, child?' Lady Penrose appeared genuinely surprised. 'Surely you're not one of those who still disapprove? Why, it has been danced even here in this staid old place for quite some time at private functions!'

'Oh, it isn't that. It's merely that I've never learned how,' Abbie hurriedly explained.

'Oh, well, that is easily remedied,' her godmother returned, rising to her feet as nimbly as any seventeen-year-old girl. 'Providing Mr Cavanagh is willing to remain to offer assistance, that is?'

'I am completely at your disposal, ma'am,' he assured her promptly. Which left Abbie wondering what irritated her more: her godmother's satisfied smirk or the look of unholy amusement on Bart's face for having comprehensively spiked her guns.

Admitting defeat with as much grace as she could muster, she helped clear an area for dancing, while her godmother, seating herself at the fine instrument in the corner of the room, selected various pieces of music, with Kitty's assistance.

The embarrassing moment when she and Bart took up their positions could not be long delayed, and Abbie braced herself for that bodily contact the dance demanded. What she was totally unprepared for was her instant reaction to the gentle masculine clasp on her waist and fingers. What she ought to have felt was revulsion, not a pleasantly warm sensation slowly spreading across every inch of her skin. She risked a glance up at him through her lashes, and then promptly wished she had not, for the slight twitch she detected at one corner of his mouth was proof positive that he was very aware that she wasn't as indifferent to his touch as she was striving so hard to appear.

As dancing had always been one of her favourite pastimes, Abbie swiftly managed to channel her thoughts once the tuition was underway. She mastered the steps with relative ease, though she was forced grudgingly to admit that, for someone who by his own admission danced only rarely, Bart was an extremely adroit teacher. Consequently within a relatively short space of time they were swirling about the room together in complete harmony, as though they had danced together on scores of occasions before.

'That was excellent,' Lady Penrose announced, clapping hands that only moments before had moved expertly over the keys. 'Would you like me to select another tune so that you may practise a little more?'

'Oh, no,' Abbie answered promptly, thereby denying Bart the opportunity to decide. She became aware that he still retained a hold on her hand and withdrew it. 'There's nothing further Mr Cavanagh can teach me.'

'Certainly not about the waltz,' he murmured for her ears only, and then chuckled as she took a few hurried steps away from his side. 'I believe we must be on our way too, Lady Penrose,' he added, turning his attention to her. 'Otherwise Kitty's fond mama will imagine the worse—that I've strangled her daughter in a fit of rage.'

'You have my deepest sympathy, Kitty,' Abbie told her, even though the girl appeared to have taken her brother's teasing in good part. 'If Bart is a prime example of how brothers treat their sisters, I'm heartily glad that I was never cursed with one.'

'Husbands can be as bad,' Bart warned, 'if not a good deal worse.'

'In that case, I'm equally glad I have decided to eschew matrimony.'

Abbie had meant it in jest, but it was clear from the reactions of her listeners that not one of them was amused by the untruthful declaration. Lady Penrose seemed shocked, Kitty ridiculously disappointed and Bart looked nothing so much as downright angry. Then his expression changed, and he merely appeared thoughtful while he helped return the pieces of furniture to their former positions.

'Well, that was a most—er—fortuitous visit, wouldn't you agree?' Lady Penrose remarked, the instant her guests had taken their leave.

'Unexpected, certainly,' Abbie answered, before she turned to find her godmother regarding her keenly.

'Were you surprised by it? How strange!' Smiling at some private thought, Lady Penrose sought refuge in her favourite chair. 'I, on the other hand, would have been amazed had Mr Cavanagh not made a visit soon after his return.'

The following evening, as she accompanied her godmother into the house the Cavanaghs had rented for the duration of their stay in Bath, Abbie experienced a degree of trepidation at the ordeal ahead of her. And an ordeal was precisely how she had come to view that promised dance with Bart!

Although she had seen nothing of him since his visit the day before, he had continued to intrude into her thoughts, if anything, more than ever. More disturbing still was the uneasy suspicion that Bart himself now strongly suspected that she wasn't as impervious to his masculinity as she might wish to appear.

The warmth that immediately sprang into his eyes the instant he caught sight of her approaching strongly suggested that he wasn't indifferent to her either. She couldn't recall him ever looking at her in quite that way years ago, and found herself experiencing a flutter of mingled excitement and satisfaction knowing that he found her very much to his taste. Yet at the same time she felt that it would be foolish beyond measure not to keep a firm control on her emotions where he was concerned. She must never forget that his dealings with her sex could not withstand too close a scrutiny. Yet, surely it could do no harm for them to become...just friends?

'Has something occurred to disturb you?' he asked softly, the instant Lady Penrose had turned from him to exchange a few words with his stepmother.

Abbie looked up to discover warmth still lingering in eyes that had become searching. He had evidently detected something in her expression to betray her slightly troubled state. If anything, it was increasing with every passing second he retained that gentle hold on her fingers.

'If I appear a little concerned, it is only the prospect of having to perform the waltz in public for the very first time,' she said, with a flash of inspiration.

'There's no need for you to feel anxious' he assured her, his gaze straying from her face to take in every detail of her appearance.

She knew she was looking her best in a new gown of spider gauze over pale blue silk, with matching accessories. Her hair had been beautifully arranged by Felcham in a mass of bouncy curls into which the skilled abigail had fastened a tiny spray of artificial forget-me-knots. To complete the ensemble Lady Penrose had kindly loaned her a pair of sapphire earrings and a sapphire pendant, the end of which almost reached the cleft between her breasts. His gaze was like a soft caress as it lingered there momentarily, bringing an extra glow to her cheeks which she could only hope he would attribute to the contents of a rouge pot.

'I'm no monster, Abbie, no matter what you might think,' he added, when at last he raised his eyes again to hers. 'I'll not roar at you if you should happen to step on my toes. In point of fact, I would consider it a small price to pay to have you partner me in a waltz.'

For some obscure reason Abbie was finding it a little difficult to breathe, and nigh on impossible to control her suddenly erratic pulse. It wasn't as if she was unused to receiving admiring glances from the opposite sex. Somehow, though, this man's regard was both unnerving and exciting at one and the same time.

'Why, sir, I do believe you are attempting to flirt with me,' she responded archly, in a valiant attempt to conceal her increasing confusion.

'I never flirt,' he countered, his voice little more than a husky whisper. 'And if I were ever tempted to try, be assured it would never be with you.'

Fortunately the arrival of more guests made it possible for Abbie to move on, but not before she had glimpsed the twitch at one corner of that far too attractive masculine mouth, which suggested strongly that he had detected her faint sigh of relief.

No sooner had she and her godmother found themselves two vacant chairs by the wall, than Kitty surprisingly joined them, looking bright-eyed and excited, and very pretty in a new gown of ivory silk.

'Bart said I might leave him and Mama to greet the rest of the guests, as the dancing will commence soon.' She gazed in a vague way about the crowded salon, decorated for the occasion with vases of flowers and several graceful potted palms. 'I must say Mama is very clever at organising this sort of thing. Even Bart admits that she's an extremely good hostess. And he isn't one to pass too many compliments, especially where our sex is concerned.'

Kitty then seemed to recall to whom she was speaking, and favoured Abbie with a furtive glance. 'I don't think he holds females in general in very high esteem, except the odd one or two. And you, definitely, number among those exceptions.'

Unfortunately Abbie, who at that moment had just happened to take an unwary sip from a glass of fruit punch, pressed upon her by a passing footman, dissolved into a fit of coughing.

'What rot!' she exclaimed when she was able.

'Oh, no, my dear,' Lady Penrose surprisingly countered. 'Kitty is absolutely right. Assuredly, her brother does admire you. From the first, I suspected that he was one of those gentlemen who have little patience for megrims and vapours. And for all that you are intensely feminine, you have inherited your grandfather's strength of character, as well as, I strongly suspect, a certain degree of his stubbornness too.'

Abbie wasn't certain whether this was intended as a compliment or not. From odd things Lady Penrose had let fall in recent days, she had gained the distinct impression that her godmother didn't hold Colonel Augustus Graham in the highest esteem. Which wasn't unduly surprising in the circumstances, she decided. She and her godmother had formed a close bond in a short time. It was perhaps understandable, therefore, that, given the Colonel's behaviour towards his granddaughter in recent years, Lady Penrose would have taken him in dislike.

Rudely brought out of these reflections by an unexpected squeal of delight from Kitty, Abbie turned her head to see what had induced her young friend to become so animated. Two young gentlemen had just entered the room, both dressed in the height of fashion: one startlingly so in primrose and lavender; the other more soberly in a black long-tailed coat and buff-coloured breeches. By the dour expression on Bart's face she considered it reasonable to suppose that he wasn't altogether pleased by the appearance of one, or perhaps both, of them.

'Why, it is! It's Cousin Cedric!' Kitty exclaimed, clapping her hands delightedly. 'I wonder what could have brought him to Bath? Do excuse me, I must go across and welcome him.'

'Now, which of them is Cousin Cedric, do you suppose?' Abbie murmured, having found it impossible from that distance to detect any similarity between the cousins. 'Is it the dandy who seems unable to move his head because of the ridiculous height of his shirt points, or the faultlessly groomed gentleman beside him?'

'I suspect it is the overdressed young sprig,' Lady Penrose answered bluntly, thereby betraying her opinion of his attire. 'The Adonis, unless I much mistake the matter, is none other than Charles Asquith, the Dowager Lady Marchbank's nephew.

From what Hermione Marchbank tells me, her young ne'er-do-well of a nephew is frequently in dun territory. He only ever pays her a visit when payment of debts becomes pressing. The foolish creature usually bails him out eventually.'

Abbie could not help but smile at this frank disclosure. There wasn't a great deal Lady Penrose didn't know about the comings and goings that went on in Bath. Evidently she didn't hold the Dowager Lady Marchbank's nephew in the highest esteem. There was no denying, however, that he was very pleasing on the eye. Definitely the most handsome man in the room, Abbie swiftly decided, as Kitty steered the gentlemen towards them and she was able to study his perfectly chiselled features and the expert arrangement of guinea-gold curls more closely.

'So what brings you to Bath, Ceddie?' Kitty asked, after making the introductions, and surprisingly focusing her attention on her cousin, rather than his striking companion.

'My friend Charles, here, fancied a change of air, so I agreed to bear him company while he paid a visit to his favourite aunt.'

'Definitely in dun territory. The young care-for-nobody!' Lady Penrose muttered.

Fortunately no one except Abbie appeared to have heard, as Cedric Cavanagh had at that moment been admitting to having been a trifle bored with life in the capital of late. 'The same old round of balls and parties, and Mama parading every new debutante before me,' he went on, stifling a yawn. 'Really, it was becoming quite tedious.'

'Oh, I know I shan't find it dull at all,' Kitty responded. 'I'm looking forward to my come-out next year. I would have liked a Season this spring, but Bart flatly refused to entertain the notion. Said I needed practice in how to comport myself in polite society.'

Cedric drew an ornate snuffbox from the pocket of his nip-waisted jacket, and with a very affected air extracted a pinch of its contents. 'Loath though I am to agree with my big cousin on anything, I do believe he has a point there. Hoydenish behaviour ain't tolerated in town, especially among the debs. And I shouldn't like for you to disgrace the proud name we bear.'

Abbie, exerting masterly self-control, managed not to laugh. She didn't quite know what amused her more—her godmother's expression of comical dismay, or the darkling glance Kitty bestowed upon her dandified cousin.

She raised her own eyes in time to catch a touch of merriment flitting over handsome features, and decided that, although Lady Penrose might well have his measure, and he was possibly little more than the pleasure-seeking wastrel she considered him to be, Mr Asquith at least possessed a sense of humour.

'Ceddie, old boy, I'm surprised at your lack of *savoir-faire*,' he said. 'I shall certainly have to think seriously about excluding you from my circle of friends if you show signs of becoming boorish.'

Cedric's look of outrage was almost Abbie's undoing. 'I shall take leave to inform you, Charles, that my conduct and manners are held to be above reproach. Which is more than can be said for certain other members of my family. If Kitty's behaviour on occasions gives rise for concern in certain quarters, I for one could appreciate why, and never blame her. Her brother could hardly be considered a suitable role model. A positive brute!' A shudder ran through his wiry frame. 'I cannot tell you how it grieves me to think that Bart will one day become head of our family.'

'Taking my name in vain again, Cedric?'

Bart, having approached them completely unnoticed, had a wry grin on his face too. Abbie could only assume that, far from being annoyed, he had attained a deal of unholy amusement from overhearing his dandified cousin's strictures on his behaviour. Amazingly enough, Cedric made no attempt to deny it. More surprising still, he returned his much taller cousin's sardonic look without so much as a blink.

'I have never made any secret of the fact that I think you totally unsuitable for the role, Bartholomew,' he reiterated, withdrawing his gaze momentarily to remove an infinitesimal speck from his sleeve.

'No, not unsuitable,' Bart corrected, 'merely lacking the ambition to inherit the title. Unlike you, who covet nothing more. And in case it has escaped your memory,' he went on, not offering Cedric the opportunity to deny the accusation. 'our esteemed uncle took a second wife not two years ago.'

Cedric's lip curled, but it was a poor imitation of the look of contempt on Bart's face. 'It is unlikely at his advanced age that the marriage will ever prove fruitful.'

'He isn't so decrepit as you evidently imagine, Cedric, and is still able to perform all the duties of a husband,' Bart assured him. 'In his most recent letter I was delighted to read that he's very much looking forward to the autumn, when he expects Lady Cavanagh to present him with a pledge of her affection.'

Although Cedric appeared genuinely stunned by this intelligence for a moment, he recovered quickly enough, and shrugged. 'There's no guarantee it will be a boy.'

'True,' Bart agreed, looking suddenly grave. 'But I for one do hope it is the son he desires, even though, in my eyes, the child could never replace our cousin Philip, whose demise was a great shock to us all.'

It occurred to Abbie then how ignorant she was about the Cavanagh lineage. She experienced a surprising desire to learn more. Unfortunately an awkward silence followed Bart's admission, and she was not unduly sorry to hear the musicians hired for the

evening strike up a chord to announce the commencement of dancing, and willingly acquiesced to
Mr Asquith's request to partner him.

'Have you just recently removed to Bath, Miss
Graham?' he enquired, as they took up their positions
in the set.

'I have been here almost a month, sir, as a guest of
my godmother, Lady Penrose.'

'You are not related to the Cavanaghs in any way?'

All at once Abbie became aware that several young
ladies were darting envious looks in her direction.
And little wonder! Charles Asquith was without a
doubt the most striking gentleman present.

'No, sir, although I have been acquainted with
Bartholomew Cavanagh for very many years. He is
my grandfather's godson.'

'Ah, I see! So it is unlikely that you are able to satisfy my curiosity by divulging why there is a suggestion of antipathy between Cedric and Miss
Cavanagh's brother?'

As they parted in the dance Abbie took the opportunity to glance at Bart, who was still bearing Lady
Penrose company, and was surprised to discover him
staring fixedly at the area set aside for dancing, his
brow darkly forbidding. She had noticed Kitty and
her cousin join the set, but she couldn't imagine either Cedric or Kitty was responsible for the highly
disgruntled expression. In point of fact, had she been

a fanciful female, she might have supposed that she was the object of his evident displeasure.

'No, sir, I'm afraid I cannot.' She risked a quick look over her shoulder, and smiled to herself. Cedric Cavanagh was as light on his feet as his partner. 'I cannot imagine the cousins have very much in common, though, can you?'

As the steps of the dance separated them again at that moment, he was unable to comment, and when they came together again, he voiced the hope that their arriving without invitations hadn't been responsible for giving rise to any ill feeling.

'I should think that highly unlikely, sir,' she assured him. 'I would be the first to admit that I do not know Bartholomew Cavanagh very well, but I wouldn't imagine he'd concern himself over such trifles.'

It was a timely reminder, and the instant the dance came to an end Abbie, surprisingly experiencing no reluctance whatsoever to relinquish her position as possibly the most envied female in the room to another, returned to Lady Penrose's side.

As luck would have it, Bart had by that time moved back across to the door to welcome some late arrivals, so she didn't hesitate to discover if her knowledgeable godmother could satisfy her curiosity over Bart's genealogy.

'Oh, yes. I met all three Cavanagh brothers during my very first Season. Henry, the eldest and holder of the title, was by that time married, and so too was George, to Bart's mother. The youngest brother Frederick married his wife during my second Season, if my memory serves me correctly. Each of the brothers produced one son. Again, if my memory serves me correctly, Lord Cavanagh's sole offspring, Philip, died three, or maybe four years ago in a riding accident. All very sad. As you heard Bart mention, his uncle remarried—a widow, I believe, and quite some years his junior.'

Abbie gazed across the room at their host, who at that moment happened to be conversing with a lively young matron who put Abbie forcibly in mind of a certain other female of Bart's acquaintance. She felt an uncomfortable feeling in the pit of her stomach, as though her insides were attempting to twist into knots.

'I gained the distinct impression that Bart was fond of his late cousin,' she said, in an attempt to force her thoughts in a new direction, 'though not so enamoured of Cedric. It's clear that Cedric is resentful of Bart's superior position in the family. I suspect, though, there's more to his obvious resentment than just that.'

Kitty, rejoining them a moment later, a little breathless after the dance, was able to enlighten them. 'Oh, Cedric has never quite forgiven Bart for laying about him with a riding crop,' she disclosed, grinning wickedly. 'Not that I blame Bart for doing so,' she added in her brother's defence, when her interested listeners looked appalled. 'Bart may have his faults, but no one could ever accuse him of not caring for his horses. He made it clear to Cedric that he wasn't to ride the prized hunter, but Cedric took no notice. I'm afraid when Bart discovered what Cedric had done he lost his temper.'

Kitty turned her head to find her brother heading in their direction once again. 'I must say, though, Bart's a lot more tolerant now than he used to be, but he can still become out of all reason cross on occasions.'

'Still talking about me behind my back, minx?' he quizzed her, as she twinkled wickedly up at him, and for the first time Abbie appreciated that there was a genuine bond of affection between brother and sister. He didn't wait for a response, but turned to her, reminding her that she had promised him the next dance.

'Having just discovered how brutal you can be on occasions, I'm not at all sure that I'm being altogether sensible in placing myself in your hands, even on a dance floor,' she teased, as they took up their positions in readiness for the first waltz.

He favoured her with one of his lopsided grins, which she was beginning to find most endearing, before glancing briefly across at his sister, still happily conversing with Lady Penrose. 'What has the little minx been saying to my detriment?'

'Merely that you beat your younger and much smaller cousin black and blue,' she enlightened him, surprisingly finding it no difficult matter to concentrate on the dance and converse at the same time.

'Damnable little idiot!' he growled, then smiled as perfectly arched brows rose. 'Cedric, not Kitty. No doubt you've learned why he earned my disapprobation? At best, he is merely a competent horseman. He might easily have broken his fool neck. Or worse, he might have injured my prized hunter! The trouble with Cedric is that he's too damned fond of getting his own way.'

Abbie smiled up at him in some amusement. 'That, if I may say so, seems to be a family failing.'

His bark of appreciative laughter induced several heads to turn in their direction. 'Yes, you're right. I could never tolerate being thwarted, still can't for that matter. On that occasion my father surprisingly took Cedric's part; said that I shouldn't have set about someone half my size. The black looks I kept getting from my aunt and uncle for having had the temerity to take a riding crop to their precious son didn't make the situation any easier. So I took off and inflicted myself upon you and your grandfather, something that I was inclined to do when things hadn't been going my way at home.'

Smiling ruefully, Bart shook his head, as if ashamed of past actions. 'That, as it happens, turned out to be the last time I stayed with your grandfather.

If my memory serves me correctly, it was shortly after I paid that impromptu visit to your home that I decided to offer my services to King and Country and set sail for the Peninsula.'

Lowering her eyes, Abbie stared fixedly at the diamond pin nestling in the folds of his neckcloth. As though she would ever forget that particular visit! His life had changed afterwards and so too had hers. But in her case definitely not for the better!

As their dance drew to an end Abbie somehow managed to suppress the surge of resentment the memory of that particular visit never failed to evoke. She might well have succeeded in putting it from her mind entirely had it not been for the regard Bart subsequently received from the female guest who had paid him marked attention a little earlier.

Mrs Drusilla Herbert was not a total stranger. Since her arrival in the city, Abbie had seen her, accompanied by her dull, morose husband, at two or three fashionable parties. Up until that evening, however, she had never appreciated just how strong the resemblance was between Mrs Herbert and the late Sir Oswald Fitzpatrick's vivacious widow: the blonde hair, the blue eyes, the same full, pouting lips and curvaceous figures. Yes, they were strikingly similar. And possibly shared similar tastes in their lovers too, she thought bitterly, as she watched Bart look down, with a twisted half-smile, when full breasts were pressed invitingly against the sleeve of his jacket.

Resolutely turning her head away, she swallowed hard, but was given insufficient time to ponder on the disturbing possibility that the acrid taste which had suddenly invaded her mouth might have stemmed from something other than that old, lingering resentment, for a young gentleman was standing before her, requesting her hand for the next set of dances.

Thereafter a succession of different partners kept her on the dance floor for much of the time. Sadly, though, not one succeeded in holding her attention, at least not for long. Nor did any one of them manage to revive that tiny flutter of mingled excitement and pleasure that she had experienced when swirling round the room with Bart. This, and the fact that the host himself made no attempt to ask her to dance a second time, did little to combat her increasing ill humour. Consequently she didn't hesitate to slip quietly out of the French windows on to the terrace at the first available opportunity to be alone with her thoughts.

Considering that it was growing increasingly warm in the salon, Abbie was surprised to discover no one else taking advantage of the fresh air, and didn't hesitate to avail herself of one of the wicker chairs, tucked away in the shadowy corner of the terrace.

For a few moments she attempted to pierce the gloom and study the garden. She could just make out the outlines of various shrubs, and neatly clipped hedges, but could detect no movement, certainly nothing to suggest that she wasn't alone. Everyone else, it seemed, was happy to remain inside, enjoying the dancing and companionship of the other guests. So why wasn't she deriving much pleasure from the evening? It was so unlike her to fall prey to moods of despondency. Yet there was no denying she had, and deep down she knew precisely why.

She shook her head, wondering at herself, but refused not to face up to the truth. Unbelievably she had not attempted to prevent herself from becoming increasingly fond of a man whose manners and morals left much to be desired. She had believed…hoped, maybe, that he had changed, that he wasn't the same self-seeking, callous creature he had been in his youth. A forlorn hope, she thought bitterly. Any man who could flirt openly with another man's wife, in full view of the cream of Bath society and, worse still, with the lady's husband standing not six feet away, was past praying for! A debauched lecher he was and would remain. And it was utter madness to suppose he might ever change!

'Ah, Miss Graham,' a smooth voice drawled. 'So this is where you've been hiding yourself.'

Startled, Abbie swivelled round in her chair to discover Mr Asquith standing not three feet away. Evidently he had been looking for her, but the knowledge that her company was sought by the best-looking man at the party did little to revive her spirits, a fact that her smile quite failed to disguise.

'Has something occurred to upset you, ma'am?' he

asked, sounding a trifle aggrieved, as though accustomed to a more fulsome response from the objects of his attention. 'Would you prefer to be alone?'

'Not at all, sir,' she answered promptly, if not entirely truthfully. 'I merely wished for a breath of air, and became lost in thought.'

Perfectly moulded lips lifted into the most attractive masculine smile Abbie had ever seen, and yet surprisingly it did not even give rise to the slightest fluttering in her breast. 'Won't you sit down, Mr Asquith, and bear me company for a short while? Or did you seek me out at someone else's behest...my godmother's, perhaps?'

'It was entirely on my own account,' he admitted, seating himself, like the perfect gentleman, at a discreet distance so that not so much as a fold of her skirt brushed against his immaculate attire. 'I was hoping that you would favour me with the final dance before supper and allow me to bear you company during the meal afterwards, or are you promised to another?'

She could so easily have been, as numerous gentlemen had requested her company. But, foolish creature that she was, she had resolutely left that space on her dance card clear in the hope that Bart would wish to write his name there. What a bird-witted female she was to be sure!

Again she was forced to do battle with a surge of pique tinged with jealousy, before she could utter with any degree of conviction, 'I should be delighted to have you bear me company, sir, even though I know it shall make me the object of envy where most of the young ladies present are concerned.'

'Your appearance alone, my dear Miss Graham, would ensure that,' he murmured, before raising her hand and brushing his lips lightly across her fingers.

Although unaccustomed to such displays of gallantry, Abbie didn't feel in the least embarrassed, or even shocked. In fact, if anything, the handsome Mr Asquith's behaviour rather amused her. All the same, she thought it might be prudent not to offer further encouragement to a person who was undoubtedly a master of the art of dalliance, and was on the point of uttering a mild reproof, when she caught a sudden movement. A moment later their host was emerging from the shadows, and in no good humour, if his deeply furrowed brow was any indication.

'I trust I do not intrude.' Bart's voice, though level, distinctly betrayed the fact that he didn't care a whit if he were *de trop*. He moved slowly towards them, as stealthily as a predatory beast, his gaze no less menacing either as it remained fixed on Abbie's companion. 'I believe you are engaged for the next dance, Asquith. Do not let us detain you.'

For several unnerving seconds Abbie feared a confrontation. Mr Asquith's admiring expression had faded and he appeared as grim now as their host. 'May I escort you back to the protection of Lady Penrose's side, Miss Graham?'

As Abbie had no intention of becoming involved in an unpleasant scene, she made up her mind to intervene the instant she observed the muscles along Bart's jaw tighten still further.

'There's no need for you to trouble yourself on my account, sir,' she answered, rising swiftly and placing herself between the two. 'Be assured I shall return in time for our dance.'

'What the devil do you mean by skulking out here with a man of his stamp, my girl?' Bart demanded, the instant Mr Asquith had sauntered back into the salon.

Abbie swung round to face him, the guard on her own temper weakening with every passing second. 'Where I go, and with whom, is entirely my own concern, Mr Cavanagh. Kindly remember that I am not Kitty, and therefore not obliged to defer to your dictates.'

Lips curled back into a smile that bore little resemblance to Mr Asquith's charming offering of minutes before. 'Had you been my sister, Miss Graham, you wouldn't be standing there with that expression of childish defiance, but would have been locked in your room by now, nursing a sore rear.'

By the glint in his eyes, Abbie was under no illusion that he would have derived immense satisfaction from carrying out the humiliating punishment, and was obliged to use every ounce of self-control she possessed not to take a hasty step away, and to school

her features into an expression of unalloyed contempt.

'No doubt such brutish, cavalier antics appeal to
the type of female on whom you choose to dispense
your favours, Mr Cavanagh. Let me assure you that
I, on the other hand, am completely unimpressed by
such behaviour.'

'Is that so?' he husked. 'Perhaps a display of raw
masculinity is precisely what would do you the most
good, Miss Abigail Graham.'

The threatening gleam in his dark eyes intensified,
a distinct warning that she foolishly chose not to
heed. The next moment her arms were imprisoned
behind her back, both wrists held captive in long fingers, while her chin was thrust up and held fast in his
other shapely hand. There was a flash of white teeth
as his gaze, softening noticeably, focused on her
mouth.

Swiftly accepting that it would be futile to struggle, Abbie refused to demean herself by engaging in
an undignified attempt to free herself. His face drew
ever nearer, his intent clear, and she braced herself
for the penance he was determined to exact.

For several moments shock held her rigid. Instead
of the hard, punishing kiss that she had anticipated,
his lips were gently arousing, skilfully so, exerting
only sufficient pressure to force hers to part and
mould themselves perfectly to his. Instead of revulsion, she experienced a wave of tactile pleasure, a

wealth of unfamiliar sensations that left no part of her immune. Never would she have believed it possible to experience such delight in the mere contact with a masculine mouth. Now she wanted him to free her, but not to run away. Quite the opposite, in fact. She longed to place her arms around him, to experience more than just contact with his lips.

As though he were able to read her every thought, he released her chin to run his hand down the length of her neck to the fine bones of her shoulder, his feather-light touch arousing a further surge of foreign sensations that had rapidly achieved precedence over conscious thought. In those few blissful seconds, when his lips followed the burning trail of his exploring fingers, and she heard the guttural sound rising in his throat, she was aware only of him and of the desire for this man alone to satisfy a rapidly increasing need.

Then, unbidden, that humiliating memory returned with a vengeance—Bart's ardent fondling of naked breasts before fumbling beneath skirts. She could even hear those same low moans of pleasure as clearly now as she had six years before, when his all but naked companion had slid her fingers beneath his breeches' flap.

Never would Abbie have believed it possible for shame to replace pleasure or disgust crush desire so comprehensively, or so swiftly, had she not experienced it for herself in those next wholly degrading moments when reality returned with a vengeance.

Easily escaping from the hold on her wrists, she stepped back, a surge of anger filling the void that disbelief had left in its wake. Before she realised what she was doing, her arm had swung in a wide arc, and her hand had made contact with a resounding slap. She saw the resulting flash of anger in Bart's dark eyes, but didn't remain long enough to witness the mingled bewilderment and sadness that swiftly replaced it.

Chapter Six

Gazing longingly at the lace-edged box on the table beside her chair, Lady Penrose once again summoned up sufficient will-power not to remove the lid and sample the delicacies within. To be sure, her god-daughter was proving a marvellous influence, she decided. Undeniably she was more inclined to take exercise, and she consumed far fewer glasses of her favourite tipple, port, these days. Furthermore, she had substantially reduced her daily intake of choco-lates and sweet biscuits, with the result that she had lost several pounds in weight and was feeling a good deal better for having done so. She just wished that Abbie was deriving as much benefit and pleasure from her sojourn in Bath, as she herself was in hav-ing her as a guest under her roof.

Oh, undoubtedly the girl was contented enough, Lady Penrose reflected, resting her head against the chair and gazing absently up at the plaster-work ceiling. But contentment was far short of real happiness, and dear Abbie deserved her share of that after what she had endured in recent years.

She felt again that stab of resentment towards Colonel Graham for treating his granddaughter so unfairly, for not taking account of her wishes and feelings. Yet, at the same time, she was forced to own that she was increasingly taking the view that the Colonel's godson might indeed be the very one for Abbie. When the girl set aside her understandable resentment, she and Bartholomew Cavanagh rubbed along together very well. They were remarkably well suited and had, she very much suspected, more in common than either of them as yet realised. One thing was certain, though—Abbie, not in the least in awe of him, wasn't afraid to speak her mind, and Mr Cavanagh, Lady Penrose suspected also, rather admired her for it.

Unless she was very much mistaken too, their relationship had taken something of a turn for the worse the previous evening. Smiling to herself, she recalled the thunderous expression on Bart's face when he had spotted that handsome ne'er-do-well, Mr Asquith, heading for the terrace shortly after Abbie herself had taken refuge out there. She hadn't been best pleased herself, for although she was sure that her goddaughter was far too discerning to be beguiled by a handsome face, she had no intention of allowing her to become the butt of malicious gossip,

and had been about to go after her, when Mr Cavanagh had gone striding past, heading purposefully
towards the French window.

Just what had taken place outside after Mr
Asquith's return to the salon was anybody's guess.
All the same, their host's subdued mood, and her
goddaughter's forced gaiety during the latter part of
the evening, gave one every reason to suppose that
something untoward had occurred.

A light tap on the door, quickly followed by the
housekeeper's entrance, succeeded in restoring Lady
Penrose to the present. Vaguely she recalled having
heard the sound of the door-knocker, and assumed
this must be the reason for the interruption.

'It's a gentleman wishing to see Miss Abbie, my
lady. I wasn't certain whether she'd returned. Shall I
inform Mr Cavanagh that she's not at home?'

'No, don't do that,' Lady Penrose countered, her
mind working rapidly. 'Just show him up... Oh, and,
Mrs Bates,' she added, checking the housekeeper's
immediate departure, 'when my goddaughter returns,
just ask her to come straight up here to me. There'll
be no need to mention we have a visitor.'

Lady Penrose had every faith in her loyal housekeeper to carry out the instructions to the letter.
Which was perhaps just as well, she decided, for it
was highly likely that Abbie would avoid the drawing-room like the plague if she discovered the visitor's identity. And that would serve no useful purpose

at all, especially if Mr Cavanagh's sole reason for calling was to attempt a reconciliation.

In point of fact, Lady Penrose's assumption was only partially correct. Bart had indeed decided to call with the intention of offering the olive branch, but he was also determined to discover just what it was that made Abbie decidedly wary of him.

He had spent the majority of the night staring blindly at the canopy above his bed, turning over in his mind certain aspects of their association since her arrival in Bath, most especially the events of the previous evening.

Once he had mastered his annoyance at being dealt a sound box round the ear, he had swiftly acknowledged he'd been at fault in presuming to criticise her behaviour, even though he still felt it incumbent upon him to stand her protector in the absence of her grandfather.

As far as the rest of the interlude on the terrace was concerned, he couldn't find it within himself to regret what had taken place between them. What had come as a complete surprise, however, was the feeling of overwhelming tenderness that had gripped him from the moment his lips had touched hers. Abbie too had not been indifferent to their very first embrace either; of that he felt sure. The rigidity had soon left her and her response had been sweetly satisfying. He had loosened his grasp and she had made not the least attempt to break free. Then, perversely, she had chosen to do so.

So what had happened? What had wrought the drastic change? He shook his head, at a loss to understand. If he had attempted to take his lovemaking a good deal further, he could have understood her becoming fearful or resentful. Only it was neither fear nor resentment her expression had betrayed the instant before she had lashed out at him like an avenging virago. No, it had been revulsion and anger.

The housekeeper's reappearance had the same effect upon him as it had had on her employer minutes before. Half-expecting to be denied an interview, he was pleasantly surprised when he was invited to follow her up the stairs. All the same, he couldn't quite disguise his disappointment when he entered the drawing-room to find only Lady Penrose present.

Her eyes twinkled at him, a clear indication that she hadn't failed to note his fleeting look of dissatisfaction. 'Mr Cavanagh, how nice to see you!' she greeted him, holding out her hand for him to bow over, which he did with remarkable grace for a man of his size. 'I do realise that it was my goddaughter whom you really wished to see. However, I am more than happy to entertain you until her return.'

After nodding dismissal to the housekeeper, she turned her attention to Bart again. 'Do help yourself to a glass of something, Mr Cavanagh. There's a particularly fine burgundy in the tall decanter over there.

And whilst you're about it, perhaps you'd be good enough to pour me a glass of port. I've been remarkably good of late, but it cannot hurt to suffer a little relapse now and then. After all, life would be very dull if we didn't indulge in the odd little vice, would it not?'

His fleeting disappointment having now receded completely, Bart couldn't help smiling to himself as he went over to the decanters. He rather liked Lady Penrose, a roguish matron of great charm and character, who was certainly not lacking intelligence.

'You do not appear surprised by my visit, my lady,' he remarked, after handing her her chosen tipple, and seating himself in the chair directly opposite.

'After your—er—disagreement with my god-daughter, I would have been astonished had you not called, Mr Cavanagh,' she divulged, startling him somewhat.

He regarded her in silence for a moment over the rim of his glass. 'Should I infer from that that Abbie has confided in you, ma'am?'

'You would be grossly mistaken if you did. Should you be fortunate enough to come to know my god-daughter a good deal better, sir, you will discover that she's one to keep her own counsel for the most part. And she's most definitely no talebearer.'

Lady Penrose took a moment to sample the contents of her glass and to place the delicate vessel down on the table beside her elbow, before favouring him with her full attention once more.

'I, for one, am very grateful to you for your prompt intervention last night. Abbie understandably would not have been, however.'

He was suddenly alert. 'Then she does resent me for some reason, ma'am…I suspected as much.'

Lady Penrose didn't attempt to deny it. 'I have no intention, Mr Cavanagh, of betraying my goddaughter's trust by repeating what she has told me. But I shall tell you this much… It is my belief that she has not confided in me fully, and that the real cause of her resentment…mistrust, call it what you will…lies very much deeper. If your intentions towards her are in any way serious, then you'd do well to discover what has fuelled those negative feelings towards you.'

Although intensely puzzled, Bart couldn't suppress a rueful smile. Up until that moment he hadn't fully appreciated the depths of his own feelings. Lady Penrose, on the other hand, had been a deal more discerning, and had suspected that his regard had been rapidly increasing. All the same, given that for some reason Abbie did bear him a grudge, was it possible to win her love?

Lady Penrose caught his attention by raising a warning finger. Then he heard it too: the light tread along the passageway. The next moment the door opened, and Abbie swept into the room, her sweet smile disappearing the instant her eyes fell upon him.

Lady Penrose was not slow to fill the breach. 'Ah, so there you are, dear! Did you manage to get everything you wanted in the library?'

With only the merest inclination of her head to acknowledge Bart's presence, Abbie came forward to give the two books she was carrying to her godmother. 'All except the Jane Austen novel you wanted, which I've been assured will be available for collection tomorrow.'

Bart, who had risen to his feet, was about to request a few minutes' private conversation with Abbie, when he detected the hint of warning in Lady Penrose's expression. Evidently she didn't think he would meet with much success, and undoubtedly she was right. Abbie, who had not attempted to sit down, looked as if she had every intention of departing at the first opportunity.

Lady Penrose managed to forestall her by saying, 'I'm so very pleased Mr Cavanagh has called, aren't you, dear? It grants us the opportunity to thank him for a most pleasurable evening.'

It was as much as Bart could do to maintain his countenance when a pair of violet eyes pierced him with a dagger look. There was a suspicion of a twitch, too, about Lady Penrose's mouth, before she added, 'And we are destined to enjoy many more pleasurable evenings during the forthcoming weeks. I received several invitations this morning.' She paused to look about her in a vague manner. 'I must have left the cards in the downstairs parlour. What a scatter-brain I am! Do be a dear and fetch them for me. I really ought to respond to one or two without delay.'

Abbie seemingly needed no further persuasion. She had reached the door before her godmother had finished speaking, and departed without uttering another word.

'Well…?' Lady Penrose smiled roguishly up at Bart. 'What are you waiting for? It will not take her long to discover the invitation cards are not in the parlour.'

Requiring no further prompting, he departed after the swiftest of farewells. As he descended the stairs he saw Abbie entering the room where they had conducted the interview with the groom a couple of weeks before, and didn't hesitate to follow.

She swung round as she detected the click of the door, her eyes hardening as she saw his hand still grasping the handle. 'What are you doing here? Surely even you are not so insensitive as to suppose that I've any desire to converse with you?'

'No, I don't suppose you have. But I've an earnest wish to speak to you. If only to say how very sorry I am for my behaviour yesterday evening.'

Bart could see at a glance that he had taken the wind out of her sails. The implacable look was replaced by one of surprise, before she turned to stare out of the window. Clearly she hadn't expected an apology. Had she thought him incapable of making one, too high in the instep ever to consider himself in the wrong? His objective would be hard indeed to attain if she thought so poorly of him.

'You are not entirely to blame,' she said softly. 'My own behaviour left much to be desired. I should never have lashed out at you that way.'

Truth to tell, at the time he had not been best pleased, but now he could appreciate the amusing aspect of it. Not many men would successfully have broken through his guard. 'You pack a powerful wallop, ma'am. My ear stung for a considerable time afterwards.'

Although a watery chuckle greeted this sally, she looked genuinely repentant as she turned back to face him. 'Even so I shouldn't have done it, not after you had come out to the terrace merely to offer protection.'

Evidently he wasn't the only one to have passed a restless night. The interlude had obviously preyed on her mind also, and she was gracious enough to accept her share of the blame. He could not help but admire too the way she had remained at the party, and not feigned some trifling ailment in order to escape, like a frightened child, as most females of his acquaintance would undoubtedly have done.

'But there was no need for you to put yourself to the trouble,' she added, her tone marginally harsher.

'Lady Penrose had already put me on my guard concerning Mr Asquith. And be assured I'm no green girl to be beguiled by a handsome face. Besides which, it's rumoured that he's on the look out for an heiress, so he's hardly likely to concern himself with me.'

'Don't be ridiculous, girl!' Bart snapped, momentarily forgetting his resolve to keep a tight rein on his temper. Fortunately she didn't seem unduly put out by the reprimand. If anything, she appeared faintly amused by it. Nevertheless he decided it might be wise to try to choose his words with more care from this point in time.

'He could easily have discovered last night that you are closely related to Colonel Augustus Graham. Although your grandfather might not have gone into society too often in recent years, the fact that he's well-heeled is common knowledge.'

The amused glint in blue eyes intensified. 'But what isn't common knowledge, and what I shall not hesitate to make clear if Mr Asquith proves a nuisance by singling me out for particular attention, is that my grandfather has as good as told me that he intends to disinherit me.'

If Abbie had needed further proof that Bart was in complete ignorance of the situation which had existed between her and her grandfather for the past six years, she was being given it now. His expression was a mixture of astonished disbelief and anger.

'The devil he has!' he barked. 'I don't believe a word of it. The Colonel absolutely dotes upon you.' She shrugged, before turning again to stare sightlessly through the window. 'Believe it or not, as you will. It is true, all the same. We have become estranged, Bart. And I cannot foresee that situation changing.'

'But why, Abbie?' He could not have sounded more genuinely puzzled, or troubled by what he was hearing, had he tried. 'What caused this rift between you? You used to be so very close.'

'Yes, we were,' she agreed, after several moments of doing battle with her conscience, debating whether or not to tell him, and finally deciding that he would discover the truth eventually anyway. 'Unfortunately, though, my grandfather could never find it within himself to forgive me for refusing to marry you.'

When no response was forthcoming, Abbie turned to discover him staring fixedly at the carpet, his expression difficult to read, until finally he raised his eyes and she noticed that normally alert gleam shadowed by an emotion bordering on despair.

'So, that's it,' he surprised her by murmuring. 'That's why you bear me a grudge, harbour resentment. Yes, it is reason enough to dislike me.'

She experienced a strong impulse to rush over and place her arms about him, but curbed it. 'I do not dislike you, Bart,' she assured him softly. 'In fact, there have been times in recent weeks when I've liked you very well. But I cannot deny there have been many occasions when I've felt very embittered. As a girl, I resented my grandfather's obvious affection for you. And I very much resented the fact that he never attempted to take account of my feelings when he proposed that ridiculous union between us.'

Brown eyes narrowed at this, but, whatever had crossed Bart's mind, he chose not to share it with her, and merely asked, 'So what do you intend to do now? Remain with your godmother until he comes to his senses and sees reason?'

Her shout of laughter contained precious little mirth. 'For six years I hoped, prayed he would do just that, would come to acknowledge that my feelings should be taken into account. But I refuse to delude myself any longer. His attitude won't change. And I refuse to live in a house where I'm virtually ignored for the most part, and treated with no more respect than a servant. No…' she shook her head '…he'll not change. His arranging my visit to Bath at a time when he knew for certain you'd be here is proof enough of that.'

His sigh was audible. 'So, will you remain with your godmother? She's clearly very fond of you.'

'Yes, she's wonderful company, and I like her very well, only…'

'Only what?' he prompted.

'I do not wish to become her pensioner. Ideally I would like to set up an establishment of my own, be independent. Unfortunately that cannot happen until I'm five-and-twenty, and receive the inheritance left to me by my mother. I suppose I could repay Lady Penrose's kindness by becoming her companion. Only I do not think she would agree to it. And I know she would be hurt, not to say insulted, if I engaged in some genteel occupation in order to pay my way. The only other possibility is for me to take up painting in earnest, and hope to earn a little money that way.'

Without realising it, Abbie had spoken of an idea she had been nurturing for quite some time, and was surprised when she discovered Bart regarding her thoughtfully, disquiet etched in every contour of his face.

'Do not concern yourself on my account, sir. I shall come about. At least I now reside in a house where I'm treated with affection and respect, and am made to feel welcome.'

'Confound the Colonel!' Bart exploded, his temper having got the better of him again. 'How long does he intend to remain away?'

'I'm not altogether sure. It all depends on how long he remained in Yorkshire. He intended to spend some time with his nephew, Sir Montague Graham. Why?' She looked suspiciously across at him. 'You do not propose to pay him an impromptu visit, surely, because of what I've just told you?'

'Damned right, I do!' he answered, not attempting

to moderate his language. 'And he'll find a missive, clearly stating my own views on the matter, awaiting him on his return.'

Abbie was beside him in an instant and, without conscious thought, placed her fingers on his arm. 'Don't, Bart...please don't do anything you might one day come to regret. I've no desire to be the cause of an estrangement between you. The matter is none of your making, none of your concern.'

'On the contrary.' If possible, he looked more doggedly determined than before as he stared at the tapering fingers resting lightly upon his sleeve. 'It is very much my concern. I owe you a debt of gratitude I could never hope to repay,' he astounded her by admitting. 'But for you I would have undoubtedly remained that wholly selfish care-for-nobody I was in my youth. I truly believe your refusing to marry me was the making of me, Abbie. I wouldn't attempt to suggest that I am now without fault, but at least I've learned to consider the feelings of others during these past years. Whilst I benefited, you were made to suffer. To me that's intolerable!'

Although moved by the stance he had adopted, she couldn't help but feel saddened that she might easily be the cause of a rift between two gentlemen who had been as close as father and son.

'If you make contact with my grandfather, Bart, then do so on your own account, for it shall not benefit me,' she said, in a last attempt to sway him. 'Believe me when I tell you that I'm content enough here, and have no desire to return to Foxhunter Grange.'

She half expected him to suggest that she might think differently in time. What she did not anticipate was the blunt question he did ask. 'Why did you refuse to marry me, Abbie?'

Unable to return that penetrating gaze, she lowered her eyes, before taking refuge before the window once more. The silence lengthened between them, forcing her to give him an answer. 'We were too young… We would not have suited.'

'I agree with you, at least in part,' he responded, moving slowly across to the door. 'Your godmother will be wondering what has become of you, so I'd best take my leave.'

A few moments later, Abbie heard the front door close and saw him emerge from the house, appearing lost in thought, in a world of his own. Had he believed her? she wondered. Or had he suspected that she'd not been totally honest? And why hadn't she told him the complete truth? She shook her head, uncertain in her own mind just why she hadn't done so. She only knew that, for some reason, it didn't seem so important any more. What she had witnessed on that certain afternoon six years ago belonged to the past. Yes, Bart had changed. Why had it taken her so long to appreciate the fact?

* * *

The following day saw Abbie in the lending library again. She had accompanied her godmother almost to the Pump Room, when she had remembered the book, and had slipped away before Lady Penrose could voice any protest.

As promised, the librarian had the novel already wrapped, awaiting collection. She placed it into her reticule for safety's sake, and was about to retrace her steps, when her way was blocked by a tall figure looming in the doorway.

'Good heavens, Bart!' She smiled up at him a little tentatively, as he wasn't looking best pleased about something. 'I'm about to visit the Pump Room. I didn't expect to see you here.'

'And I didn't expect to come upon you without so much as a maid to bear you company,' he responded tersely. 'What's Lady Penrose about, permitting you to go about the city unescorted? I'll have a thing or two to say about that when next I see her.'

Inclined to be more amused than anything else by this blatant interference in her affairs, Abbie merely suggested that they remove themselves, as they were beginning to attract attention, not to mention succeeding in preventing others from entering the premises.

'Really, you are the outside of enough on occasions, Bart!' she told him, as they set off in the direction of the Pump Room. 'It will be all over Bath by tomorrow that you're taking an uncommon interest in my welfare. That was none other than Lady Crowe attempting to gain entry to the library. She's reputed to be one of the city's most notorious gossips.'

The broad shoulder that rose in a shrug of indifference was proof enough that he wasn't unduly troubled, even before he said, 'Well, what of it? It's no less than the truth. I do take an interest in you... Damnation!'

Abbie wasn't sure which surprised her more: the admission itself, or the forceful expletive that swiftly followed. The next moment her arm was taken in a vicelike grip and she was thrust none too gently down a side road, and into a doorway.

'What on earth are you about, Bart? This isn't the way I wish to go at all.'

'I know. But it's the only way to avoid meeting that confounded Herbert creature!' he snapped. 'That's the one big fault with residing in this confounded place—you cannot avoid bumping into those people you least wish to see! And I cannot abide clinging females. The wretched woman has been casting out lures since the day we first met.'

Bart watched Abbie's blue eyes widen in astonishment. 'What...? Don't tell me she's a particular friend of yours?'

'No. But I thought she was one of yours,' Abbie admitted, after she had recovered sufficiently from the shock. 'You appeared to be enjoying her company the other evening, at any rate.'

'If you are referring to our party,' he responded, not slow to follow her train of thought, 'then let me remind you that, as host, I was obliged to make all my guests welcome. Had I had my way, she wouldn't have been invited in the first place, only I left all that side of things to Eugenie.'

He risked a glance over his shoulder. Then, deciding it was safe enough to do so, guided Abbie back towards the main street. 'Now what were we talking about…? Ah, yes, I remember! Your welfare.'

Again he received that startled wide-eyed look, and smiled. 'I've been giving a deal of thought to what you were saying yesterday, Abbie,' he admitted, 'and am pleased to say that I'm in a position to help.'

She merely looked suspicious now. 'What do you mean?'

'I should like to commission you to paint a portrait.'

'Whose?'

'Mine.' His shout of laughter induced several passers-by to stare in their direction. 'I cannot imagine why you're regarding me as though I've just sprouted a second head. Why shouldn't I have my portrait painted? I'm a man of means. It's high time I had my likeness done again.'

For several moments all she did was to gape up at him. 'Are you in earnest?'

'Completely,' he assured her. 'It would mean, of course, your returning to Cavanagh Court with us next week. For reasons which I'll not go into, I've been forced to shorten our stay in Bath. Lady Penrose is most welcome to bear you company, if she chooses to do so, but her presence is not essential. My stepmother will be happy enough to act as chaperon in your godmother's stead.'

When she made no attempt to respond, Bart looked down to discover her staring thoughtfully ahead, evidently willing to give the suggestion some consideration. 'Take a few days to think it over, and let me know your decision at the end of the week.'

Chapter Seven

It was midway through the afternoon, when the carriage turned off the road and into a tree-lined driveway, that Abbie caught her first sight of Cavanagh Court. Built in the mellow Cotswold stone, the leaded glass in its mullioned windows glinting in the sunlight, the Tudor manor house was, as she had frequently heard her grandfather remark, the most delightfully situated country residence for a gentleman of means.

As she followed Kitty and her mother into the entrance porch, Abbie had a brief glimpse of well-tended gardens, before her attention was again claimed by the house itself. As though by some intangible force, it drew her into the entrance hall. Its atmosphere, warm and friendly, wrapped itself around her, making her feel instantly at home, though it was left to the master himself, who, travelling in his curricle, had arrived a short time before, to utter the verbal welcome.

'I trust you will be very happy here, Abbie. If there's anything you require, do not hesitate to ask. I insist you treat my home as your own.'

The warmth in his eyes fading marginally, he turned his attention to his stepmother. 'I'll leave you to ensure that our guest is made comfortable, Eugenie. There are one or two matters requiring my immediate attention.'

Abbie was instantly aware of the change in Mrs Cavanagh's demeanour. All at once she seemed a little unsure of herself, nothing like the calm, sensible companion she had proven to be throughout the entire journey from Bath.

'Oh, yes, of course…but… Oh, where to put her? Are you certain you have no preference?'

'Oh, for heaven's sake!' Bart snapped, experiencing the usual stab of annoyance whenever his stepmother fell into one of her twittering moods. Then he noticed a perfect brow marred by a frown of staunch disapproval, and amazingly found his irritation waning. 'Why not put her in the blue bedchamber?' he suggested, before he bethought him of something else, and turned to his aged butler who had remained, awaiting possible instructions. 'Is the back bedchamber in the east wing still empty of furnishings?'

'Indeed, yes, sir. No decision has yet been made on a possible new colour scheme.'

'In that case, Eugenie, I would definitely suggest the blue bedchamber. That adjoining room can then function as a studio for Abbie.' The warmth instantly returned to his eyes as he fixed them on his guest. 'I shall leave you in Eugenie's capable hands, and look forward to seeing you at dinner, if not before.'

'I must say you have a wonderfully soothing effect on my brother, Abbie,' Kitty murmured, having studied his recent behaviour with interest. 'I thought Bart and Mama were reaching a better understanding whilst we were in Bath, but it seems I was wrong, and things really haven't improved at all.'

As it happened, Abbie wasn't left to puzzle over the surprising disclosure for long, for Mrs Cavanagh, after issuing instructions to her maid, took it upon herself to escort Abbie to the allotted bedchamber, a light, airy room, the furnishings of which were in varying shades of blue, and which boasted a commanding view of an ornamental lake.

'Oh, this is charming!' Abbie declared, casting her eyes over the powder-blue bed hangings and matching drapes. 'How lucky you are to be mistress of such a delightful house!'

She took a moment to cast a glance across at the door that she assumed led to the adjoining chamber, which was to function as her studio, before turning in time to catch a wistful expression flitting over her companion's face.

'Yes, you're right. This is a pleasant house,' Eugenie Cavanagh agreed at length. 'Yet, I must confess that, although I've been very happy living here, most especially when Bart's father was alive, I've never felt wholly mistress of Cavanagh Court.'

She gave an uncertain little laugh as she went over to study the view from the window. 'That must seem strange to you, my dear. This has been my home for eighteen years, and still I find it difficult to issue instructions to the servants, most especially to those who were here when Bart's mother was alive. And I've never attempted to effect many changes. I realise now the mistake I made—I shouldn't have striven so hard to become a second mother to Bart, but ought to have concentrated my efforts on becoming mistress of this fine house.'

Abbie wasn't at all sure just why she had been designated the role of confidante. It was true that, from the start of their journey from Bath, Eugenie had suggested that all needless formality should cease between them and they had rubbed along together very well. All the same, it did not automatically follow that they were ever likely to become close friends.

Perhaps, though, Abbie mused, seating herself on the edge of the bed, Eugenie felt some explanation was due for her show of diffidence in the hall a short time earlier. Abbie had to admit she had been surprised by the uncharacteristic behaviour, and more so by Bart's unfortunate reaction to it. She knew well enough that he could be quite abrupt on occasions, and wasn't the sort to suffer fools gladly, but even so, from what she'd witnessed while in Bath, Bart had always treated Eugenie with the utmost respect.

Not quite knowing what to think, she asked, 'Are you trying to suggest that Bart resents your being here?'

'Oh, good heavens, no!' Eugenie didn't hesitate to assure her. 'At least,' she amended, 'I do not believe he does so any longer.'

'Which means that he did at one time,' Abbie prompted, when Eugenie came to sit beside her on the bed.

'Well, that was only to be expected, wasn't it?' Eugenie responded, betraying a wealth of sympathy and understanding. 'Poor Bart was still a boy when his mother died. They were very close, sadly much closer than he and his father were ever destined to become. Within twelve months his father had married me, which I think Bart took as a kind of betrayal, an insult to his mother's memory. Kitty's birth the following year certainly did nothing to improve matters. Relations between Bart and his father went from bad to worse during that period. He was punished regularly for his rudeness to me, which I considered made the situation so very much worse.' A sigh escaped her. 'Ashamed though I am to admit to it, I felt enormous relief whenever he went to stay with you and your grandfather. I'm sure Bart was much happier there.'

Perhaps he was, Abbie mused, smiling to herself. But she most certainly was not! She could recall how much she resented his visits, so it wasn't too difficult to appreciate the resentment Bart harboured towards his stepmother, even if the poor woman had done little to merit it.

'But Bart's attitude did change, surely, as he grew older?'

'Oh, yes,' Eugenie didn't hesitate to confirm. 'He certainly became more tolerant of the situation here. And whenever he came home on leave during his years in the army, he couldn't have been kinder to me, and openly admitted how glad he was that I had married his father and made him happy during his declining years. Yes, he has mellowed in many ways. Yet he remains a strong-willed man who continues to find my displays of hesitancy a little trying.'

The wistful expression once again fluttered over Eugenie's kindly face. 'One of my dearest wishes is to see him happily married. I sincerely hope his future bride possesses the strength of character, which I sadly lacked, to make this house her home, and not maintain it as a shrine to his mother, which I foolishly always did.'

Abbie was at a loss to understand just why Eugenie should wish to share her concerns, unless it was because, misguidedly, Eugenie believed that she

could influence Bart to make changes to his house
and lands so that his future bride wouldn't feel, as
clearly Eugenie had always done, as though she were
living in the shadow of the late Elizabeth Cavanagh.
If so, Eugenie was destined to be disappointed, for
although Abbie felt she and Bart had developed a better understanding and had, against all the odds, become friends during their weeks together in Bath, she
wouldn't dream of attempting to interfere in matters
that were none of her concern. She was here to paint
a portrait, not involve herself in the personal concerns
of the various members of the Cavanagh family.

A housemaid entering with a pitcher of warm water
spared Abbie the necessity of having to formulate
some non-committal response. Eugenie immediately
left her in the capable hands of the young maid who,
after ably assisting her out of her travel-creased garments and into a lightweight muslin gown, was in the
process of repairing the damage the journey had
wreaked on the silky black hair, when the bedchamber door opened yet again, and Kitty came skipping
lightly into the room, appearing none the worse for
having spent several hours in a closed carriage.

'Well, I must say, Kitty, you look wonderfully restored after the journey.'

'Oh, travelling never tires me. Mama said you
would want to rest for an hour or so before dinner.
But I said that was fudge, that you weren't in your
dotage, and would enjoy a tour of the house.'

Once again Abbie found herself at a loss to know quite how to respond. If the truth were known, she would have welcomed an hour's rest, but rather than be considered an ancient, she refrained from admitting as much, and merely instructed her seemingly tireless young friend to lead the way.

The tour commenced with an inspection of the bedchambers in the east wing, all of which, though tastefully furnished, were betraying varying signs of wear. Wallpapers and curtains in several rooms were sadly faded, proof that little had been changed over the years.

They then proceeded to the west wing, and even though she was assured that the master of the house was still ensconced in his library, Abbie was reluctant to view the main apartments. She was certainly not disposed to linger either when she found her eyes returning again and again to the room's most imposing feature: a huge four-poster bed, adorned with claret-coloured hangings. Consequently she had no hesitation in agreeing to Kitty's suggestion of viewing the kitchens next.

'It will give you the opportunity to meet Cook,' Kitty added, as she led the way out of the room and along the passageway. 'Figg is a dear. She'll prepare anything you fancy, providing she thinks the lord and master will enjoy it too. Like all the older servants, she's a soft spot for Bart. His preferences always come first with them.

'We'll use the back stairs. It will be quicker,' she added, opening a door at the end of the passageway, which led on to a stairwell.

'I assume this leads to the servants' quarters,' Abbie said, gazing up at the flight of stone steps.

Kitty nodded. 'And out on to the roof. This part of the house is newer than the rest. Bart's grandfather enlarged the property about forty years ago. You can gain access to a limited part of the roof only, but there's a tremendous view of the surrounding countryside. Would you like to see?'

Abbie needed no second prompting, and as she followed up the stone steps, and out on to the leads, she was forced to acknowledge just how ignorant she still was about Bart's family history. 'You see, Kitty, I assume, from what you were just saying, that the house and lands once belonged to his maternal grandfather?'

'Yes, that's right—the Bellinghams. Bart was named after his grandfather. Mama remembers old Bartholomew Bellingham. She says Bart resembles his grandfather in character.'

Abbie's eyes began to twinkle. 'Ahh, I see! So he was an irascible gentleman too, was he?'

Kitty gurgled appreciatively. 'Oh, Bart isn't so bad. And at least he's fair. There isn't a person working in the house or on the land, as far as I'm aware, who doesn't have the utmost respect for him. He's really looked after this place since Papa died. The love of the land is in his blood, I suppose. He adores it here.'

While Kitty had been speaking, Abbie had been admiring the glorious landscape. Except for the moderate-sized park surrounding the property, the farmland stretched out as far as the eye could see. 'Yes, I can well understand why he does,' she said, drawing her attention away from the tremendous view to gaze absently down at one or two cracks in the masonry near her hand. 'And do you enjoy living here too?'

'Oh, yes,' Kitty didn't hesitate to assure her. 'Mama's youngest sister married a clergyman and still lives in the local parsonage, which was Mama's home before she married, so I've always had my cousins for company. I very much enjoyed our stay in Bath, but I'm not sorry to be back.'

Abbie frowned at this. It had occurred to her during the journey that Kitty had seemed surprisingly cheerful considering her visit to Bath had been shorter than planned. 'I must confess your attitude surprises me a little. After all, returning here has meant that you've been forced, for the time being at least, to relinquish any hope of a speedy engagement between Miss Whitham and your brother.'

All at once Kitty seemed to find it necessary to study the nails on her left hand. 'Oh, well, I can't be too disappointed about that. I was forced to come to the conclusion you were right all along. Caroline

Whitham is pretty enough, but Bart would soon have tired of her. He needs someone who isn't afraid to stand up to him.'

Evidently mother and daughter thought alike where the master of the house was concerned, Abbie mused, smiling to herself as she accompanied Kitty back down the stairs to a stone passageway, by which one gained access to a sizeable courtyard at the back of the house and also the kitchen area.

After being introduced to most members of the household staff, Abbie was taken on a tour of the downstairs rooms, ending with a visit to the library, where they found Bart, seated behind his desk, reading through a pile of correspondence.

He looked up as they entered, and raised his hand, dismissing his sister's apology for disturbing him. 'I've dealt with everything I intend to do today.' He looked directly at Abbie. 'Did you manage to rest after the journey?'

'Good heavens, you're as bad as Mama!' Kitty scolded. 'Abbie isn't in her dotage quite yet. She doesn't need to rest.'

There was just a suspicion of a twitch at one corner of his mouth as Bart rose to his feet, and gathered together the letters. 'Dare I ask what you have been up to then since your arrival?'

'I've been showing Abbie round the house,' Kitty answered, her gaze straying beyond her brother's shoulders towards the window, where there remained clear evidence of a recent fire. 'How do you suppose it started, Bart? One of the servants being clumsy? Barryman is getting old, you know. It's high time he retired.'

'He's still more than capable of performing all his duties,' he countered, after watching Abbie's brow furrow as she examined the window. 'It was he, after all, who discovered the fire. He raised the alarm, and managed to have it put out before it had taken too firm a hold.'

He had tried to sound sublimely unconcerned, and was thankful when his sister didn't pursue the matter. 'If you're not too fatigued after your tour of the house, perhaps you'd both care to join me for a stroll in the garden? I could do with some fresh air.'

Kitty appeared to consider for a moment. 'Er—no, I think I'll bear Mama company for an hour before dinner. I know I can safely leave Abbie in your capable hands, brother dear,' she said, casting him a wickedly provocative grin before departing.

Bart couldn't help smiling too as he watched the door close behind her. His sister might be a confounded little minx on occasions, but she was no fool. Unless he was greatly mistaken, she already suspected that his reason for inviting Abbie to the Court had little to do with a desire to have his portrait painted.

He transferred his attention to the female who had come to occupy his thoughts far more than any other had succeeded in doing to find her still gazing avidly at that certain telltale spot on the window frame. It was obvious that she suspected something; suspected that the explanation given for the damage to the carpet, curtains and a sizeable section of wall covering was not the true one. He ought he supposed to feel aggrieved that she doubted his word, but he didn't. In fact, he was happy to confide in her, for he knew instinctively that she could be trusted.

'Is it your intention to study that window until it's time to go in to dinner? I'm sure you'd find a tour of the gardens a far more pleasant way of occupying yourself.'

'W-what?' She turned, that troubled frown still very much in evidence.

'What is it about my library window that causes you such concern?' He raised one dark brow in a quizzical arch. 'It could do with a coat of paint, I grant you.'

'It would benefit from some slight repair too. The wood around the catch has been gouged out. Recently, I suspect. The hallmark of an attempted break-in, I should say.'

When his only response was a crooked half-smile, Abbie guessed the truth at once. 'So none of the servants was to blame. It was an intruder. Have you discovered any valuables missing?'

Bart shook his head. 'No. Robbery, I do not believe, was the motive.'

She was not slow to understand. 'You mean the fire was started deliberately?'

Without responding, he came to stand so close beside her that the sleeve of his jacket brushed against her arm. Although his nearness brought vividly to mind that unforgettable interlude on a certain Bath terrace, Abbie experienced not the smallest qualm in being alone with him, and didn't attempt to put a seemly distance between them by taking a step away either.

Tall and strong, he could overpower her in a trice, just as he had done on that memorable evening not so long ago. Even so, some inner feminine wisdom assured her that, although he was certainly no saint, he would never force his attentions on an unwilling female, and would never take advantage of her vulnerability while she remained a guest under his roof.

Raising her eyes, she studied the line of his firm jaw. Yes, the rugged contours of his face undoubtedly betrayed his strength of character, intelligence and determination. Yet she could detect nothing to indicate that he was lacking compassion. If anything, the tiny lines about his eyes betrayed a sense of humour, and although there was nothing weak about the set of his mouth, the sensual curve to his bottom lip suggested a passionate nature rather than a cold-blooded one.

'Since the war there has been much unrest,' he began at last, and Abbie found it no difficult matter to concentrate on what he was saying. 'Hardly surprising when one considers that men who fought bravely for their country have come home to find themselves surplus to requirement. Without work they are unable to support their families. Discontent among the poor is widespread, and seems particularly prevalent hereabouts.'

He took a moment to stare across the park at the field where cows were grazing. 'I'm by no means the only one to have suffered loss of livestock and damage to property. Lord Warren, my nearest neighbour, has been a victim of the unrest too. But, for reasons which escape me completely, I seem to be the prime recipient of the surge of malcontent in this area that began earlier in the year. Which I find hard to understand, as I'm one of the few landowners hereabouts who have spoken out vociferously against the high corn prices. The torching of my library curtains and carpet was merely the latest in what I very much fear will turn out to be ever-increasing attacks.'

'So what do you intend to do?' she asked, sure in her own mind that he had already taken steps to protect his property. He did not disappoint her.

'As you heard Kitty mention a short while ago, our butler, Barryman, is no longer young, but remains conscientious. It's largely thanks to him the damage was minimal. All the same, a man of his advanced years cannot be expected to keep a constant vigil. That, in part, was the reason I shortened our stay in

Bath, so that I could be on hand should anything else untoward occur. I have men now patrolling the grounds at night. Lord Warren is also arranging for a peacekeeping force to be sent to the area. Having a company of soldiers riding about the countryside will possibly deter many from engaging in unlawful acts, but it will prove no lasting solution to the problem of unrest.'

He drew his attention away from the view beyond the window to look down at her, and his features were instantly softened by the warmth of his smile. 'But all is far from doom and gloom. Besides which, the intruder, though it wasn't his intention, has served me a good turn. The library has been looking increasingly shabby for years. The fire has meant that I cannot postpone the redecorating any longer. So I should appreciate some advice on what new carpet and curtains to select.'

Abbie didn't attempt to hide her astonishment. 'It's Eugenie you ought to consult.'

He raised one brow in a sceptical arch. 'My stepmother has made few changes since she came to live in the house.'

'No, I know she hasn't.' Abbie didn't wish to be a talebearer by repeating what Eugenie had said to her in confidence. All the same she could not resist adding, 'Has it never crossed your mind to wonder why?'

Narrow-eyed, he regarded her in silence for a moment, then suggested they begin their tour of the garden, and said nothing further until they were outside, enjoying the warm, rose-scented air.

'I was not always kind to Eugenie,' he admitted, pausing to examine several particularly fine blooms. 'In fact, during those first years of her marriage to my father I was downright cruel, needlessly so, for she did nothing to warrant my antipathy. I very much resented her taking my mother's place, and made my feelings brutally clear. It's only in recent years that I have come to appreciate her fully, to acknowledge what a really fine person she is. But the damage, I'm afraid, was already done. She remains to this day a little nervous in my company, and her attacks of diffidence, her reluctance to make decisions, irritates me on occasions. If I did ask her to choose new furnishings for the library, I know she would be plaguing me constantly for assurances that I approve her choice.' He smiled wryly. 'And I'm not a man renowned for his limitless patience.'

He was nothing if not brutally honest, and Abbie couldn't help admiring him for this. 'You do not, if what I have been told is true, resemble your late father in character. I seem to remember someone, possibly my grandfather, saying he was a restrained, tolerant gentleman.'

'He was,' Bart concurred, that wry smile in evidence again. 'But I tried his patience to the limits on more than one occasion over my attitude towards Eugenie. No one regrets that more than I. And not only for the beatings I justly received.' He shook his head, as though at some private thought. 'Eugenie proved to be his ideal mate. She suited my father very well, more so, I suspect, than my mother ever did. Like myself, my mother inherited that determined Bellingham streak. Yet she had a gentler side too, especially where I was concerned. It was she who planted the rose gardens here.'

'She certainly favoured the colour pink,' Abbie said, then realised when he frowned that he might possibly have taken the simple observation as criticism.

'You're right,' he agreed after a moment. 'There isn't much variation in colour. What would you do to improve it?'

'Maybe alternating squares of deep red and pink would look striking. And beyond the box hedge the same arrangement with white and yellow, perhaps.'

Bart caught sight of a slightly stooped figure, busily removing the dead flower heads, just beyond one of the dividing hedges. 'Figg,' he called, 'I want some changes made to the rose garden.'

By the deep lines of disapproval etched in the weather-beaten face, Abbie suspected the good Mr Figg didn't approve of change. As he came along the path towards them, he favoured her with a rather hard, suspicious look before touching his forelock and gazing up at his master.

'It be true, sir, that one or two of the bushes be getting old, but they still produce fine blooms, as you can see.'

'It's neither the quality nor the quantity of blooms that is at fault, Figg, merely the lack of variation in colour. So you will make yourself available tomorrow morning to discuss some alterations with Miss Graham, here. She has offered some splendid suggestions that I wish you to put into effect as soon as possible.'

Abbie wasn't certain which annoyed her more—Bart's lofty assumption that she would be happy to redesign his garden, or the openly hostile look the head gardener darted in her direction before he acknowledged his master's instructions and trudged away.

'I cannot imagine why you might suppose, Mr Cavanagh, that I should wish to involve myself in improvements to your gardens during my time here at the Court? Moreover, that I have the least desire to work hand in hand with such a surly, unpleasant fellow as your head groundsman?'

The haughty tone was completely wasted on him. 'Oh, you'll not be able to start the portrait until all the materials you require have arrived, which won't be for several days. In the meantime you'll not wish to be idle. And I have no intention of allowing you to become bored. Or slaving over a red-hot palette from dawn till dusk, for that matter. And as far as

Figg is concerned, you'll have him eating out of your hand in no time.'

Abbie wasn't so sure, but decided not to pursue the matter and merely asked, as he calmly entwined her arm through his and they set off down a different path, whether the gardener was any relation to the cook.

'Brother and sister. Although neither is married, Cook is addressed as though she were. Both of them are unfailingly loyal.' His lips twitched. 'That is why I'm prepared to overlook my head gardener's—er—surliness. And the fact that he's good at his job, as are all those in my employ...with perhaps one exception.'

They had by this time arrived at the courtyard at the back of the house, from which one gained access to the stabling block and several large barns. There seemed a surprising lack of activity, the reason for which was soon explained when Bart's head groom emerged from the stable, leading a handsome chestnut stallion.

'The lads be over at the 'ouse, sir, sampling Mrs Figg's plum cake. Young Josh has joined 'em too, miss, if you were wanting a word wi' 'im,' Hackman added, smiling in approval at the way Abbie came fearlessly forward to make the acquaintance of his master's prized mount. 'He can be a mite skittish on occasions, miss. But you seem to 'ave a way wi' beasts.'

'And so she should, Hackman,' Bart remarked. 'She's lived round horses most all her life.' He detected a certain wistful expression flitting over her delicate features. 'But that doesn't mean I'll permit her to ride this one. You are at liberty to saddle up any mount in my stable for Miss Graham, except for Samson.'

'Understood, sir,' Hackman acknowledged, but Abbie merely smiled, a wickedly provocative smile that lent an added sparkle to her most striking feature.

'Don't you dare even think about it,' Bart warned in a voice that was all the more threatening because of its softness. 'I know well enough that you are a fine horsewoman. But Samson is headstrong, and no mount for a lady.'

Abbie thought it prudent not to tease him further, but could not resist saying, 'And what makes you suppose that I'll avail myself of any of your hacks? With all the other tasks you've set me, there will be little time for riding.'

'There'll be ample opportunity,' he countered, once again entwining her arm through his, as he guided her back across the courtyard. 'I've every intention of showing you round the whole estate.' The troubled frown returned. 'Just promise me, Abbie, that you won't attempt to go off on your own.'

She had thought it strange when he had insisted on bringing her groom to the Court. Now, however, she understood, and didn't hesitate to assure him. 'Yes, with the unfortunate happenings hereabouts, it's quite understandable why you wanted Josh along.'

'It's not just the unrest, Abbie,' he admitted. 'I could trust Hackman to take excellent care of you. But he'll not always be available, and I haven't much faith in that lad I employed a few months back. His father worked on the estate, and was trustworthy, and hardworking. I cannot say the same for his son. Hackman isn't happy with him, and I trust his judgement.'

They had by this time reached the path that led to the front of the house. Abbie paused to admire a fine wisteria that covered a substantial area of the side wall, thereby forcing Bart to stop also. The next moment a sizeable piece of masonry hit the ground with a resounding thud, a mere few yards away from where they both stood, causing Abbie to gasp in alarm, and Bart to frown heavily as he gazed above his head.

'My God!' he muttered. 'If you hadn't stopped when you did, Abbie… I'd better send someone up there tomorrow to effect necessary repairs.'

Chapter Eight

Thankfully, during the following days no further unnerving incidents occurred, and once the materials required to undertake Bart's portrait had arrived at the Court, Abbie quickly settled into a pleasurable routine.

Taking full advantage of Bart's kind offer, she availed herself of one of his horses. Most mornings, weather permitting, would see her riding out across the estate on the lovely dapple mare that had quickly become her favourite mount. Bart himself, more often than not, would bear her company, and whenever he was unavailable, Kitty was always more than ready to enjoy the exercise and fresh air, though she never once attempted to do so when she knew her brother was free.

Unfortunately he seemed less eager to make himself available in the afternoons, when Abbie would retreat to the makeshift studio to work on his portrait.

After he had condescended to turn up for the first few sittings, during which she managed to complete a few preliminary sketches, he began to show a disinclination to remain for more than twenty minutes or so. And sometimes didn't concern himself to turn up at all!

When eventually she had felt it incumbent upon her to draw his attention to the fact that his seeming reluctance to sit for his portrait would result in her remaining at the Court longer than had been anticipated, he had merely shrugged those broad shoulders of his and had said, 'Well, what of it? There's no urgency for you to return to Bath, is there?' To which she had had no answer, for if the truth had been known, she had swiftly grown to enjoy the comfortable life at Cavanagh Court.

From the very first the servants had treated her with the utmost respect, making life so very agreeable that she had been forced to give herself an inward shake more than once, to remind herself that the Court wasn't her home and that she would be returning to Bath long before summer had given way to autumn. Even Figg, after an initial display of resentment, had done a great deal to make her feel welcome whenever she had ventured into his domain. In general, after having listened intently to any schemes she had put forward to improve certain areas, he had shown genuine enthusiasm, and on one or two occasions had even gone so far as to voice ideas of his own. Which he had felt sure would meet with approval, providing Miss Graham would be willing to put the suggestions before the master herself.

Figg's sister too had proved no less accommodating, and had sent regular messages via the maids, assuring Miss Graham that should there be any particular dishes she would like prepared, she had only to ask. As Abbie had found nothing wanting in the estimable Mrs Figg's culinary skills, the message she had continued to send back was that she had been very well pleased with what had been set before her at mealtimes.

Nevertheless, she was destined to discover one morning, after she had been at the Court almost three weeks, that her efforts not to cause any of the servants undue work had not met with universal approval.

'Cook's right put out,' Rose, the young housemaid, announced, as she entered early as usual with the pitcher of warm water. 'Taken it into her head that you don't think she's capable of preparing any fancy dishes just because she ain't employed by some titled gentleman, and don't work in some posh London house.'

In face of this alarming disclosure, Abbie thought it prudent to adopt a different tack and, the instant she had completed her toilette, made her way directly down to the kitchens in order to soothe any ruffled feathers.

* * *

Unfortunately she discovered that evening, when joined by Kitty and her mother, that it was impossible to please everyone.

'Oh, dear,' Eugenie muttered, clearly dismayed, after Abbie had disclosed that one of her favourite dishes, chicken in a delicious creamy sauce, would be on the menu. 'Bart isn't at all fond of rich food nowadays. I think it must be the result of those years of privation, when in the army and forced to go without. He now much prefers simple fare.'

Abbie had by this time come to the conclusion that Eugenie wasn't so much in awe of her stepson as determined to do all she could to avoid those unpleasant confrontations she had been forced to endure years before.

Never had Abbie known such a good-natured, unselfish soul. Yet she could understand now just what induced Bart's occasional bouts of impatience where his stepmother was concerned. She had come perilously close to losing her own temper when she had consulted with Eugenie over the new décor for the library. Eugenie would agree wholeheartedly in one breath, then shed doubt in the next; until Abbie, having decided only firm action would serve, had taken it upon herself to make the final decision. Appearing harassed, she had marched resolutely into the library to attain Bart's signature on the order form, only to receive an 'I told you so' look from the master of the house.

'If he doesn't choose to sample the dish, no one is going to force him to do so,' Abbie responded, betraying her indifference with a shrug. 'Mrs Figg has cooked for him long enough to know his likes and dislikes. She'll have provided an alternative, I'm sure. Besides which,' she added, 'pandering to the whims of strong-willed gentlemen is highly inadvisable. Believe me, I know! You run the risk of turning them into totally selfish autocrats.'

Kitty gurgled with laughter. 'You're not in the least afraid of my brother, are you, Abbie?'

'And why should she be?' queried a smooth voice, and they all turned to discover Bart standing in the doorway, his eyes, like his sister's, twinkling with amusement. 'She is far too sensible to go out of her way to annoy me.'

'Don't be too sure of that,' Abbie herself countered. 'I was unable to avoid a lengthy encounter with your gardener this morning, and succumbed to an imp of pure mischief. You'll never guess what I've managed to persuade him to grow in the shelter of the walled garden.'

'Oh, do tell!' Eugenie prompted, after Abbie had given way to a wicked chuckle.

'Dahlias.'

Bart's brows rose. 'What…? Not that newfangled flower?'

'Strangely enough, that is more or less what Figg

himself said,' Abbie revealed. 'But believe it or not, he now fully intends to grow a large bed of them. What a pity I shan't be here to view the results when all his plans have been put into effect! I guarantee you'll have flowers enough to fill every room!'

Only Bart didn't appear to find the prospect pleasing. Abbie watched the smile leaving his eyes the moment before he turned and headed across the room in the direction of the decanters.

It crossed her mind to wonder whether he might be annoyed because she had taken it upon herself to suggest rather more changes in the garden than he deemed necessary. If so, his irritation certainly didn't last very long, for during dinner he barked with laughter, when she called him a contrary so-and-so, after he had helped himself to a second substantial portion of her favourite chicken dish.

He was disposed not to linger over his port either that evening, once the meal was over, and rejoined the ladies in the drawing-room in time to sample a dish of tea.

'I've been wondering, Eugenie,' he said, after settling himself beside Abbie on the sofa, as had become his custom, 'whether you would care to spend some time with your sister Mildred in Brighton this summer, as our stay in Bath was shorter than originally planned?'

Eugenie's expression of delighted surprise faded

when her gaze slid to the person seated beside him. 'I should dearly love to, Bart. But, in the circumstances, I do not think I should leave at this time.'

He was quick to appreciate the reason behind her reluctance. 'Do not concern yourself over the proprieties. Abbie will be suitably chaperoned. All I need do is write to Lady Penrose. She informed me before I left Bath that she would be only too delighted to join us here at the Court should Abbie's stay turn out to be longer than originally planned.'

Abbie flashed him a look of exasperation. 'Which I can safely promise will be the case, if you continue to find excuses not to sit for me in the afternoons. I've been here for three weeks and have barely made a start.'

Although he smiled, he refused to be drawn, and turned his attention once again to his stepmother. 'So you may spend time by the sea with a clear conscience, my dear. I'm sure you and Kitty will find the change of air beneficial.'

Eugenie was very taken with the idea. Surprisingly enough, though, Kitty betrayed little enthusiasm, the reason for which became clear the instant her mother had departed in order to dash off a quick note to the sister of whom she saw little.

'It isn't that I don't wish to go, Bart,' she assured him when he commented on her lack of interest. 'It's just that I thought we might hold a party here for Mama at the end of the month. It's her fiftieth birthday, and I thought she'd like to celebrate with her neighbours and friends. If you're agreeable, I thought perhaps Abbie and I might arrange it so that it would be a surprise.'

'I think it a splendid notion,' he didn't hesitate to assure her. 'There's absolutely no reason why you cannot delay your departure by a few days, and if your mother should question the delay, all you need say is that Lady Penrose is unable to leave Bath before the end of the month.'

Abbie wasn't proof against the entreaty in Kitty's eyes, and didn't hesitate to offer her help.

Later, however, when she retired to her bedchamber, she wasn't altogether sure that she had been wise to involve herself further in the Cavanagh family's affairs.

After changing into her nightwear, she padded across the room and settled herself on the window seat, where she could gaze across the park at the moonlit waters of the lake.

How she loved that view! How quickly she had grown to love the whole place: the gardens, the house; and most especially the company of its master. It was pointless not facing the fact that, incredible though it was, she had by imperceptible degrees grown excessively fond of Bartholomew Cavanagh.

Smiling, she shook her head, unable to believe that just two months ago she had viewed him as the bane of her life, the person responsible for causing her so much malcontent. Now, though, she was forced to acknowledge she had been sadly at fault to denounce him as the villain of the piece. What had he done, after all? Nothing, she decided, except make a cuckold of her grandfather's most influential neighbour. And as Lady Penrose had once sagely pointed out— one shouldn't blame a man for behaving like a man. There was no denying either that Lady Sophia Fitzpatrick had been a willing participant in the affair. What still rankled, though, what she still, after all these years, found hard to forgive or forget, was that not two hours after his rendezvous in the summerhouse, he was voicing his earnest desire to marry her.

She shook her head, finding it difficult to equate the master of Cavanagh Court, solid, reliable and considerate, to that unfeeling, care-for-nobody who had heartlessly proposed marriage to her, while still wearing the very clothes he had worn when he had set off earlier to keep that assignation with Lady Sophia.

Something moving among the clump of trees by the lake caught her attention, putting an end to the unsavoury reflections. For a few moments, as the moon emerged from behind the clouds, it was possible to see quite clearly, and yet nothing now stirred.

It must have been pure imagination, she decided, before clambering into bed.

The following afternoon she was favoured by a visit from the master of the house, who condescended to sit for his portrait. Whether or not she had managed to prick his conscience the evening before was anybody's guess, though she began to think it highly unlikely when he soon betrayed signs of unrest.

'No one could accuse you of being a restful gentleman, Bart,' she told him, when he cast a longing look over his shoulder in the direction of the window. 'I believe I must resign myself to sessions of no more than fifteen minutes. And be thankful for small mercies, I suppose!'

Her dry humour never failed to bring a smile to his lips. 'Oh, it's too nice a day to be stuck indoors, Abbie. Let's go for a walk. I promise I'll give you a further half-hour later, but if I don't move soon I'll be as stiff as a varnished eel.'

Abbie was in two minds. She knew she ought to work on the portrait. Yet, Bart was right, it was too fine a day to remain inside, and the grounds beckoned. Furthermore Figg, an accurate forecaster of no little renown, had predicted change in a day or two, so it seemed such a pity not to take advantage of the clement weather while she may.

'I've only to collect my parasol. I'll join you downstairs in a few minutes,' she assured him, her decision made.

As good as her word, she met up with him again in the hall, winning herself a smile of approval for not keeping him kicking his heels before they set off across the sloping front lawn down to the lake.

By this time, of course, Abbie had explored most every area of the estate, either on horseback, or on foot. Undoubtedly her favourite haunt was the neat, well-tended gardens, most especially the shrubbery, where she could hide herself among the foliage for half an hour or so, and gain the solitude to read a book.

The lake too was high on her list of preferred spots. On two or three occasions she had ventured down to the water's edge and surprised the odd frog lurking among the reeds. She had never, however, made use of the wooden bridge to gain access to the far side, and decided to do so now in order to admire the view across the park from the shelter of the folly nestling among the trees.

The footbridge was not sufficiently wide to allow two people to walk side by side without brushing against each other at frequent intervals, so Bart, permitting her to lead the way, paused to study the reedbed, which yearly had been encroaching further into the lake.

'It's no good,' he announced, his frown betraying his displeasure as he studied the far bank. 'I'll need to arrange for some men to clear most of this lot out. I taught Kitty how to swim here. It would be downright dangerous to attempt to do so now, with this lot snaring at your feet.'

'Ahh! So there are some advantages in having an older brother,' Abbie declared, 'especially having one who's willing to give of his time to teach something useful.'

Observing that now familiar wickedly teasing sparkle before she turned and strolled away, Bart couldn't forbear a smile of his own. What an absolute darling she was! he mused, studying the graceful way she moved. Blessed with lovely, regular features, a trim, shapely figure and a ladylike air that was completely natural and blessedly free from those annoying affectations adopted by too many of her sex nowadays, she was for him the epitome of womanhood. It was no mere physical attraction either, he was forced to concede. He admired her ready wit; this coupled with an abundance of sound common sense made her the ideal companion.

Perhaps, though, he was just a besotted fool in thinking her so perfect, merely a hapless male trapped in the toils of an emotion that had been steadily increasing since the night of the Fergussons' party, where they had come face to face again after so many years? Well, if this were indeed the case, he was forced silently to own that he was highly satisfied with this imprisoned state, and experienced not the remotest desire ever to regain his freedom.

Smiling still, he eased his elbows off the wooden handrail, and set off in pursuit. He slowly increased his pace and was within yards of her when it happened. One moment Abbie was standing there, appearing as though she hadn't a care in the world as she stared across the park in the direction of the village church, where Eugenie's father had once conducted the services; the next there came the sound of splintering timber, and she was disappearing through a large hole.

Bart made a valiant dive to reach her, but only succeeded in saving the now torn and misshapen pink parasol from suffering a similar fate. Without pausing to remove even his coat, he vaulted over the wooden handrail to land only a matter of feet away from where Abbie, gasping and spluttering, was endeavouring to keep her head above water. He had her on her back in a trice, one hand securely under her chin keeping her afloat. Terrified though she undoubtedly was, she thankfully obeyed his command not to struggle. It was an easy matter then for him to get them both safely back to within a few yards of the bank.

Bart soon discovered that negotiating a safe passage across the reed bed was to prove more difficult. Half-dragging, half-carrying Abbie, he found it as much as he could do to keep them both from sinking knee deep in the mud each time he moved. In the end it was only by making use of the gnarled roots of an overhanging tree that he managed finally to get them both safely on the grassy bank.

Exhausted, Abbie dropped to her knees, and it was several minutes before she could find breath enough to thank him for saving her life, for she was in no doubt that he had. Even if by some miracle she had managed to flounder her way to the water's edge, she would never have negotiated a path through the area of stinking, slimy mud.

When he made no attempt to respond, she glanced up to find him staring down at her, his expression an impenetrable mask. Then he slipped off his sodden, mud-streaked jacket and placed it about her shoulders, insisting that she keep it on; the reason for which Rose wasn't slow to make embarrassingly clear a short time later, when Abbie had reached the sanctuary of her bedchamber.

'Cor blimey, miss! You can see clear through that gown o' yourn where there ain't no mud a-clinging!' the little housemaid declared, betraying a deal more honesty than tact.

One glance in the full-length mirror was sufficient to confirm this humiliating fact. Abbie, having allowed Bart's jacket to slip from her shoulders, could feel the heat glowing in her cheeks as she saw the clear outlines of breasts, hips and thighs. The fact that her hair resembled nothing so much as a collection of rats' tails, and that her face, like the veritable urchin's, was streaked with dirt, were as nothing when compared to the knowledge that her charms had been revealed, if only for a brief period, to Bart's experienced gaze.

Peeling off the soiled gown, she tossed it aside, with the fervent hope that it was ruined beyond repair so that she might be spared the mortification of seeing it hanging again in the wardrobe, a taunting reminder of a humiliating episode she would far rather forget.

Once the bath had arrived she wasted no time in restoring her appearance, and was sitting patiently whilst the maid pinned the last few strands of hair into place, when there was a light scratch on the door and Kitty entered, carrying a sheet of paper in her hand and an expression of real concern on her face.

'Bart's just told me what happened. I can hardly believe it!' she exclaimed, plumping herself down on the bed. 'I told him it might so easily have been me who received a soaking. I went for a walk the other morning, when you and Bart were out riding, and came back over the bridge.'

'You would have fared rather better than I did, Kitty,' Abbie wasn't slow to point out. 'You, I understand, can swim.'

'Well, yes,' Kitty was forced to concede. 'But it would have been no easy matter, hampered by petticoats, to reach the bank.'

An appalling possibility occurred to Abbie. 'Surely you were wearing clothes when your brother taught you?'

'Well, yes. But a deal less than I'm wearing now.' Kitty chuckled at Abbie's expression of prim disapproval. 'You forget he is my brother, after all.'

But he isn't mine! Abbie silently countered, instantly banishing the foolish notion of asking Bart to teach her to swim from her mind, and then promptly changed the subject by inquiring the whereabouts of Eugenie.

'Oh, she took it into her head to call and see her sister at the vicarage. She hasn't done so since our return from Bath, so it's more than likely that Aunt Clara will persuade her to remain for dinner. I didn't accompany her because I wanted to make a list of those we must invite to her party.' Kitty glanced across at the maid, who was busily picking up the soiled garments to take downstairs for laundering. 'Don't forget it's supposed to be a secret, Rose. So don't go saying anything in front of Mama.'

'I won't forget, miss,' the maid assured her. 'It'll be nice having a large party here again. Cook especially is looking forward to it, though I did hear her say the sooner you can spare time to discuss menus for both dinner and supper, the better.'

Kitty cast a look of earnest appeal in Abbie's direction. 'You'll help me do that, won't you?'

'Of course I shall,' Abbie readily confirmed, feeling slightly guilty because she'd done nothing to help thus far. 'But surely you don't want to consult with Cook now? We can do so tomorrow. You've been indoors most all the day. Wouldn't you prefer to go out for a ride?'

'Yes, I would,' Kitty admitted. 'Dinner's been put back an hour because Bart wants to examine the damage to the bridge, so there'd be time enough. Only he told me you were to rest until dinner, and I wasn't to trouble you.'

Torn between a feeling of gratitude for Bart's concern for her well-being, and annoyance over his dictatorial attitude, Abbie hovered for a moment before announcing that she was more than capable of deciding whether she felt able to go out or not. 'And a good canter across the park would do us both some good, so I'll meet you in the stable-yard in half an hour.'

As Abbie had only to slip off a robe to don her habit, she arrived before the appointed time. Josh, she quickly noticed, was occupied in saddling the dapple mare she always chose to ride, and the youngest member of Hackman's staff, Tom, was busily cleaning out one of the stalls, while Ben Dodd, unkempt as usual, his mouth twisted by an unpleasant smirk, just stood there, leaning on his broom.

This was by no means the first time Abbie had caught him shirking his duties. She knew too that Hackman didn't hold this particular underling in high esteem, and could fully appreciate why. Yet it was not so much Dodd's work-shy attitude that Abbie found objectionable as his surly manner.

Unfortunately she had been forced to tolerate his company on the odd occasion when she had gone out for a ride with Kitty, for Dodd had been employed as Kitty's personal groom. Just what Kitty's opinion of him was was difficult to judge, for the girl seemed oblivious to his presence most of the time. How Abbie wished she could say the same! Unfortunately, she had too frequently caught a lascivious gleam in that shifty gaze of his, and had gained the distinct impression that he had been attempting to judge what she and Kitty would look like without their shifts.

Today, however, she was determined not to put up with his presence, and was almost upon him before he realised she was there. 'As you're clearly fatigued today, Dodd, Josh shall deputise for you and accompany us out.'

For once his eyes met hers, albeit fleetingly, and there was no mistaking the resentment lurking there. He looked for a moment as though he might argue, then he shrugged. 'As you like, miss,' he muttered before slouching away.

Kitty, when they rode out of the stable-yard, didn't appear to notice that they were being attended by a different groom. Nor did it seem that she had any clear destination in mind. In this, however, Abbie swiftly realised that she had misjudged her companion, when Kitty announced her intention of calling upon the most influential family in the neighbourhood.

'Lord and Lady Warren are in residence, because I know for a fact that Bart has ridden over to see them since our return from Bath. Lady Warren happens to be my godmother. She's very kind and will help us arrange things for the party so Mama doesn't find out about it.'

In this Kitty was absolutely correct. Lady Warren was delighted by the impromptu visit and greeted her goddaughter warmly. 'Of course I shall do anything to help, my dear,' she assured her the instant she discovered the reason behind the visit. 'You leave the invitation cards with me and I'll ensure they're all delivered, and enclose a little note of my own to say that replies must be sent back here to me. Not that I think too many will refuse. It has been some considerable time since a party was held at the Court.'

She then turned her attention to Abbie, running an expert eye over the stylish habit. 'And you are a friend of Kitty's, Miss Graham? You must find time to dine with us one evening during your stay in the county.'

'Oh, Abbie isn't my friend, Godmama,' Kitty announced ingenuously, thereby denying Abbie the time to thank Lady Warren for the invitation. 'Well, she is now. But she was Bart's friend long before she was mine.'

Abbie couldn't mistake the speculative gleam in Lady Warren's kindly grey eyes, but before she could disclose that the master of Cavanagh Court was none other than her grandfather's godson, and that she had been acquainted with Bart since childhood, her attention was captured by three gentlemen who unexpectedly entered the drawing-room. It was not so much her first glimpse of the tall, distinguished master of the house, or the young man who resembled him too closely not to be his son and heir that had her very nearly gaping in astonishment as the unexpected sight of the exquisitely attired young sprig entering in their wake.

'Great heavens!' Kitty exclaimed, nowhere near as successful as Abbie at concealing her surprise. 'What in the world are you doing here, Cedric?'

Appearing far from offended by his cousin's less-than-gracious greeting, Cedric seemed delighted to be the cynosure of all eyes, and took a moment to remove a speck of something from his sleeve before revealing that he and Richard Warren had attended the same school.

'Bumped into each other quite by chance when Ricky was staying overnight in Bath, breaking his journey after escorting his maiden aunt back to Somerset. When I happened to mention that I was already quite weary of that devilish dull place, he kindly invited me to return with him here.'

'And has Mr Asquith accompanied you?' Abbie couldn't resist asking, knowing full well that Bart wouldn't be best pleased if he had. Cedric, however, shook his head.

'No, he was quite content to remain with his aunt.'

Abbie couldn't forbear a smile at this. It was much more likely that Mr Asquith was paying avid court to some heiress, and Cedric had grown heartily sick and tired of trailing after him. Bart's cousin might have had his faults, but he was certainly no fortune-hunter.

Cedric might well have remained basking in the sunshine of her approval if he had not a minute or two later, after discovering the reason behind her visit to the Court, allowed the lingering resentment he harboured to surface.

'My, my, having his likeness painted, is he?' Cedric's weak mouth was twisted by an unpleasant smirk. 'For all his protestations to the contrary, it would seem my cousin is preparing himself for the day when he might hold a higher position in the family.'

Not surprisingly Lord and Lady Warren exchanged puzzled glances, as did Kitty and their son. Abbie, however, was under no illusion to what Cedric was alluding, and found herself instantly coming to Bart's defence.

'You are labouring under a misapprehension, Mr Cavanagh,' she told him, her voice as level as her gaze. 'In this instance Bart's actions stemmed from altruism, not ambition.'

If anything, this pronouncement appeared to puzzle everyone even more, Cedric included. All the same, Abbie refused to elaborate, and changed the subject by enquiring whether he would be remaining long enough in the locale to attend Mrs Cavanagh's birthday celebration.

He appeared much struck by the notion. 'Do you know, Miss Graham, I rather think I shall. Needless to say a country party wouldn't be my first choice of entertainment,' he admitted with quaint snobbery. 'But even though I stayed at the Court on several occasions in the dim and distant past, I cannot recall ever attending a large party there. It might well prove to be amusing to see how well Bart succeeds in entertaining his neighbours.'

It needed only that to fire Abbie's determination to ensure that Eugenie's birthday party turned out to be a memorable occasion, not the tedious little affair that Cedric clearly expected it to be.

A short while later, when she and Kitty were returning to the Court, she began to suggest others who might be persuaded to attend.

'I'll write to my godmother as soon as we get back to the house, and inquire if it's possible for her to leave Bath in time to attend the party. She'll be of invaluable help in keeping your mother entertained whilst we organise things. I wonder too,' she added as the Court came into view, 'whether Giles Fergusson might be persuaded to come.'

'Oh, what a splendid notion!' Kitty exclaimed. 'He's stayed with us on numerous occasions in the past. I'll ask Bart to write to him.'

Kitty's evident delight at the prospect of having Giles to stay in no way amazed Abbie. She had observed them together often enough while she had been in Bath to be very certain that Kitty held Giles in the highest regard. What did come as something of a surprise, however, was the sudden, unmistakable glow in her young friend's dark eyes. She had watched her conversing with Richard Warren a short while before, and it was clear to see that they were easy in each other's company, but even so that certain look had been absent from Kitty's expression.

'You're very fond of Giles, aren't you, Kitty?'

'Oh, yes. I liked him from the first,' she unblushingly admitted. 'I prefer the company of older gentlemen. They're not silly as younger men sometimes are. And I especially like Giles. He's interesting to talk to. What's more, he doesn't treat me like a child, as Bart tends to do. Though he's been heaps better of late,' she added, casting Abbie a sidelong glance. 'He's not nearly so sharp, either. You're a marvellous influence on him, you know?'

Whether this was true or not, Abbie would have been hard pressed to say. She was forced silently to acknowledge, though, as they rode into the stableyard to find him standing there, impatiently tapping his crop against the side of one boot, that if her presence did have a beneficial effect on his temper, it was in no way foolproof.

He swung round the instant he detected the sound of hoofs on cobblestones, his thunderous expression evidence of his frame of mind.

'Where the hell do you suppose you two have been!' he bellowed, uncaring that the youngest stable-lad was staring at him in open-mouthed astonishment.

Chapter Nine

Unlike Kitty, who appeared dismayed by her brother's angry outburst, Abbie felt the first stirring of her own temper. Having lived with a brusque ex-army colonel for most of her life, she was well used to a gentleman's bouts of ill humour. Nevertheless, for all that her grandfather could be an irascible so-and-so on occasions, and not one to mince words either, he had never once taken her to task in the presence of others.

Out of the corner of her eye she detected the satisfied smirk on Dodd's unpleasant, weasel-like face as he led Samson from the stable. Obviously he had overheard his master's outburst, and was undoubtedly hoping to witness the female who had dared to dispense with his services so summarily earlier being taken down a peg or two. Nothing could more surely have strengthened her resolve to thwart Bart's intention of venting his spleen in public.

Drawing the mare alongside the mounting block, Abbie slid nimbly from the saddle, and then immediately turned her attention to Kitty. 'If you hurry, you'll have time before dinner to add those few names to your list of guests.'

Seemingly needing no further prompting, Kitty departed the instant she had placed her mount in Josh's charge. Abbie too handed the reins over to her groom, before walking serenely away in the direction of the garden. Whether her calm handling of the situation had momentarily left Bart speechless, she had no way of knowing. All the same, she couldn't say she was unduly surprised to hear the sound of rapidly approaching footsteps directly behind her a few moments later. The sudden clasp on her shoulder, before she was spun round none too gently, came as no real surprise either. Nor, for that matter, did his expression of barely suppressed rage.

'How dare you walk away when you know full well that I wish to speak with you?'

Although nowhere near as composed as she was attempting to appear, Abbie was determined not to make matters worse by losing the grasp on her own temper. 'You did not wish to speak to me, Bart,' she countered, maintaining the praiseworthy control. 'What you wished to do was vent your ill humour by browbeating me. And worse, you were prepared to do so in the presence of others. Your sister and stepmother are accustomed to your boorish manners, and seem willing to overlook them. I, on the other hand, am not. You were born a gentleman. You would do well to remember that in future, especially in your dealings with me.'

At this he appeared, if anything, more murderous than before. The muscles along the powerful jaw tightened visibly, and she could almost hear him counting slowly up to ten under his breath. Yet to do him justice he made no attempt to grasp her again and shake her until her teeth rattled, an action which, she didn't doubt for a second, would have afforded him the utmost satisfaction.

Instead, he merely ran impatient fingers through his hair whilst he raised his eyes to the patch of azure sky directly above his head. 'If…if my forceful enquiry in the stable-yard offended your delicate sensibilities, then I apologise,' he began, now exercising commendable restraint himself. 'However, you would do well to remember, Abbie, that even gentlemen are apt to give way to their feelings on occasions, most especially when their sound advice has been imprudently ignored.'

She neither misunderstood, nor was she reticent to air her own views. 'I am neither headstrong, nor insensible to your concerns for my well-being,' she assured him softly. 'And neither am I a child, Bart. I am quite capable of deciding whether I feel able to go out for a ride. Good heavens! You must think me a poor creature indeed if you suppose that such a trifling accident, as happened earlier, would be likely to overset me to such an extent that I must take to my bed.'

His expression became guarded, markedly so, and all at once she knew that far more lay behind his show of ill humour than she had supposed. As had happened before, she reached out to place her fingers on his arm. 'What is it? What's wrong?'

'What happened at the lake was no accident, Abbie,' Bart admitted at length, after giving the matter of whether to confide in her or not a few moments' intense thought. 'I returned to the bridge with Hackman to check for further signs of wear. The timbers weren't rotten, as I had supposed. They had been sawed through quite deliberately.'

When no response was forthcoming, Bart raised his eyes to discover her staring fixedly at a fine specimen of a pink rose, and was immediately struck by her lack of reaction.

'You'll forgive me for saying so, Abbie, but you do not appear unduly surprised.'

This succeeded in briefly recapturing her attention, before she took advantage of the bench conveniently situated directly behind her. 'In truth, sir, I'm not,' she confessed. 'You've already disclosed that you have suffered more damage to your property than the other landowners hereabouts—hayricks burned, fences pulled down and the fire at your house. It would seem that since your return from

Bath the miscreants have decided to increase the frequency of their unlawful acts against you.'

Bart considered this for a moment as he settled himself on the bench beside her. 'It would be wrong to conclude that on the evidence of what has happened today.'

One fine brow rose in a sceptical arch. 'You think so?'

'Yes, I do,' he affirmed. 'After all, we cannot be sure just when the damage to the bridge was effected.'

'Well, I can tell you this much—' Abbie didn't hesitate to enlighten him '—Kitty herself mentioned that she had walked over the bridge just the other day. Furthermore, last night, I thought I saw someone lurking in the clump of trees by the lake. At the time I dismissed it as a mere trick of the moonlight. Naturally, after what happened today, I'm inclined to believe my eyes had not deceived me.'

For the first time she betrayed deep concern by frowning heavily. 'I'm not at all sure that that chunk of masonry, which happened to fall just as we were walking down the path beside the house, was a mischance either.' She held his full attention. 'You see, shortly after our arrival at the Court, I was up on the leads with Kitty. I noticed sections of masonry were betraying signs of wear. But when I rested my hand against the stonework, I detected no movement whatsoever. And I remember quite clearly that there wasn't so much as a breath of wind that day.'

For several moments Bart sat quietly digesting what Abbie had revealed, and more importantly what he strongly suspected was occurring to her as a very real possibility, but before he could voice his own thoughts, the sounds of an altercation succeeded in capturing his full attention.

'What the deuce…?' he muttered, rising instantly to his feet.

Although it was impossible to keep pace with his long-striding gait, Abbie didn't hesitate to follow, and arrived in the stable-yard, only moments after Bart himself, in time to witness her groom plant a flush hit to Ben Dodd's jaw, the force of which sent him sprawling in the dirt.

It would have afforded her much gratification to have been able to carry out such a feat herself, for she couldn't deny she had taken the ill-favoured Dodd in dislike. All the same, she was forced to own it wasn't the behaviour she had come to expect from her groom, whose disposition she had always considered placid. Moreover, it was an unequal contest, her groom having the advantage of both height and build, though it was much to Josh's credit that he made no attempt to follow up his advantage while his opponent remained on the ground.

'What the devil's going on here?' Bart demanded, striding forward and thereby effectively putting an end to hostilities. 'Well?' he barked, after waiting in vain for an explanation.

As neither groom appeared willing, or able, to meet his disapproving gaze, and both continued to stare dumbly at some spot on the ground, Bart turned his attention to his youngest employee, whose snub-nosed face he at last perceived peering round the stable door. 'What's this all about, lad?'

Even from where she stood Abbie could see the boy was trembling, and thought for a moment that it must be the presence of his master which had quite overset him, until she caught the glance he directed at Dodd.

Seemingly Bart had not been oblivious to the look of terror in the boy's eyes either, for in the next breath he assured him he had naught to fear if he told the truth.

'Them's bin brawling, sir.'

'Yes, I saw that for myself, lad. But why did they fight?'

Once again terrified eyes shot a fleeting look in Dodd's direction. Abbie at least could guess the reason why the boy was reluctant to speak: Tom was fearful of repercussions should he reveal what he knew. After all, Hackman was not always on hand to ensure that both his underlings toed the line, and she strongly suspected that the work-shy Dodd was not above resorting to bullying tactics in the head groom's absence.

Abbie had no wish to interfere in a matter that was essentially Bart's concern, even though her own groom was involved. Yet she knew only too well that there was a limit to his patience, and that he wouldn't wait indefinitely for an explanation. She cast a look in Josh's direction, and thankfully he wasn't slow to interpret the unspoken request in her eyes.

'I started the fight, Mr Cavanagh,' he admitted, thereby instantly gaining everyone's attention. It was clear, none the less, by his suddenly intense look that Bart, like Abbie, suspected far more lay behind the scuffle than a mere difference of opinion.

'Why? What did my groom do to incite your wrath?'

Amazingly enough not only did Tom understand the question, it was he who supplied the answer. 'Mr Dodd were setting about your 'orse, sir, wiv a crop.'

As Dodd scrambled to his feet, Tom sought the protection of Josh's side, an action that told its own tale and which instantly ignited a spark of understanding in the eyes of his master.

'It were nothing, sir,' Dodd muttered. 'You know 'ow skittish Samson be when he don't get no exercise. It were a lick or two I give him, that were all.'

Either Bart did not believe a word, or the explanation had come too late, for his expression had grown darkly uncompromising. 'Go and collect your belongings. And don't set foot on my land again.'

* * *

There was a noticeable improvement in the atmosphere in and around the stable block after Dodd's departure. Abbie frequently detected the sound of Tom's gleeful chuckles during the following days, and Josh too whistled as he went about his work. Precisely what Kitty's views were on the loss of her personal groom Abbie found difficult to judge, for Kitty made no comment within her hearing. Hackman, on the other hand, was not at all reticent to air his views.

'Never could take to the lad, Miss Abbie, and that's a fact,' he openly admitted, one morning, when she was returning to the house by way of the yard, and had paused to pass the time of day with the iron ruler of the stables. 'The master liked old Dodd and was prepared to give his son a chance. A big mistake to be sure, and a rare one for the master to make, for in general he's a good judge o' men, so he is.

'Came as no surprise to me, neither, that the young wastrel were mistreating the stock,' he went on, pausing in his grooming of one of the carriage horses. 'I had my suspicions. Not that I ever caught him doing so myself, more's the pity. I'd 'ave enjoyed placing a well-aimed kick to the seat of his breeches. Aye, there's a definite mean streak in that little runt, and no mistake, and we're well rid of 'im.'

'Had Dodd worked here for long, Mr Hackman?' Abbie asked, as he seemed disposed to chatter.

He shook his head. 'I mind he started in early

spring, a month or so after the old groom had passed on.'

'I doubt Dodd will find it easy to obtain another position, given that he left without a reference.'

'Well, I don't know about that, miss,' he surprised her by responding. 'I did 'ere tell he'd been taken on by that there stranger who bought the tavern on the Evesham road early in the year.' He tutted. 'Don't drink there no more, m'self. Don't care for the company. Rum lot you get in there nowadays, if you ask me. Should suit Dodd fine. Be in good company, I'm thinking.'

'Well, you certainly do not appear to be missing the extra pair of hands,' Abbie remarked, after gazing about the recently swept yard.

'That we ain't, miss,' Hackman agreed. 'The work still gets done, though the master will need to think about taking someone else on afore too long. I'll be off to take the mistress and Miss Kitty to Brighton in a few days, and no one can expect little Tom to cope on his own. That groom o' yourn be a fine lad, though. Taken to 'im in a big way, so I 'ave. I'd be happy enough to leave him in charge while I'm away. But I don't expect you'll be staying too much longer yourself, miss.'

Up until that moment Abbie hadn't looked ahead to the day when she would be leaving the Court. Eugenie's birthday was looming large on the horizon, Giles and her godmother were due to arrive at the end

of the week, and it stood to reason that once Eugenie and Kitty had left for Brighton, her days at the
Court would be numbered. At least they certainly
would be if Bart had his way, she decided, entering
the house and making her way upstairs to her makeshift studio.

Since the mishap at the bridge, Bart had undergone
something of a change and had found time to sit most
every afternoon, with the result that the portrait was
all but finished. That, she now realised, as she removed the protective sheet to study the subject of the
painting, had been his goal. Of course it had. And she
had been a simpleton not to have realised before! He
wanted her away from Cavanagh Court as soon as
possible.

Smiling wryly, she went over to one of the windows to stare out at the lake, and the bridge, which
had now been repaired. Undoubtedly she would have
felt deeply hurt if she had supposed for a moment that
it was her company of which he had grown tired, but
she knew this was not so. Good relations between
them having soon been fully restored after their little altercation on the day of Dodd's departure, Bart
had continued to seek her company frequently. No,
it was much more likely that he desired her swift departure for her own safety. But what of his own?
Surely he must suspect, as she did herself, that maybe
something very sinister, perhaps some very personal

revenge, lay behind these malicious acts perpetrated against him?

Detecting the click of the door, Abbie turned, and was not unduly surprised to see the subject of her thoughts entering the room, on time yet again for the sitting. His smile as he stared across at her was as warm as ever. Yet, wasn't there just a touch of concern in his expression too? How she wished he would share his troubles with her. How she wished she could remain at the Court to help uncover the identities of those responsible for the malicious acts, but she knew Bart well enough by now to be sure that he would never entertain the notion.

'Now what, I wonder, could be responsible for bringing that wistful look to your pretty face, my sweet?' he asked, resorting to one of those endearments which he was wont to use with such frequency that she was hardly conscious of them any longer. Only this time she was very aware, and something inside lurched painfully.

'I was merely thinking that, with this magnificent show of enthusiasm on your part to see the portrait finished, my stay here will soon be at an end,' she admitted, seeing no reason to conceal the truth, and watched as he took up his usual stance before the far window so that the light played about his hair, highlighting the rich chestnut tones, something that she had attempted to bring out in her painting.

Something flickered too in the dark depths of his

eyes, but so fleetingly that she was given insufficient time even to attempt to interpret what it might have been. 'And do you find the prospect of a return to Bath not wholly pleasing?'

Abbie was in two minds. Once again she saw no reason to lie, while at the same time she had no intention of revealing just how depressing she found the mere thought of leaving the Court. 'I wouldn't attempt to pretend that I do not prefer life in the country,' she disclosed at last, choosing her words with care. 'But I am resigned, and very sensible too of how kind my godmother is to offer me the opportunity of sharing her home.'

'Had you agreed to marry me, the Court would now be your home,' Bart reminded her, 'and there would be no need for you to return to Bath.'

Whatever Abbie might have expected him to say next, it certainly hadn't been that. He had taken her completely off guard, and it showed. Unable to meet his suddenly intense gaze, she sat herself before the easel. Unfortunately her hand shook so much that she dared not attempt to continue with the portrait, and very reluctantly raised her eyes to discover an odd, almost smugly satisfied smile playing about his mouth.

'For quite some time I have suspected that more lay behind your refusal to marry me,' he admitted at length, his eyes momentarily straying to the trembling fingers of her right hand. 'Now, I'm firmly convinced of it.'

'We—we were both too young,' she responded, her voice as unsteady as her hand, and knew by the quizzical lift of one dark brow that he would no longer be satisfied with that explanation, even before he said,

'Very true. But neither your grandfather nor I wished for the marriage to take place immediately. I was more than happy to wait a year or two before tying the knot. In fact, I would have insisted upon it, had you agreed.'

His gaze once again grew intense, and she found it impossible to draw hers away. 'But you didn't agree, did you? You wouldn't even entertain the notion. In fact, after increasingly thinking back to that time, I honestly believe the mere thought of marrying me was abhorrent to you. And I cannot help asking myself why? What did I ever do to gave you such a disgust of mc?'

Why in the name of heaven was he alluding to that period in their lives now? she wondered, somehow managing to suppress a groan. Why now, when the reason she had been so set against marrying him had been increasingly diminishing in importance? It wasn't that she was prepared to overlook his past behaviour—far from it, in fact; but at least she was mature enough now to appreciate why it had taken place.

'Come, Abbie,' he continued, after waiting in vain

for a response. 'I would like to think that we have become…friends, that we now have a better understanding of each other. If…if there can never be anything else between us, at least let there be total honesty.'

His words, though almost casually uttered, were a revelation, forcing her at last to acknowledge, if only to herself, that her decision not to entertain even the idea of marrying him years ago might yet prove to be a grave error of judgement on her part. Against all the odds she had come to look upon him as a friend, certainly one of the best, if not the best she'd ever had. She would always treasure his friendship, and had no intention of repaying the kindness he had shown towards her by evasion or lies.

'You asked me to marry you because my grandfather desired the match, did you not?' she said softly. 'You were no more in love with me than I was with you.'

Thankfully he made no attempt to deny it. Yet his honesty, if anything, only made what she knew she must reveal next far more of a difficult task. 'When I was a child I can recall my governess reminding me often that self-esteem was a sin. Evidently she was aware that I suffered from a surfeit of pride. Indeed, I did, and still do, for that matter. Even now I would find it immensely difficult to welcome a gentleman into my arms, when another woman's odour still clings to his person.'

She didn't allow his expression of complete bewilderment to discourage her. She had come thus far, and was now determined to confess all. 'Cast your mind back to that last visit you made to Foxhunter Grange, Bart,' she ordered softly. 'Can you not recall what you were doing just an hour or two before you made your oh, so very gallant proposal of marriage? Can you not recall precisely where you were, and with whom?

'No?' she added, when his expression merely grew thoughtful and she received no response. 'Well, I'm no expert in such matters, but I wouldn't have considered the floor of a summerhouse the ideal place for—er—tupping.'

Had she not witnessed it with her own eyes, Abbie would never have believed it possible for healthily tanned skin to lose every vestige of colour in a matter of seconds. Never had she seen a gentleman appear more stunned, so completely devastated. Only minutes before she had believed that he had every right to know why she had rejected his suit so comprehensively; now she would have given almost anything to be able to retract the confession.

The memory of what she had witnessed on that spring afternoon so many years ago no longer had the power to overset her, as it once had. Only before she could assure him of this, Barryman entered with the intelligence that Lord Warren and an officer of dragoons awaited him in the library.

Bart appeared not to hesitate to grasp the excuse to leave, legitimate though it was, and strode from the room without uttering anything further.

Chapter Ten

When she discovered they were to be deprived of masculine company that evening, owing to the fact that Bart had accepted an invitation to dine with Lord Warren, Abbie didn't attach too much importance to his absence. When he didn't put in an appearance at the breakfast table the following morning, however, and she discovered he had broken his fast early and had already left the house, she couldn't help wondering whether he was deliberately attempting to avoid her as much as possible, and that her leaving the Court at the earliest opportunity might be the best course of action, given that he might well be feeling uncomfortable now with her continued presence under his roof.

In the meantime she at least would strive to behave as normally as possible, just as though she had never made that wretched confession. She had planned to visit the nearest town in order to purchase a birthday present for Eugenie, and had hoped that Bart might accompany her. As this was out of the question now, she had no choice but to secure the services of her groom.

Although the town was several miles away, they made good time on a morning that was both dry and pleasantly warm. It didn't take Abbie long to discover the ideal gift for Eugenie; even though her funds were limited, she had sufficient in her purse to buy the matching set of three crystal containers in which perfumes could be stored.

Well pleased with her purchase, for she felt certain Eugenie would appreciate the gift, Abbie returned to where Josh was awaiting her with the horses. She would dearly have liked to remain for a while in order to explore the narrow cobbled streets in the town, but didn't delay her return, for there was something that she wished to discuss with Bart, an ideal solution to a problem that she was amazed had never occurred to her before.

She cast a fleeting glance at the tall figure riding alongside. Whistling a popular ditty, Josh looked very contented. No one could ever accuse him of having a morose disposition. Even when they had been in Bath he had always appeared very well pleased to accompany her about the city. Yet he, like herself, seemed just that fraction more relaxed in the country. He had certainly seemed at ease during his time at the Court, more so since Dodd's departure.

Hackman thought well of him too. So surely there was no need for Bart to engage another groom when the ideal person was at hand?

She turned to look at him again, about to suggest that he might like to remain at the Court after her departure, and was surprised to discover deep lines etched across his forehead. The reason for the grim expression was not difficult to locate. Propped against the front wall of a poorly maintained tavern just a short distance ahead, a straw dangling from between his lips, was a very familiar figure.

As he detected the sound of hoofbeats he turned his head, the length of straw falling as his mouth curled into a sneer. 'Glad to see they're keeping you hard at it, Arkwright,' he jeered, as they drew nearer. 'Keep in Cavanagh's good books and you might even get old Hackman's job one o' these days. Being at some master's beck and call is all you're fit for. But some of us were born for 'igher fings.'

Abbie had no intention whatsoever of even paying Dodd the common courtesy of acknowledging his presence, and would have ridden past without favouring him with so much as a second glance, had she not detected what had now become a very familiar accent.

The next moment a swarthy individual, whose appearance was as unkempt as his tavern, emerged from the doorway. At least Abbie assumed it must be the landlord, for Dodd instantly set about moving the barrel that had stood by the wall beside him.

'Ah've just bethowt missen—' Catching sight of Abbie, the new arrival ceased speaking abruptly. Then dark eyes, set in a thin, sallow face betraying a lifetime's dissipation, favoured her with a long, insulting stare as she drew abreast of him.

'Good day to 'ee, ma'am,' he called, raising a decidedly grubby hand to the matted black hair at his temple. 'And a reet fine morning it be too.'

'Indeed, it is,' she felt obliged to acknowledge, even though she had no intention of pausing to exchange further pleasantries.

'What a coincidence, Josh, to find someone hereabouts from your neck of the woods,' she remarked, once they had ridden on a few yards.

'Nay, Miss Abbie, he don't come from my part of Yorkshire. He be a West Riding man.'

'I stand corrected,' she acknowledged, prior to glancing back over her shoulder to discover Dodd and his employer deep in conversation, still standing at the front of the inn, staring fixedly in their direction. Perhaps Dodd was revealing precisely who they were. If so, his companion for some reason appeared very interested.

A shudder ran through her as she turned to look at the road ahead. There was something decidedly unpleasant about that stranger. It was not just his filthy, unkempt appearance that was distasteful. There was something in his expression that was ugly, menacing. Little wonder Hackman didn't patronise the inn, she mused. She couldn't imagine too many travellers would risk sampling mine host's hospitality either, if the state of the exterior was an indication of what one would discover within.

The chance encounter with Dodd ought to have kept Josh's future in the forefront of her mind. Strangely it did not. Once they had ridden round the bend in the road and the tavern was no longer visible, her thoughts immediately turned to the last-minute arrangements for Eugenie's party, and it wasn't until she had arrived back at the Court, and discovered from Barryman that the master of the house had also returned, that her mind once again began to dwell on her groom's future.

Only for a moment did she hesitate before knocking on the library door and entering to discover Bart seated behind his desk, staring fixedly through the window. If, indeed, he was feeling slightly awkward now with her presence in the house, at least she could prove that she was not similarly afflicted. She had carried the secret of his affair with Lady Sophia Fitzpatrick around with her for six long years, for heaven's sake, and it hadn't prevented her from finally coming to look upon Bart as a friend! And she had no intention of allowing a past indiscretion to thrust a wedge in their friendship if she could do anything to avoid it, either! she thought determinedly, closing the door, and moving further into the room.

It was a moment or two before he took the trouble to discover who had entered. Then he was on his feet in an instant, his expression betraying mild surprise, but certainly no degree of embarrassment.

'Kitty told me you'd gone out to buy a present for Eugenie,' he said, after gesturing her to the chair on the opposite side of the desk, which she took as an indication that at least he was in no hurry for her to leave. 'Did you enjoy your visit?'

'Very much. I would have liked to explore for a while, but there are one or two matters I must attend to before the party on Friday, the main one being to beard the lion in his den and persuade him to part with some of his splendid blooms so that I have something with which to decorate the large salon, and the dining-room.'

'I don't suppose you'll have much trouble with Figg,' he assured her, smiling briefly before his expression grew sombre and he began to gather together the papers that littered his desk. 'Did you have a particular reason for wishing to see me?'

'Yes, I did,' she answered, refusing to be daunted by his abrupt change of tone. 'I wondered whether you'd already found a replacement for Dodd and, if not, whether you might consider Josh for the position?'

If anything, his expression grew more serious, but

at least she had succeeded in regaining his full attention. 'I'd be the first to admit to making a mistake in taking on Dodd, and I have no intention of making another, Abbie, not at the present time when I need to be especially careful. What do we know about Josh Arkwright? Nothing,' he went on without waiting for an answer. ' I maintain that it's a mistake to employ people without references. Dodd's a prime example.'

'True,' she was forced to agree. 'But surely you don't imagine that Josh had anything to do with the damage to the bridge, or that masonry falling from the roof? Why, it's ridiculous! What possible motive could he have? He isn't even from around these parts, so he cannot hold a grievance against you.'

Bart found himself smiling despite the seriousness of the conversation. 'I agree it does seem unlikely. The lad couldn't have been responsible for starting the fire, either. But then neither could Dodd. They were both in Bath at the time.' A sigh escaped him. 'I'm afraid at the moment, though, I'm suspicious of most everyone, looking at people I've known for years and wondering.'

'I would be less than truthful if I didn't own to the fact that it had crossed my mind to suspect someone close to you, someone who can gain access to the house. Someone who, moreover, would not seem out of place wandering about the grounds.' She shook her head. 'But I couldn't begin to imagine who it might be. Most all those you employ have been with you for years. So why all this sudden ill feeling towards you now?'

Again he found himself smiling. 'So you, like the Major who was here yesterday, are inclined to believe that something quite personal is the motive for the recent incidents?'

Abbie moved uncomfortably in the chair. 'Well, yes… Don't you?'

'If I didn't before, I'm certainly considering the possibility now,' he freely admitted. 'I discovered from Major Wetherby that there are certain factions among the poor openly voicing malcontent. And who can blame them? Times are hard. Perhaps, more significantly, he also confirms that instances of damage to property are confined to this area alone, the vast majority perpetrated against me. Which, of course, we already knew. So he's proposing to station half his men in the vicinity. There are plenty in the area willing to take them in. Personally, though, I'm not altogether sure that it's the solution.'

Abbie had no difficulty in understanding his reservations. 'You suspect that whoever is responsible will merely postpone any future unlawful action until the soldiers have moved on.'

A hint of respect sprang into his dark eyes. 'Yes, that's precisely what I expect will happen. The Major will be unable to keep his men here indefinitely. As soon as their services are required elsewhere they will move on.'

Bart easily identified the lingering expression of concern, before Abbie rose to her feet, effectively bringing the brief tête-à-tête to an end by announcing that she simply couldn't offend Eugenie's sensibilities by going in to luncheon smelling of the stables, and must therefore hurry and change her attire.

'For the time being we should be safe enough, with the Major's men billeted close by,' he assured her, arresting her progress across to the door. 'So put it from your mind. You've enough to think about with the party. Oh, and, Abbie,' he added, as she was about to withdraw, 'be sure that I shall give some serious thought to offering Josh a permanent position here.'

Although they did not travel together, Lady Penrose and Giles arrived within a matter of minutes of each other the following afternoon, and instantly Abbie was conscious of a different atmosphere in the house. Her godmother's easy manners and lazy good humour made her a popular house guest no matter where she stayed, and Eugenie's welcome could not have been warmer. Quite naturally Bart was delighted to have Giles residing under his roof, if only for a few days, so that he could enjoy some masculine company for a change, and Kitty too didn't attempt to conceal her pleasure at seeing her brother's close friend again.

Although promising faithfully to look in on her godmother later, Abbie had no intention of interfering in the duties of the hostess, and happily stepped aside so that Eugenie, ably assisted by her daughter, could fulfil her role in the household by ensuring her guests were comfortably settled in their respective bedchambers. Lady Penrose, Abbie felt sure, would appreciate a rest after the journey. She felt equally certain that Giles, once he had changed his attire, would wish to seek out Bart's company again in the library. Consequently Abbie wasn't slow to avail herself of the opportunity of slipping quietly away to the garden, where she could be alone with her thoughts.

It was all very well for Bart to suggest that she shouldn't concern herself with his troubles, she decided, once again availing herself of that conveniently positioned bench halfway along the path. But for heaven's sake, how could she not! When he had put in an appearance at luncheon the day before, she had known she had been fanciful in supposing that he had been attempting to avoid her. He had been excellent company throughout the remainder of the day, behaving just as he had always done. Well, almost, she amended silently. Kitty and her mother might suppose that he wasn't unduly troubled by the series of unfortunate occurrences. But she had detected that expression of concern, which had returned in unguarded moments.

Surely there must be something she could do during the time she remained at the Court? After all, one might have supposed that, as an outsider, she would be able to view things more objectively than Bart; except, when she had been checking over the menus for the party with Cook the previous afternoon, and had raised the subject of the recent happenings, she hadn't doubted for a moment that Mrs Figg's concern for her master's safety had been genuine.

Yes, indeed it was difficult to believe that any one of the servants could have been involved in the unfortunate happenings. Yet, at the same time, the person responsible for the most recent misdeeds must surely have been someone who hadn't aroused suspicion by his presence at the Court?

'Now, miss, what's all this?' a rough voice suddenly demanded to know, instantly drawing Abbie out of her brown study. 'You ain't a-fretting yourself on account of the flowers, now? I won't let you down, miss.'

'Oh, hello, Figgie,' she acknowledged, easily managing a smile. Of all Bart's people she had, amazingly enough, grown most fond of this occasionally irascible old man. 'No, I know I can rely on you. Sit down, won't you? I'd like to ask you something.'

He neither showed reluctance to comply, nor did he attempt to stop puffing on his pipe, as he knew she didn't object to his smoking. 'What's worrying you, miss?'

Abbie couldn't prevent a further smile. One of the old man's most endearing qualities was his bluntness. He always said precisely what was on his mind. 'What's your opinion of the recent happenings here, Figgie?'

'Rum goings on, and no mistake. Mind you, miss, the one who did the bridge must be a right knock-in-the-cradle, if t'were the master he were aiming to 'urt.' His shoulders shook as he gave vent to a wheezy laugh. 'The master can swim like a fish, so he can.'

'Now that is something I hadn't considered,' Abbie admitted, more to herself. 'Everyone who works for Mr Cavanagh must surely know that he can swim.'

'Those that 'ave worked 'ere for some time would, miss,' he agreed, 'and that's most everyone. 'Cepting that groom o' yourn. But 'ee's a good lad. Brings me round a barrow load o' the good stuff most every day and puts it on the pile, yonder.'

His approval of Josh came as no surprise. Everyone seemed to like him. Which, she sincerely hoped, would act in his favour if Bart was seriously to consider employing him.

'What about the people employed on the land, Figgie? Are they all content working for Mr Cavanagh?'

'You'll not find one who'd say a word against him, miss, and that's a fact. Like his father and grandfather afore 'im, he be well liked.'

'Not by everyone,' she countered.

'Well, miss, I don't reckon anyone born and bred in these parts would bear 'im a grudge. He's fair to his people, and he's always done business with local tradesmen. Now I ain't saying the master's ain't put a nose or two out of joint in his time. He ain't afeared to speak his mind. Bound to 'ave rubbed someone up the wrong way. But I reckon there be more to it than that. Besides…'

Abbie detected the sound of approaching footsteps too, and turned to see Bart, closely followed by his sister and Giles, entering the garden by way of the wicket gate.

Bart was not slow to observe her either, or his head gardener, for that matter, and raised his brows in exaggerated surprise. 'What's all this then, Figg? Resting on your spade again, I see. I shall seriously need to consider turning you off at the twelvemonth if you continue neglecting your duties in this shameful manner.'

Abbie could not help smiling at Figg's wicked chuckle, as he rose to his feet and hobbled away to continue with what he had been doing. He was a canny old man whose knowledge stretched a deal further than the confines of the garden he tended so well. Perhaps there was something in what he had said, she mused, and the answer to Bart's present troubles would not be found here at the Court, but somewhere in his past.

'Would you care to bear me company?' Bart invited, smiling crookedly as Kitty and Giles walked past them, chattering happily together and seemingly locked in a world of their own. 'Otherwise, I very much fear that I'm likely to be ignored for the most part.'

'I, for one, wouldn't be at all surprised if you were,' Abbie declared, rising to her feet and automatically allowing him to entwine her arm through his without giving the matter a second thought. 'You know Giles is in love with her, of course?' she added, successfully maintaining a slow pace and forcing Bart to do likewise so that a discreet distance was maintained between them and the couple in front.

Once again those dark brows rose, only this time his surprise seemed genuine. 'Evidently you didn't realise.' She was unable to suppress a wicked smile of satisfaction. 'And here I have been misguidedly thinking you omnipotent! Seemingly it is much easier to be objective when one is not closely involved.'

'Don't be smug, baggage! It doesn't suit you,' he scolded, trying his utmost to look severe, but failing quite miserably. 'What makes you suppose my friend's affections are engaged? Has he confided in you?'

'Good heavens, no! If Giles is likely to confide in anyone then it will be you, Bart. But I doubt he'll ever broach the subject himself. I strongly suspect he considers himself far too old for her, and therefore unlikely ever to be in the running, as it were.'

'There's no denying there's a disparity in age, though I've always known that he's dashed fond of her.' He stared intently at the couple under discussion, as though attempting to view them in a different light. 'Kitty has never once hinted that her feelings might be engaged.'

'I'm not altogether surprised,' Abbie returned. 'I don't believe she realises it herself yet. But she will in time. She's openly admitted to me that she prefers the company of older men.' Her lips twitched. 'Which is quite amazing, considering from whom she has gained the majority of her experience of the more mature male.'

Clearly he was under no illusion as to precisely whom she was referring, and his low growl in response very nearly sent her into whoops of laughter. 'And females, of course, mature more quickly,' she continued, maintaining her self-control. 'Kitty might still be young, but she's neither frivolous nor shallow. When she returns from Brighton, you will have a clearer indication. She'll be granted the opportunity to meet many young men there, and of course in London too when she goes in the spring. But I shall be very, very surprised if she betrays a partiality for any gentleman's company.'

Although he made no attempt to discuss the matter further, Abbie knew she had given him much to mull over, which she considered no bad thing in the circumstances. It could do him nothing but good to think about something other than the disturbing incidents at the Court.

Consequently Abbie returned to the house, feeling very well pleased with herself. Parting company with the others in the hall, she went directly upstairs to fulfil the promise she had made to her godmother, and discovered her reclining on the *chaise longue* in her bedchamber, a plate of sweet almond biscuits and a glass of ratafia at her elbow.

Swinging her feet to the floor so that Abbie could sit beside her, Lady Penrose noted with satisfaction the healthy bloom in her goddaughter's flawless complexion. 'A bucolic existence evidently agrees with you, my dear. You look quite disgustingly healthy.'

Up until that moment Abbie had not appreciated just how much she had missed her godmother's lively company and wry good humour. Eugenie Cavanagh was undoubtedly one of the most good-natured females one could ever wish to meet. Nevertheless, it could not be denied that her conversation sadly lacked that special stimulating sparkle. Only with Bart could she enjoy a joke and engage in a little harmless verbal fencing.

'All things considered, I have very much enjoyed my stay here at the Court,' Abbie wasn't reticent to admit. 'I felt very comfortable here from the first. It's a lovely old house. In need of a little refurbishment here and there, as you can see,' she added, gazing about at the faded soft furnishings in the bedchamber, 'but its slight imperfections seem only to enhance its character and charm.'

'Like its owner, perhaps?' Lady Penrose suggested, grinning wickedly, and Abbie didn't pretend to misunderstand.

'Very well… Yes, I have come to view Bart in a new light,' she freely acknowledged, though for some obscure reason she didn't seem able to meet her godmother's knowing gaze. For some reason too she had developed the sudden urge to pluck at the folds of her skirt, like a diffident child suddenly thrust into the presence of an imposing stranger. 'But that was only to be expected in the circumstances, given the kindness he has shown towards me in recent weeks.'

'Very true,' Lady Penrose agreed. 'Although I might have wished he'd refrained from encouraging you in the idiotic notion of becoming a professional artist. I'm not denying that you have a natural talent, Abbie,' she thought it tactful to add, after receiving a brief, reproachful look. 'But you must face facts, my dear. No one who can afford to pay generously for a portrait to be painted will seek the services of an unknown. Almost all would wish for an acknowledged master to undertake the work.'

No matter how much she might resent it, Abbie had silently to acknowledge that what her godmother had said was true. Bart too would have known this, would have known that she would find it nigh impossible to support herself as an artist, especially as she had received no professional training. So why on earth had he encouraged her?

'I expect Bart was just trying to be kind,' she murmured, 'and didn't wish to be the one to crush my foolish hopes.'

Although she smiled at this, Lady Penrose refrained from comment, and merely asked how his portrait was progressing.

'All but finished,' Abbie told her, wishing with all her heart that it was quite otherwise, for she had no valid reason now to delay her return to Bath, and she felt sure that Lady Penrose would not wish to remain for more than a week.

She suddenly felt very low, and was relieved to see Felcham enter the room in order to help her mistress dress for dinner, because it gave her the excuse she needed to seek the sanctuary of her own bedchamber.

Going immediately over to the window, Abbie stared out at the view she had swiftly grown to love. Why was it that she had been able to accept that in all probability she would never become a successful professional artist, when she simply couldn't bear to think about the day when she would leave Cavanagh Court...and its master?

Chapter Eleven

Fortunately for Abbie she was kept far too busy throughout the following day, ensuring that everything would run smoothly for the surprise party, to dwell too frequently on her return to Bath. Which was perhaps just as well, she reflected, adding the finishing touches to her toilette, because she hadn't been at all successful in shrugging off her mood of despondency throughout the previous evening and had caught Bart regarding her intently on two or three occasions.

'You look lovely, miss,' Rose announced, placing the lightweight silk shawl about Abbie's shoulders, while at the same time studying the arrangement of her silky black locks. 'I watched very closely to how Miss Felcham did your hair, miss. I'm sure I could do it myself next time.'

'I'm certain you could too,' Abbie agreed. From her first day at the Court she had been more than satisfied with the young housemaid's services. 'I'm afraid, though, it's unlikely you'll be granted the opportunity to try. There'll be no more large dinner parties before your mistress leaves for Brighton. And I shall be returning to Bath myself at the end of next week.'

Determined not to fall victim to a fit of the sullens again this evening, Abbie did her best to ignore the return of that painful spasm beneath her ribcage. 'In the meantime, you could do no better than try to pick up a few tips from Felcham. She's an extremely competent lady's maid. Which I'm sure you will be one day.'

This brought a smile to Rose's face. 'That's what I'd really like to be, miss, though it ain't likely to happen unless the master marries. Still, I don't suppose he'll leave it too much longer before he takes a wife.'

A pain, far more acutely searing than anything she had suffered thus far, shot through Abbie, and for a moment she felt the need to grasp the back of a chair for support. It was bad enough having to come to terms with leaving the Court; Bart's marrying was something she simply didn't wish to contemplate, now or ever.

Only by tapping into that deep well of inner strength, which had been steadily increasing during recent years, did Abbie manage to restore sufficient composure to take herself downstairs to the drawing-room where everyone had congregated. Thankfully

Kitty was enthusing over the lovely amethyst set Bart had presented to Eugenie for her birthday, and Abbie was able to slip into the chair beside her godmother before anyone noticed she was there.

She was further aided by the arrival of the first guests; by the time she had taken her seat in the dining-room, and had worked her way through several delicious courses, she was feeling a deal more composed. Even so, she could scarcely bring herself to peer up at the head of the table, where Bart sat happily conversing with Lady Warren and another close neighbour's middle-aged wife.

'You and Kitty must have worked very hard this afternoon to arrange all the flowers, Abbie,' Lady Penrose remarked, sidling up beside her goddaughter the instant they had returned to the drawing-room.

'Yes, I'm rather pleased with the way things have gone thus far,' Abbie freely admitted, glancing across at the door, where Eugenie was stationed beside her stepson in readiness to welcome the first of the guests who had been invited just to the party. 'Of course Kitty and I realised at the outset that we would be unable to keep the event a secret, so we merely informed Eugenie that Bart had suggested a few people should join us for dinner this evening by way of a celebration, though it was clear she hadn't been expecting quite so many at table. And the party, of course, has come as a complete surprise to her, for which we have you to thank. It was a marvellous idea of yours to take her out in the carriage, keeping her away from the Court for much of the day'

'I thoroughly enjoyed myself,' Lady Penrose declared. 'Although I reside permanently in Bath now, I do not know this part of the country at all well. It was most agreeable seeing the sights. There's some lovely countryside round here.'

'I've done a deal of exploring whilst I've been here,' Abbie disclosed. 'I've never been at a loss for something to do. Bart has seen to that.'

Lady Penrose subjected her goddaughter to a prolonged stare before her attention was captured by a familiar figure. 'Good heavens! Where did he spring from? I thought he'd returned to London.'

Abbie turned in time to see Eugenie's eyes widen as she greeted Bart's cousin, and couldn't say she was altogether surprised by the reaction. Cedric Cavanagh's attire could never be described as sober, and this evening he was more startlingly arrayed than usual in a primrose-coloured coat, with matching knee breeches. The preposterously large nosegay fixed in his lapel was no less dazzling than the emerald nestling between the folds of the most intricately tied cravat Abbie had ever seen.

'Oh, dear me,' she murmured unsteadily. 'Just look at Bart's face. I do hope he manages to refrain from saying something cutting to his cousin throughout the evening. But I wouldn't lay odds on it.'

'What an utter twiddle-poop the boy is!' Lady Penrose exclaimed, not mincing words. 'Little wonder Bart doesn't hold his cousin in high esteem.'

Abbie was forced to agree. 'Cedric has been a guest at the Hall for almost three weeks. But this is the first time he's visited the Court. Bart has shown no interest in seeking his cousin's company either. Although I was somewhat surprised to learn from Bart, after he had dined with the Warrens the other evening, that Cedric would not be dining with us this evening, owing to the fact that he was accompanying Richard Warren to watch a mill.'

Lady Penrose was amazed and did not attempt to hide the fact. 'Well, well, well! Who would have supposed a fribble like Cedric would have been interested in the manly sport of boxing?'

Abbie frowned at this. 'Yes, perhaps he isn't quite what he seems,' she responded, before giving her godmother's arm a warning squeeze. 'Have a care, ma'am. I do believe the popinjay is heading our way.'

'Why, Mr Cavanagh, this is a surprise!' Lady Penrose greeted him. 'Bath has quite lost its sparkle since your departure. And little wonder! You whisked it all away, I see, in the folds of your cravat.'

Abbie almost choked, but Cedric appeared very well pleased as he attempted to peer down at the glinting emerald. 'Yes, it's a splendid stone, is it not? Mama presented it to me on my last birthday.' He then turned his attention to Abbie in order to secure her promise for a dance, and then, much to her intense relief, sauntered away in order to pay his respects to his favourite cousin.

Lady Penrose frowned as she watched him present the nosegay to Kitty. 'Well, at any rate, he appears to have a genuine fondness for her. I sincerely trust it is no more than cousinly affection, though. I cannot envisage Bartholomew Cavanagh ever being persuaded to sanction a marriage in that quarter.'

Abbie smiled to herself. 'I cannot imagine he'll ever be called upon to do so. Unless I'm grossly mistaken, Kitty finds Cedric amusing, nothing more.'

She refused to divulge more than this by betraying Kitty's regard for a certain other gentleman, even though she half suspected there was no real need for her to do so, for her godmother was no fool, and noticed a deal more than most people imagined.

On another matter, however, she had come perilously close to attaining her godmother's opinion. Undoubtedly Lady Penrose would have been the ideal person with whom to share her concerns over Bart's future well-being. All the same she had refrained from doing so, simply because she could not envisage any further incidents occurring during the remainder of her stay at the Court, most especially not now, when there was a company of dragoons stationed in the locale.

It just so happened that Bart had invited several of the young officers to the party, their smart dark blue uniforms making a pleasing contrast to the more sober black coats worn by the majority of the gentlemen present. Most all the younger female guests were eyeing the officers with favour, and Abbie too was not slow to accept Major Wetherby's invitation to dance, although her eager acceptance had little to do with a preference for gentlemen sporting dashing regimentals.

The Major wasn't slow to divulge that he had made Bart's acquaintance whilst out in the Peninsula. Something in his tone strongly suggested that their association had not been altogether amicable, but Abbie tactfully refrained from attempting to discover if she was right, and merely asked if any progress had been made in uncovering the identities of those involved in damage to property.

'No, ma'am,' he answered. 'And I'm not particularly hopeful that we shall bring any to book.'

'Oh, and why not, Major?'

'Because our inquiries thus far have come to naught. A reward is usually inducement enough for someone to reveal what he knows. But in this instance we have drawn a blank, which has only served to strengthen my belief that the unrest is not so widespread in this area, but an isolated pocket of perhaps two or three troublemakers who have a particular target in mind.'

Before the steps of the dance separated them, Abbie noticed his head turn fleetingly in the direction of the door, where Bart, stoically maintaining his role as host, still bore Eugenie company. Had it not been for the slight tightening of the muscles she perceived about the Major's full-lipped mouth, his expression would have been difficult to read. As it was, she was now firmly convinced that there was no love lost between him and Bart, and didn't hesitate to pick up the threads of their conversation when the steps of the dance brought them together again.

'You were referring to Mr Cavanagh, Major, I believe. That someone bears him a grudge also occurred to me,' she freely admitted. 'Yet I also know that he is well respected in these parts.'

'That I also have discovered. He had a reputation for fairness when in the army, ma'am. But one still makes enemies, and Cavanagh is no exception. You, I understand, have known him for some years. Therefore you must be well aware that he isn't always diplomatic, and isn't afraid to speak his mind.'

'True,' she was forced to concede. 'But I hardly think that sufficient inducement to attempt to burn down his house, or make attempts on his life.'

As the dance came to an end the Major drew her aside. 'Clearly you are in Cavanagh's confidence, ma'am, so I shall speak freely. Knowing him as I do, it's my belief that the answer to the conundrum lies in some action of his in the past, something he did to someone at some point. And that someone is now bent on revenge. I suggested this to Cavanagh the other night, when we dined with Lord and Lady Warren. I wasn't altogether sure that he had taken the possibility seriously. If you value his friendship, ma'am, I would strongly suggest that you persuade him to think long and hard about the past and the enemies he might have made. I cannot remain in the locale indefinitely to offer protection.'

It was at this point that Bart, having maintained thus far an amiable resignation to his duties as host, began to grow a fraction weary of waiting for the last of the guests to arrive, and glanced about the room at those who had had the common courtesy not to force him to kick his heels by the door. He found it no difficult matter to locate Abbie among the throng. He was surprised to detect what appeared suspiciously like a look of concern on her delicate features, and couldn't help wondering what had been said to bring about the evident disquiet.

'Damned Provost,' he muttered darkly, as his glance strayed to the gentleman bearing her company, whom he had never held in high esteem, and didn't realise his voice had carried until he noticed his stepmother regarding him with a marked degree of uncertainty.

'You do not need to remain with me, Bart, if you would prefer to bear the gentlemen company. I'm quite happy to linger here to welcome the last of the guests.'

He found it no difficult task to summon up a smile. It had taken him too many years to recognise his stepmother's fine qualities. Her displays of diffidence would always irritate him, he supposed. At least, though, she wasn't totally lacking intelligence, and her kindness more than compensated for her slight faults.

'I wouldn't dream of deserting you, Eugenie, on such an occasion as this.'

She blushed becomingly, like a girl embarking on her first Season. 'It was so very thoughtful of you to organise this for me, Bart. We haven't held a large party here in such a long time. It's delightful having all our neighbours and so many friends about us.'

Bart was surprised how much enjoyment he was deriving from the occasion too. Apart from the few weeks they had spent in Bath, they had done little socialising since his father's demise.

'It's Kitty and Abbie you have to thank, Eugenie. All I did was agree to the party, which I did most willingly. One should celebrate such a milestone in one's life. Though looking at you tonight, my dear, no one would suppose for a moment that you'd blessed this earth for half a century.'

He noted the second becoming blush his gallantry had engendered, but his satisfaction was short-lived, for a moment later he caught sight of Abbie again, dancing this time with Cedric, her expression, if anything, more troubled than before.

'Perhaps it's time we both mingled with our guests,' he suggested. 'We can rely on Barryman to locate our whereabouts in the event of yet more late arrivals.'

As she seemed only too willing to comply, Bart escorted her to the corner of the room, where several ladies of her own age had congregated. He then took himself off to the adjoining parlour, which had been set out for those wishing to play cards, and immediately joined his closest friend, avidly watching the play at one of the tables.

'The duties of amiable host are beginning to pall, are they, old fellow?' Giles quizzed him, as Bart reached his side.

'I'm resigned, dear boy. Besides which, I'm fully conscious that I owe it to Eugenie to ensure the evening is a pleasurable one, and shall therefore fulfil my role by entertaining the more mature matrons present. The younger guests, with my irrepressible sister's assistance, will undoubtedly succeed in entertaining themselves.'

Giles regarded him for a moment in silence. 'I notice a great change in you, my friend. You appear far more contented than I've ever known you.'

Bart couldn't forbear a rueful smile at this woefully inaccurate observation. 'Then it would seem I missed my vocation in life. I should have become an actor. No, I'm not wholly content,' he admitted. 'And in the circumstances it's hardly surprising just why I'm not.' He reached out to lay a hand briefly on Giles's shoulder. 'We'll talk again later. But for the time being I must leave you to your own devices as my presence, it would appear, is required to make up a fourth at whist.'

He was happy enough to join the three ladies whose fondness for gambling had proved something of a trial to their respective husbands in recent years. He was happier still to relinquish his place a short while later to yet another female neighbour whose fondness for the game of chance was well known in the locale.

He then returned to the salon where most of the younger guests were engaged in a set of lively country dances, and was somewhat surprised not to find Abbie enjoying the exercise, for he well knew that she rarely missed an opportunity to step out on to the dance floor.

He eventually discovered her amidst a group of younger matrons, not appearing, it had to be said, totally engrossed in the conversation taking place. A moment later she moved away, and although she paused from time to time to exchange a few words with several of those whose acquaintance she had made since her arrival in the county, her intention was clear.

Bart had deliberately refrained from seeking her company thus far, simply because he knew well enough that to single her out for particular attention would only give rise to further speculation. He was fully aware that her presence at the Court during the past weeks had already caused a deal of gossip among his neighbours. This in itself would not have troubled him unduly had it not been that her future role in his life was far from certain. He could not have been more sure of his own feelings; of hers he was not so confident.

All the same, he was not prepared to ignore the fact that the woman he loved, the only woman he had ever truly loved, was worrying over something, most especially if confiding in him could ease her troubled mind.

Hence, hc didn't hesitate to follow her example by escaping from the crowd by way of the French windows, and caught sight of her almost at once, standing in one corner of the terrace, staring out at that part of the garden where lanterns had been hung from the branches of trees.

At the sound of his footfall she turned, that wonderful, spontaneous smile of hers instantly diminishing his fear that all was not as it should be with her, but not completely. 'Feeling a little unsociable this evening, are we?' he quizzed, deliberately keeping his tone light.

'Not at all,' she answered. 'Merely taking advantage of a little fresh air.'

He wasn't at all convinced, but thought better of pressing her further, especially as their conversation might easily be overheard by anyone strolling in the garden. Besides which, he was finding it a mite dif-

ficult to prevent his thoughts from turning to that
one other time when they had been alone on a shadowed terrace, and he had allowed desire to take control. He had never been able to forget those moments
of sweet response before his advances had been summarily rejected. Now, of course, he could understand
the reason behind the eventual rebuff. The wonder of
it was that she tolerated him at all. Yet she did, and
against all the odds she had, he felt sure, grown to
trust him and, yes, had come to look upon him as a
friend.

'And what brings you out here? Not tired already
of playing the host?'

'Not at all. I am enjoying this evening.' He bridged
the distance between them, and experienced a degree
of satisfaction, when at last he stood so closely beside her and their bodies almost touched, that she
didn't attempt to draw away even so much as an inch.
'You and Kitty have worked so hard to make this an
enjoyable occasion. When Kitty and her mother return from their Brighton trip, I'll suggest we entertain more often.'

He would have expected her to approve of this, and
yet surprisingly she frowned. 'Is there some reason
why you have refrained from doing so in the past?
All your neighbours seem so personable.'

'They are,' he readily concurred. 'Although I'd be
less than honest if I didn't admit to liking some a deal
more than others.' He shrugged. 'I suppose I've been

too involved in the running of the property to concern myself about much else, least of all socialising. I should have considered Eugenie and Kitty more. It was selfish of me, I suppose.'

'No, you're not selfish, Bart,' she countered softly. 'A little thoughtless on occasions, perhaps, but not selfish.'

Only the very real possibility that he might jeopardise that surprisingly sweet rapport which had sprung up between them prevented him from covering that provocatively smiling mouth with his own. Friendship was a poor substitute for what he really wanted. Yet it would be foolish not to accept the heartrending possibility that he might never be offered more.

'If you're sufficiently restored, perhaps you'd allow me to escort you back into the salon before our absence gives rise to comment,' he suggested, taking a hasty step away before his self-control was too severely tested.

Although she acquiesced readily enough, he thought he detected a look akin to disappointment flit over her features the moment before she turned and moved back across the terrace.

He shook his head, wondering at himself, as he followed her back into the salon. It was possibly complete madness on his part to suppose that one day her friendship might deepen. Even so, he found himself clinging to the faint hope. It somehow sustained him

and made the remainder of the evening far more pleasurable than it might otherwise have been. Nevertheless he wasn't sorry to bid the last of his guests a
fond farewell and seek the company of the one person in whom he was happy to confide his present
troubles.

'Unless you wish to follow the ladies' example and
retire, perhaps you'd care to join me in the library for
a nightcap?' he suggested.

Giles was only too happy to oblige. 'You never
cease to amaze me, old fellow,' he confessed, after
accepting the goodly measure of brandy, and watching Bart make himself comfortable in the chair opposite. 'For someone who has always thought little
of social graces, you're an accomplished host.'

Smiling to himself, Bart stared down into the contents of his glass. 'As you yourself remarked earlier
this evening, age has undoubtedly mellowed me. I am
far less intolerant of my fellow man.'

One sandy brow rose in a quizzical arch. 'And I do
not think we need look far to find the beneficial influence.'

Bart refrained from comment, and with an abrupt
change of subject voiced the wish that his friend
could make a longer stay. 'Of course I fully appreciate why you must leave tomorrow. How long do you
propose to remain with your uncle?'

Giles was suddenly grave. 'Until the end. Sadly
he'll not be with us much longer, a matter of a few

weeks only, and it's the least I can do. After all, I am his closest relative, and heir.'

Having enjoyed a close friendship with Giles since boyhood, Bart knew a deal about his background. Giles had never evinced a desire to follow in his father's footsteps by studying law, and had gone into the army, once his education was completed, in the full knowledge that one day he would inherit his uncle's sizeable property in Somerset. Throughout his life he had maintained strong ties with his uncle, with whom he had enjoyed a far closer relationship than he had with his own father.

'I do appreciate how much you'll miss the old man,' Bart said softly. 'I know also that you'll take great care of your inheritance. Of course,' he added, striving for a lighter note, 'coming into a property does have some disadvantages. One instantly becomes a matrimonial prize.'

The ploy worked, for Giles's smile returned. 'Oh, I believe I'm capable of taking a leaf out of your book, old fellow, and succeed in keeping all the little darlings at bay.'

'What, all of them?' Bart quizzed gently. 'Or am I right in thinking there is one with whom you would happily share your life?'

Although clearly taken aback, Giles didn't attempt to deny it. 'How on earth could you possibly have known? Not even my mother has ever guessed.'

'You certainly succeeded in concealing your feelings from me,' Bart admitted. 'It was someone far more discerning than I who brought it to my notice. Since then I have been observing your behaviour towards my sister, and realise that my confidante, perceptive little darling that she is, had spoken no less than the truth.'

'Abbie, of course,' Giles murmured, before a glimmer of hope flickered over his features. 'Do you suppose Kitty might possibly have said something to her?'

'Abbie is of the opinion that Kitty, as yet, does not appreciate the depths of her feelings towards you, and I'm inclined to agree with her. Needless to say it didn't go unnoticed by me that my sister ensured that you were placed beside her at dinner, and also that she chose you as her escort in to supper.'

Only for a moment longer did the glint in Giles's eyes remain, then he shook his head. 'I know she has a fondness for me, Bart. But I'm too old for her.'

'That was precisely my first thought, old fellow,' he admitted, his white teeth flashing in a sportive smile. 'Until, that is, Abbie remarked upon my sister's preference for the company of older men, and yours in particular.' He was suddenly serious. 'As Abbie was at pains to point out, Kitty is neither fickle nor flirtatious. But she's still young. I am therefore determined she should be granted the opportunity to meet other gentlemen. If, however, after her Season in Brighton and her visit to the capital next year, she has formed no attachment, you have my blessing to pay your address.'

A hint of colour had appeared in Giles's cheeks, surprisingly making him appear much younger than his thirty years. 'Thank you. I could ask no more of you than that. Or is it perhaps Miss Graham I ought to thank for being so perceptive and bringing to your notice my sincere regard for your sister?' He took a moment to sample the contents of his glass, while all the time staring intently across at his friend. 'I cannot help wondering, though, whether she's as perceptive with regard to you.'

If Giles had been expecting a rueful grin in response to this gambit, he was doomed to disappointment, for Bart, after several moments of stony silence, merely tossed the contents of his glass down his throat, and stalked back across to the decanters for a refill. 'I'm sorry old fellow,' he added. 'I didn't mean to pry.'

'I'm not at all certain whether she does realise,' Bart revealed, when at last he returned to his chair. 'And the truth of the matter is that I'm too much of a damnable coward to leave her in no doubt, lest her decision to marry me remain the same as before.'

Giles was silent for a moment, then said, 'But as you remarked yourself, neither of you were ready for matrimony then.'

'The truth of the matter is, old fellow, I was foolish enough to make the proposal at my godfather's behest, and experienced nothing but relief when she turned me down flat,' Bart admitted. 'If I ever gave the matter any thought at all, and I cannot recall her refusal ever preyed on my mind to any significant degree, I assumed she at least had had the sense to realise that we were too young.'

Giles gazed sagely across at him. 'Evidently you have since discovered more lay behind the refusal.'

'Oh, yes, much more,' Bart confirmed, before disclosing everything that had occurred during the last fateful visit to his godfather's home.

'Oh, my God!' Giles muttered, surprisingly igniting a spark of merriment in Bart's eyes.

'I do believe that that was more or less what passed through my mind when Abbie finally confided in me.' He shook his head, all amusement gone. 'I couldn't have offered her a greater insult had I tried— enjoying the favours of a neighbour's wife one moment, and the next professing my devotion to her. The wonder of it is she ever spoke to me again!'

'But surely she must realise the affair meant nothing, merely a young man sowing his wild oats, as it were,' Giles suggested hopefully.

'Yes, perhaps she does,' Bart agreed, staring intently at a spot on the ceiling. 'At least I believe she has come to look upon me as a friend. And perhaps I should be satisfied with that.'

'No, you shouldn't,' Giles countered, without giving the matter a moment's thought. 'You should tell her precisely how you feel about her now. You may come to regret it if you don't.'

Bart didn't misunderstand. 'If I delay, then I run the risk of losing her to someone else. Yes,' he agreed. 'That is a very real possibility now that she is to reside with her godmother. But it's a risk I must take. I cannot attempt to woo her now, especially not here at the Court and at the present time. I'll not have her put at further risk. She must leave.'

Bart was surprised by his friend's lack of response, for Giles was well aware of what had been happening at the Court in recent weeks. 'You appear doubtful,' he prompted, when Giles continued to stare silently down at the empty hearth. 'Surely you can appreciate my reasoning?'

Clearly troubled, Giles nodded. 'But has it never occurred to you to consider that it might be Abbie, not you, who is the real target? And before you dismiss it out of hand,' he added, when Bart was about to do just that, 'remember one thing. She has been with you on both occasions—when the masonry fell from the roof, and at the bridge. Furthermore, she was with you on the occasion when your curricle just happened to lose a wheel a few weeks ago.'

Bart took a moment to consider, then shook his head. 'No, impossible! No one would ever wish to harm that darling girl!' he declared, and then promptly dismissed it from his mind until the following day, when he witnessed an incident that forced him to take the suggestion rather more seriously.

Chapter Twelve

Midway through the following morning, while making use of the stable-yard as a short cut, Abbie was surprised to discover her normally hardworking groom sitting outside the largest of the stables, whittling away on a piece of willow.

Far from looking guilt-ridden at being caught idling away his time, he appeared remarkably well pleased to see her, and rose at once to his feet. 'Can I give you a hand with them, Miss Abbie?'

'I didn't expect to find you here,' she remarked, gratefully handing over the rug, and the basket of food that Cook had insisted pressing upon her in the event that she should lose track of time and miss luncheon. 'I thought you'd have accompanied Miss Cavanagh and Mr Fergusson out on their ride.'

'No, Mr Hackman's done that, miss, seeing as Mrs Cavanagh went out in Lady Penrose's carriage and his services weren't required.'

Abbie had been invited to go with the ladies on a visit to several neighbours, but had declined, mainly because she had wished to do a few sketches of the Court and surrounding park land as a memento of her stay. She had also been invited to join Kitty and Giles on their ride, and had declined that invitation too, having decided they might appreciate some time alone together before Giles returned to Somerset later in the day.

As they set off across the park towards the group of stately elms adjacent to the folly, Abbie's thoughts once again turned to the future well-being of the person striding happily alongside.

Since her arrival at the Court, Lady Penrose had mentioned that, although he had not accompanied her on the journey, her young groom was now fully recovered and undertaking his duties. Which meant, of course, that Josh's services would no longer be required. Knowing of Bart's reluctance to employ strangers—and in the present climate no one could blame him for that—Abbie had refrained from raising the matter of the groom's future employment again. Josh himself hadn't made her situation any easier. He had seemed so wonderfully contented here at the Court that she had tended to shy away from broaching the subject again. Time, however, was fast running out, and she could no longer avoid doing so.'

'I do not know whether you're aware of it or not,

Josh, but Lady Penrose's young groom is fully recovered,' she said, before she could change her mind.

'Happen her ladyship's head groom, Jenkins, did mention it, miss.'

As Josh was certainly no simpleton, Abbie found his seeming indifference a trifle disturbing. 'You do realise what it will mean, of course?' she persisted. 'Lady Penrose is unlikely to keep you on.'

'Aye, miss. Wouldn't expect her to neither.'

'But, Josh, aren't you in the least bit concerned?' She favoured him with a searching glance before shaking out the rug and spreading it on the ground. 'What will you do—try for some work round here, or return to Bath with Lady Penrose and myself on Friday?'

He raised his well-muscled shoulders in a shrug of complete unconcern. 'I hadn't given it much thought, miss. Happen summut'll turn up. It always does.'

Not knowing whether to admire this devil-may-care outlook or not, but deciding any attempt to discuss the issue further would be a complete waste of breath, Abbie settled herself on the rug, and began to sketch her favourite view of the Court. With her various drawing materials scattered about her within easy reach, she was very contented. She guessed Josh was too, for he had soon settled himself on the grass directly behind her, and hadn't been slow either to accept the invitation to avail himself of the contents of the food basket.

For a few minutes she was conscious of a steady munching sound, but certainly wasn't aware when it had suddenly stopped. She was as oblivious to the fact that a tall figure was approaching from the direction of the lake as she was of Josh, reaching for a stout stick, while stealthily rising to his feet. The distant warning cry caught her completely unawares, as did the sudden whoosh of air as the stick was brought down hard by her shoulder, narrowly missing the fingers of her outstretched left hand. She was hardly given time to assimilate the reason behind Josh's action before the sound of heavy running footsteps caught her attention. The next moment Bart, looking murderous, had Josh firmly held by his shirt front and was delivering a crushing blow to his jaw.

'Stop! Stop!'

Scrambling to her feet, Abbie clung to the sleeve of Bart's jacket for all she was worth in a valiant attempt to prevent him from following up his advantage by delivering a second punishing blow. 'Look! Look behind you!' she screamed.

For a few moments it seemed as if Bart was oblivious to her presence, or was intent on ignoring it. Then very slowly he turned his head to see the coiled, half-crushed serpent at the edge of the rug. 'Good Gad!' he muttered, releasing his hold on Josh and grasping Abbie's arms so tightly that she almost winced. 'Did it strike? Were you bitten?'

'No,' she assured him. 'Thanks to Josh. I didn't even realise it was there.'

It would have been a gross exaggeration to suggest that Bart's expression betrayed the least contrition. No one, however, could have doubted his sincerity when at last he apologised, and held out his hand to help Josh to his feet, least of all the groom himself who, if anything, appeared amused as he rubbed the swelling on his jaw.

'You've a powerful left hook there, Mr Cavanagh,' he declared, totally without rancour. 'Can tell you've done a bit of sparring afore now.'

For answer Bart smiled ruefully before turning his attention to Abbie to discover her looking distinctly pale. Instinctively he placed an arm about her shoulders and drew her close. She trembled slightly, but made not the least attempt to free herself from his gentle clasp.

'Be good enough to take your mistress's belongings back to the house, Josh, and I'll see you later,' Bart said, before entwining Abbie's arm through his and leading her gently away. 'I'm sorry about that. You must consider me a complete blockhead charging in upon you in that way.'

'No, not at all,' she hurriedly assured him. 'If there is one thing I cannot abide, though, it's snakes.' She shuddered again before something occurred to her, and she favoured him with a searching stare. 'But you hadn't seen the snake. It was Josh you attacked. You thought he was about to strike me with that stick. What on earth made you suppose he would wish me harm?'

Bart had the grace to look a little shamefaced. 'God knows, Abbie…I've not known what to think. And after what Giles said last night…'

'What did he say?' she prompted when his voice trailed away and he stopped to stare across the lake towards the house. 'Surely he didn't attempt to suggest that Josh might be responsible for the happenings of late?'

There was no mistaking the note of mocking disbelief in her voice, and he could only wonder at himself now for jumping to such a ludicrous assumption the very moment after he had seen the groom raising the stick high above Abbie's head.

'No, he didn't,' he admitted, once again fixing his attention upon her, his expression no less penetrating than hers had been a short time before. 'But what he did suggest was that I might not have been the target for these most recent attacks, and that it could possibly have been you.'

'What?' Abbie was stunned and it clearly showed. 'Giles must be all about in his head to suppose such a thing. Why, it is a ridiculous supposition! Who on earth would want to harm me…? And why?'

'That was precisely my initial reaction,' he admitted, guiding her towards the folly, where they could sit for a while, sheltered from the sun's harsh rays. 'But since then I've been giving it some thought.'

He led her across to the stone bench, and made no attempt to release the clasp on her hand as he sat down beside her. 'Since we met again in Bath,' he continued softly, 'you have done me the singular honour of confiding in me.' There was just a suspicion of tightening muscles along the length of his jaw. 'It's just possible that others might know that your grandfather has threatened to disinherit you. Could there be those with a vested interest, those who would be happy to see you disinherited, or worse—totally unable to fulfil your grandfather's dearest wish?'

Abbie did not misunderstand. 'By putting a period to my existence, you mean.' Although she felt moved by the touching concern he was betraying for her well-being, she couldn't prevent the mischievous side of her nature from coming to the fore. 'So what you are suggesting is that I must remain on my guard against the person who is most likely to benefit after my grandfather's demise?'

He regarded her steadily. 'To be blunt—yes.'

Somehow she managed to affect a look of wide-eyed innocence. 'But I'm certain *he* would never resort to such tactics.'

'One can never be sure,' Bart countered in all seriousness. 'Money is a strong inducement.''

It took a monumental effort, but somehow Abbie managed to control her mirth. As it had clearly never occurred to Bart to suppose that he might well be the main beneficiary in her grandfather's will, it would be grossly unfair, she decided, to make fun of him. Besides which, it really was no laughing matter. His actions of a short time earlier proved that he had grown concerned for her welfare, and it wasn't difficult to guess what might have given rise to his suspicions.

It was true that her grandfather had intended to break his journey to Scotland by remaining for a few days in Yorkshire with his nephew, Sir Montague Graham. It was likely, as her grandfather held his nephew in high esteem, that he might well have confided in him, revealing his dissatisfaction with his granddaughter's behaviour. Even so, she found it impossible to believe that Sir Montague, a gentleman of the highest principals, would ever attempt to turn the situation to his advantage by engaging the services of someone who would ensure that her days were numbered, and did not hesitate to give voice to this firm belief.

'Apart from his threat to disinherit me, Grandfather has never chosen to enlighten me as to the exact contents of his will. All the same, he has never given me any reason to suppose that he has any intention of leaving a substantial portion of his wealth to any member of the Graham family.'

'What…?' Bart made no more attempt to hide his

surprise than Abbie had done a short time earlier. 'Not even to his nephew, Montague?'

Abbie gained a modicum of satisfaction from knowing that she had judged his thoughts correctly. 'My grandfather is very fond of his nephew, understandably so. Monty is the most level-headed, charming man. He is happily married and, as far as I'm aware, very plump in the pocket. He spends most of the year in Yorkshire with his wife and children. According to Grandfather, he rarely visits the capital, and has never been addicted to games of chance.'

He appeared so ludicrously disappointed that Abbie could not forbear a further smile. 'Let me assure you, Bart, that if Sir Monty's pockets were to let, he would approach Grandfather for a loan, not engage the services of Joshua Arkwright to dispose of me. Which, I assume, was precisely what you did think.' She shook her head, certain in her own mind that this could not be so. 'Besides which, even if it were true, and Monty did mean mischief, it would avail him nothing, for unless I'm very much mistaken, Grandfather has every intention now of leaving the bulk of his wealth to you.'

It was all of ten seconds before Bart found his voice. 'The devil he has!' His expression was all at once hard and uncompromising. 'My God! I shall have a deal to say to him when next we meet.'

Easily disengaging her hand from his, Abbie placed her fingers on the sleeve of his jacket, slightly creased now after his totally unnecessary tussle with Josh. 'Please don't, Bart,' she pleaded softly. 'Unless I'm much mistaken, you've already gone against my wishes and written to Grandfather. Let that be enough.'

No denial was forthcoming, and when he continued staring broodingly at a certain spot on the ground, she knew he was unwilling to acquiesce to the request. She knew too that it would avail her nothing to force the issue, and so decided to return his thoughts to their former topic by asking what precisely had eventually persuaded him to suppose that she might be the intended victim.

'After all, Bart, these unfortunate happenings began weeks before I came to stay here,' she pointed out, 'and have all taken place solely on your property.'

'Not strictly true,' he corrected, rising to his feet. He paused to run a hand through his hair, clear evidence of his continuing troubled state of mind. 'Don't you remember that occasion when we experienced the mishap in the curricle?'

Although, in truth, she had never given the incident a second thought, she did so now, and had no difficulty in remembering just what had occurred. 'But surely that was just an accident, pure and simple? An unfortunate mischance?'

'Perhaps,' he acknowledged. 'But it's never happened to me before, at least not in one of my own carriages. Hackman is particularly conscientious and makes thorough checks himself before embarking on any journey. He swears the curricle was in good order before we set out from Bath.'

'So you believe the wheel was deliberately tampered with?' Abbie said, reading his thoughts accurately. 'And Josh accompanied us that day… Is that why you suspected him?'

Again he ran impatient fingers through his hair, wondering at himself for harbouring such a suspicion even for a moment. 'The lad's had plenty of opportunities to do you harm, had he chosen to do so. He's been your only escort on scores of occasions during your stay here, not to mention in Bath. And after what happened today, I'm certain he isn't responsible.'

'And I am equally certain that you're the one in danger, not I. Major Wetherby saw fit to confide in me last night. He firmly believes that those isolated incidents perpetrated against your neighbours during recent months were merely an attempt to divert attention from the real target, namely yourself.' Abbie waited in vain for some response. 'Surely it must have occurred to you that these happenings bear all the hallmarks of acts of revenge? Can you think of no one who might wish you ill in retaliation for…for something, perhaps, that you have done in the past?'

Although she had striven to keep her voice equable, devoid of the smallest hint of recrimination,

Abbie knew by that penetrating, narrow-eyed regard that he hadn't been slow to appreciate her train of thought. Ashamed though she was, she couldn't deny that, after her conversation with Major Wetherby, she had found herself studying every attractive matron attending the party, assessing and wondering if, perhaps, Bart's intimate liaisons with married women had been confined to just one.

'Righteous I am not, and have never been,' Bart volunteered, thereby putting an end to her unsavoury reflections. 'But disabuse yourself of the notion that I ever embarked on a career of making cuckolds of friends and neighbours when their wives were willing to do so.'

It took a monumental effort, but Abbie continued to hold his reproachful stare. If there was one thing she had discovered about Bart in recent weeks, it was that he had scant regard for those who lacked the courage of their own convictions and did not stand their ground. 'I cannot deny that it crossed my mind as a distinct possibility. It crossed my mind also to wonder about your cousin.' She continued to maintain her steady gaze. 'I believe I did hear him mention that he has every intention of returning to London today. But did it never strike you as odd that he should suddenly take it into his head to visit the area in the first place?'

Although he raised one brow in a decidedly sceptical arch, he made no attempt to dismiss the idea out of hand, and paid her the common courtesy of considering the suggestion for a full minute before finally giving a decisive shake of his head.

'It's true enough that there's no love lost between us, and that he resents my more senior position in the family. It's also true that he, too, is sufficiently plump in the pocket to have paid someone to perpetrate these acts against me, without sullying his own hands. But one thing I will say for Cedric—he sets great store by family honour. He would never do anything to discredit the name he bears.'

Abbie had no reason to doubt the truth of this. Yet it left her at a loss to know what else to suggest. 'Then I suppose we shall be forced to look elsewhere for the answer, maybe further in the past for the motive... At least,' she amended, rising to her feet, and moving towards him, 'you must do so, Bart, for my time here at the Court is fast drawing to a close, and I have the uneasy feeling that your particular nemesis isn't satisfied quite yet.'

She stared up at him, half-expecting to discover a slightly mocking glint in his eyes, or that look of impatience which he bestowed upon his stepmother whenever Eugenie's nerves got the better of her. She detected neither. If anything he looked rather forlorn, though whether he had taken the warning seriously or not was impossible to judge, for the next moment he raised one broad shoulder in a dismissive shrug, as though bored with the topic, and was suggesting they return to the house to enjoy a final luncheon in Giles's company.

During the walk back, Bart deliberately kept the conversation on mundane matters in an attempt to prevent her dwelling on his troubles. He was much moved by her evident anxiety, and although he would never have admitted as much, the fears she had voiced had certainly crossed his mind.

His immediate concerns, however, were not for himself but for the being who had swiftly come to mean everything to him. Abbie was possibly correct in her assertion that no one would wish to harm her. After what she had revealed, it did seem highly unlikely that she had been the intended target, and perhaps he had been foolish ever to consider it as a possibility. All the same, he could not be easy in his mind until she was safely back in her godmother's home. In the meantime the very least he could do was try to ensure that she was placed in no danger because of some possible past action of his.

After seeing her safely back inside the house, Bart went directly to the stable-yard in search of the person whom he was now firmly convinced would ably assist him in his endeavours. He quickly located Josh's whereabouts in the largest of the stables and drew him outside, insisting that he sit beside him on the rough wooden bench.

'Firstly, I want to apologise again for my behaviour, earlier. Yes, Josh,' he added, raising a hand to silence the young groom's embarrassed protest. 'I hope I never become too proud to admit I have been at fault. My assessment of your character has been sadly flawed.' He smiled to himself. 'Miss Graham, seemingly, is far more discerning than I. She trusted you from the first.'

'Well, sir,' Josh said, looking puzzled, 'I hope I've given good service.'

'You may be at ease on that score,' Bart assured him. 'But I want you to be more conscientious still during the time your mistress remains here at the Court. I want you to ensure that she never goes off anywhere on her own, not even just to take a stroll in the garden. I am entrusting you to guard her with your life.'

The frown deepened. 'Why, sir? Is something queer going on?'

'Yes, lad…something queer is going on.' Bart debated within himself for a moment, then decided to take Josh into his confidence. 'You must have heard about the deliberate damage to the bridge?'

'Aye, sir,' Josh confirmed. 'And the fire at the house.'

'Those were by no means the only instances. There have been several others, one or two of which I hope you may be able to shed some light. Firstly, I want you to cast your mind back to that outing we enjoyed whilst we were in Bath. Can you recall seeing anyone lingering near my curricle?'

Leaning forward, Josh rested his elbows on his knees while he stared at a spot across the yard. 'Well, only the grooms, sir. I seem to remember Mr Hackman and Dodd tending to the horses. But then they would, wouldn't they?'

Bart chose not to respond to this. Instead he said, 'And do you recall, on the day you arrived here, going off to the kitchen with Dodd?'

'Aye, sir. And a reet fine plumb cake it were too,' he confirmed with a boyish grin. 'Mrs Figg gave me a second bit, as I remember.'

'And Dodd went with you to the kitchen, did he not?'

'Aye, sir. He showed me the way, but…'

'But what?' Bart prompted when Josh frowned again.

'I mind he said he'd forgotten something, and went back across the yard.'

'You saw him return to the stable?'

'No, sir. I went into the kitchen. Dodd came in a while later.'

Time enough, Bart considered, for Dodd to have slipped up on to the leads, and dislodge that piece of masonry. He frowned. But why should Dodd wish him harm? Gratitude was what he should have felt at the time, surely? After all, he'd been offered a place at the Court when he'd been looking for work. On the other hand, it couldn't be denied that, except for the fire, for which he couldn't possibly have been responsible, as he had been in Bath at the time, Dodd had been on hand to perpetrate the other malicious acts. And it was true that nothing untoward had occurred since his departure. It couldn't be denied either that Dodd was the type to do most anything for money. It was not inconceivable, therefore, that he'd been working for two masters.

He shook his head, deciding to ponder over the conundrum later, and easily concentrated his thoughts on something of more import at the moment. 'How have you liked working here with Hackman, Josh? He can be a hard taskmaster, I know.'

If Josh considered the question a little strange, he certainly betrayed no sign of it, and his reply was prompt enough. 'He likes to see the work get done, sir. And there's nowt wrong with that.'

'Then you wouldn't object to taking orders from him? Naturally it wouldn't be for ever. Hackman will retire in a few years, and I'm certain that, when he does, you'll be more than capable of taking his place.'

Bart smiled at the look of open astonishment he received. 'Yes, I'm offering you a permanent position here, Josh, if you wish to take it. I would want you to accompany Lady Penrose when she returns to Bath on Friday to ensure the ladies arrive safely. Then, if you choose to return here, you may be certain there'll be a place for you. I do realise, of course, that you might prefer to go back to your native Yorkshire.'

Josh shrugged. 'There's nowt there for me now, sir.'

He took a moment to gaze across at the park land. 'Happen I could settle 'ere. Reet taken with the countryside, I am. And I ain't the only Yorkshireman to have taken a shine to this part of the world, neither.'

'Is that so?' Bart responded, more out of politeness than any real interest. 'So you've met a fellow countryman hereabouts?'

'Aye, sir, t'other day when I were out with Miss Abbie. Happen he be the one Dodd be working for now. Owns that tavern out on the Evesham road.' He shook his head. 'Didn't take to 'im, mind. Didn't like the look of 'im. West Riding man, not from my part.'

Having no real interest in learning about the divisions in Josh's native county, Bart hurriedly brought the discussion to an end and made his way back to the house. He had almost reached the front entrance before the young groom's disclosure struck him as odd, and he recalled something that had occurred to him before, when he had assisted Abbie in interviewing Josh—that it was not unheard of for people to move away from their county of birth in order to find work, but generally folk of Josh's station in life did not travel far from their roots, unless there happened to be a very good reason for doing so. So what had induced another native of Yorkshire to settle in this part of the world?

Chapter Thirteen

Even though he felt a sense relief as he watched his fine travelling carriage setting off on the first leg of its journey to Brighton, Bart accepted he wouldn't experience any real peace of mind until the young woman standing beside him had been removed by her godmother from his sphere also. That, of course, would not take place until Friday, just two days hence. In the meantime he could take some comfort in the knowledge that he had done all he could to ensure her continued safety whenever she left the house.

The thought jogged his memory. Nevertheless, he waited until Lady Penrose had returned indoors, before revealing to Abbie that he had something to impart. 'What with Giles's leaving, and all the hustle and bustle since, preparing for Eugenie and Kitty's departure this morning, it quite slipped my mind.'

The admission instantly captured her full attention. She gazed up at him enquiringly, her head slightly on one side, an expression that always put him in mind of an inquisitive kitten. 'No doubt you'll be relieved to know your young groom's future is secured. I offered him a position here, and he accepted.'

It was an impulsive action, brief and little more than a featherlight brush of lips against his cheek. Yet it left him almost rocking on his heels and stuttering like many of those raw recruits who had been under his command out in the Peninsula. 'Well…I…er…um…I'm glad you're pleased.'

The hand that impulsively touched his sleeve did little to restore his equilibrium. 'Oh, Bart, I could never begin to express my gratitude.'

'Then please don't try,' he adjured, taking a hurried step away before the desire to imprison her in his arms overmastered the iron self-control that he had somehow managed to exert over himself in recent weeks. 'Now, if you'll excuse me, I must leave you to your own devices. There's someone I must see.'

Bart delayed no longer in heading for the stable. He could almost feel those gorgeous-coloured eyes staring after him. He shook his head, wondering at himself. Stiff-necked wasn't the word for it! Supposedly a man of the world, experienced and self-possessed, he had been completely bowled over by what had been nothing more than a prolonged peck. Yet he couldn't deny that it had shaken him, possibly because her reaction had been totally unexpected, so natural and unselfconscious.

After mounting the horse his latest employee had only moments before led from the stable, Bart set off across the park, striving to keep as firm a rein on his spirits as he held on the powerful stallion beneath him.

Yes, against all the odds Abbie had grown to care for him; her reaction of a few minutes before and the touching concern she had betrayed over his well-being in recent weeks was proof of this. Amazing though it was, she now looked upon him in a favourable light and, more importantly, had grown to trust him. It was immensely gratifying. But it wasn't enough. No, nowhere near enough. Yet he was still faced with the heartrending possibility that a sincere friendship was all he might ever be offered. Only time would tell. And time, sadly, was against him at present.

Abbie must leave. He had to let her go, and yet by doing so he was in no doubt that, sooner or later, he might lose her to someone else. But better that, he reminded himself, than risk placing her in danger by inviting her to remain at the Court. All he could do to minimise the time they must spend apart was concentrate all his efforts on trying to uncover the identity of the person or persons who seemed hell-bent on making his life as unpleasant and hazardous as possible.

With this determination now very much in the forefront of his mind, Bart wasted no time in riding to the
village. He quickly discovered that Major Wetherby
had left earlier to pay a visit on Lord Warren, and had
no hesitation in turning his mount in the direction of
the Hall in pursuit of his quarry.

Fortune then favoured him, and he discovered
Major Wetherby, still happily ensconced in the well-
stocked library, enjoying a glass of port in the company of his host who, after furnishing him with a
drink, tactfully withdrew once he realised that Bart's
reason for calling was to seek an interview with his
guest.

'Your arrival is most opportune,' Major Wetherby
confessed. 'It has saved me the trouble of calling
upon you. My men will not be remaining in the locale for very much longer. I received orders to leave
early next week.'

Bart wasn't unduly surprised. 'In that case, Major,
I'm pleased to have the opportunity to speak to you
now, and shall come straight to the point. I want you
to cast your mind back four years, to the time when
you first arrived in the Peninsula and were assigned
to the Provost Marshal.'

Just a hint of a smile pulled at the Major's full lips.
'If my memory serves me correctly, Cavanagh, you
didn't hold the Provost in the highest esteem, and
were not reticent in airing your views. I seem to remember you were one of those who spoke out vocif-

erously against the method adopted for dealing with men who stole from our allies.'

'True,' Bart concurred, meeting the Major's faintly sardonic gaze with one of his own. 'I could never bring myself to countenance hanging a man for the mere purloining of a chicken. And never shall. However, during my years in the army, there was one man about whose neck I could happily have placed the noose myself.'

Having successfully gained the Major's full attention, Bart rose to his feet and went to stand before the window, his mind's eye having little difficulty in conjuring up many unpleasant images from the past. 'I understand from Miss Graham that, having uncovered no serious pockets of dissatisfaction in the area, you are firmly convinced that the instances of damage to property were motivated by revenge, directed against one person in particular—namely myself.'

'I said as much when we dined together here a couple of weeks ago,' the Major reminded him, 'and I've discovered nothing since to make me alter my opinion. However, I can tell you this much, Cavanagh, I haven't encountered anyone who has betrayed the least animosity towards you personally. Quite the contrary, in fact.'

Bart drew his eyes away from the magnificent park to cast the Major a wry grin. 'The reasons for your having come to the area must be common knowledge. Only a halfwit would betray any ill feeling he might be harbouring towards me in your presence.'

'True,' the Major agreed. 'But I do recall from our several past encounters in the Peninsula that you were never afraid to speak your mind. Therefore, unless you have changed to any significant degree, and I don't imagine you have, it's not inconceivable that you have ruffled a few feathers since leaving the army. All the same, I do recall that not only your fellow officers held you in high esteem, but also the men under your command.'

'The majority, yes. But certainly not all,' Bart enlightened him, once again turning to stare out of the window. 'After I had attained my Majority, I was assigned a company of men that included a loathsome piece of humanity by name of Septimus Searle, whom some mindless fool had seen fit to make up to sergeant.' His lip curled. 'Hardly surprising, really. By devious methods he had somehow managed to gain approval.'

'But not yours,' the Major prompted when silence lengthened between them.

'No,' Bart admitted. 'It didn't take me long to get his measure. I had him flogged, after he was caught stealing, and his stripes taken away and given to an Irishman who was far more worthy to sport them on his jacket. Soon afterwards we were involved in the capture of Ciudad Rodrigo. And we all know what took place in the aftermath of that confrontation, and then again a few weeks later at Badajoz.'

The Major shrugged. 'Not altogether shocking when you consider the majority of those who made up the army. Wellington's opinion of them was common knowledge.'

'Yes, rogues, thieves and liars. But not all were murderers and rapists. Septimus Searle, however, most definitely was. I know for a fact that he was one of those actively involved in the very worst of what took place at Badajoz. Afterwards he, like many others, deserted. And that is when you came upon the scene.'

Once again Bart experienced flashing images from the past as he continued to stare sightlessly across the park. 'The day you left camp to round up those deserters, I set out for Lisbon on some long-overdue leave. I was informed on my return to Spain that your mission had been a resounding success, that you had located the deserters' hideout, an abandoned village tucked away up in the hills. Wellington, having sustained considerable losses in recent engagements, was, I remember, prepared to allow those who gave themselves up voluntarily to rejoin the ranks, without fear of reprisals. Those who put up any resistance, if not killed in the attempt, were to be brought back to camp and hanged. I assumed, perhaps erroneously, that because he wasn't among the rank and file, Septimus Searle had received his just deserts.'

Major Wetherby gave vent to a bark of derisive laughter. 'Surely, Cavanagh, you don't expect me to remember whether this man Searle was among those brought back to camp and subsequently executed as an example?'

'Naturally not,' Bart assured him. 'But I would like you to cast your mind back and tell me everything you can remember about that particular assignment.'

For a moment it seemed as though Major Wetherby would not oblige, then his rather harsh features were surprisingly softened by a lopsided grin. 'Well, you're lucky, because I do happen to recall that particular mission very well, as it was my first.

'We located the hideout without too much trouble,' he continued, after substantially reducing the contents of his glass. 'The village was little more than a few derelict buildings, ransacked by the French some months before. Most were only too willing to give themselves up. The twenty or so who put up resistance were either shot or brought back to camp.'

Bart frowned heavily. 'Searle would never have given himself up, of that I'm sure.'

'What makes you so certain? As I told you, the French had scoured the hills only months before. There was little food to be had.'

'Maybe not. But Searle wouldn't have wanted to come face to face with me again, or the men in my company, who had more reason for despising him than I had.'

'In that case he might well have been one of those who put up a fight, or maybe…'

'Maybe what?' Bart prompted, when the Major fell silent.

'As I mentioned, many of the deserters were in a pretty poor state. It took us five days to get back to camp. On the second night, four men stole some provisions and took off. Three were recaptured and subsequently hanged. The fourth killed one of my men by slitting his throat, and then made off with his horse.'

Bart stared speculatively across at the Major. 'Aside from his loathsome character, there are two things I particularly remember about Searle—he was very handy with a knife, dangerously so, and he spoke with a pronounced Yorkshire accent. I discovered only the other day that a tavern on the Evesham Road is now owned by a man heralding from that particular county. And, unless I'm much mistaken, the new owner took possession at the beginning of the year, just prior to when all this trouble began. Although it may be mere coincidence, I think I'll pay a visit. If the innkeeper is Searle, I'll recognise him.'

'In that case, Cavanagh, you'll oblige me by delaying your visit for a while. I have one or two matters I must discuss with Lord Warren before I leave. I'll then return to the village, collect some of my men and ride directly over to you. If it is Searle, I'll be only too happy to take him into custody, doubly so if he should turn out to be the one who escaped from me four years ago, and murdered that young lieutenant in the process. He happened to be a particular friend of mine.'

'In that case, Major, I'll await your arrival at the Court.'

Abbie took a step back from the portrait to consider the finished result yet again. She had completed the work at the beginning of the week, but couldn't resist coming in every day to study the result of all her efforts. She was pleased, and hoped Bart would be too. It was a good likeness, and a fine piece of work, even though she did say so herself.

Yes, she had definitely succeeded in capturing that certain look, that softer expression he sometimes wore when he wasn't precisely smiling, and yet it was clear something had pleased him. It was high time the subject of the painting was informed that his likeness was finished and viewed it for himself. Why she hadn't informed him of its completion before she couldn't imagine. No, that wasn't strictly true, her conscience corrected. She had thought…hoped that by keeping it a secret she might succeed in delaying her departure for a while longer, but Bart seemed determined she should go. And perhaps it was for the best. The last thing in the world she wanted was to outstay her welcome; to make him think she was taking advantage of his kind hospitality.

The mere thought of going left her feeling hollow. She could deny the truth no longer—she loved this house, but nowhere near as much as she had grown to love its master.

Yes, the unthinkable had happened—she had fallen hopelessly in love with the very being whom she had vowed never to wed. What irony! she mused, steadfastly refusing to give way to the tears that might lessen the misery for a while, but could never hope to bring lasting relief to the torment she would carry with her through the years. If she had not been so proud, so naïve, so very prudish, she would indeed have been mistress of this fine house by now; married to a man who was neither saint nor depraved sinner, a man who, though annoyingly dictatorial and forthright on occasion, was essentially kind-hearted and considerate; she would have been married to a man who was so very right for her.

Through the haze of unshed tears, she stared once again at the likeness that, without being aware of it, she had lovingly created. One day soon, she hoped, it would find a permanent position, maybe in the library, above the fireplace. She would never see it hanging there. But then, she reminded herself, she would never need to. That face, that certain expression it had worn so often when they had been alone together here in this very room, would have a permanent place etched in her own memory.

Alerted by footsteps along the landing, she quickly covered the painting with its protective sheet. She had no desire to be caught, misty eyed and gazing adoringly at Bart's portrait, by one of the servants; or worse still by the master himself. No, it wouldn't do for Bart to discover how she now felt about him. Being the man he was, he just might feel obliged, out of misguided gallantry, to ask for her hand a second time. If she could be sure her feelings were reciprocated, she wouldn't need to think twice about accepting him. But the fact of the matter was she wasn't sure. And she could not, would not accept him on any other terms.

By dint of long practice Abbie was able quite easily to maintain the outward appearance of contentment when she left the room and went downstairs to join her godmother in the parlour, where they discussed plans for their return journey to Bath. When she suddenly announced her intention of going out for a ride, she didn't believe she aroused any suspicion, for Lady Penrose well knew her fondness for that particular form of exercise. Josh too wasn't in the least taken aback when she appeared in the yard, demanding her usual mount, and was soon leading her favourite grey mare and a gelding from the stable.

'There's no need for you to accompany me,' she told him. 'I've no intention of going far, at least no farther than the boundary of Mr Cavanagh's property, so if you've work to do here, Josh, then do not feel obliged to neglect it for my benefit.'

Just for an instant she thought she detected a slightly guarded expression, before he led the mare to the mounting block. 'I would be neglecting my duties if I *didn't* go with you, Miss Abbie. And I don't want to get into Mr Cavanagh's black books now I'm working for him.'

It was a timely reminder, and she didn't hesitate to assure him how pleased she was that he had secured himself a permanent position. 'I do so hope you'll be happy here, Josh.'

'Happen I will, miss. It's a nice place. Makes you feel comfortable, like.'

She knew precisely what he meant, only too well, but steadfastly refused to become maudlin. Hurriedly changing the subject, she suggested they make for the home wood, which had become, quite early in her stay, one of her favourite places to visit when out riding.

The August day was oppressively warm, and Abbie was grateful for the shelter from the sun's harsh rays the instant they entered the wooded area of land where Bart went shooting rabbits, when he could find the time. She had heard him remark on several occasions that it was one of his favourite spots. And that, she mused, as she led the way along one of the wider tracks, was perhaps why she too had become so fond of the place.

She could imagine him, gun over his arm, walking along a track, that alert gaze of his searching for any sudden movement in the undergrowth. She wished he had suggested an afternoon's shooting during her stay, but he hadn't, and it was unlikely now that she would be granted the opportunity to exhibit her own prowess with a firearm, a skill her somewhat eccentric grandsire had seen fit to impart when the bond between them had been so much closer than it was now.

The regrettable thought had just passed through her mind when Abbie caught sight of a rough wagon half-hidden among the trees. Josh noticed it too, and suggested it might be estate workers replenishing the log store in readiness for the cold autumn and winter nights. Abbie might have agreed, and not given the matter another thought, had it not been for the conspicuous absence of men at work and no sound of an axe or saw being applied to a felled tree.

Curiosity having quickly got the better of her, she rode over to take a closer look. The distinct absence of wood chippings in and around the cart suggested that it hadn't been used to transport logs, at least not recently, and the sad condition of the poor beast between the shafts did little to stem her growing unease. The cart was empty except for a pile of sacking concealing something at one end, which she did not hesitate to raise in order to reveal what was hidden beneath.

Josh, like Abbie, wasn't slow to recognise the evilly formed metal objects. 'Lord save us, miss!' he burst out. 'The master's never gone and ordered them 'eathen things set on his land?'

Concerned though she was, Abbie couldn't suppress a wry smile. If that selfsame question had been put to her several months before she would have needed to ponder long and hard before giving an answer. Now, she didn't even need to think about it at all.

'No, Josh, Mr Cavanagh would not,' she assured him, one hundred per cent certain in her own mind that she was right. 'Your master might be concerned about what has been happening in recent months, but he would never risk maiming an innocent man or animal by laying such barbaric devices. Which makes one wonder,' she added, 'why these mantraps are here on his land? Who brought them here and why, if not to set them?'

Grim-faced, Josh had dismounted before Abbie had finished speaking. 'Happen I should take a look around, miss, and see if I can't discover someone about who shouldn't be.'

Abbie didn't attempt to dissuade him as she was of a similar mind. 'But be careful, Josh,' she adjured. 'We don't know how many of these dreadful things have been set already.'

Waiting until her groom's broad form had disappeared from view, Abbie slipped to the ground and once again turned her attention to the poor beast between the shafts. If she had needed absolute proof that Bart had not ordered the setting of mantraps, she was looking at it now. Half-starved and bearing marks of further needless cruelty across its flanks, the gelding took the morsel in her outstretched hand, the treat she had intended giving to the mare after her ride. She proceeded to stroke the gelding's dusty neck as it munched away on the offering. It betrayed no sign of enjoyment at the show of affection. But then, Abbie reasoned, perhaps he had experienced so few acts of kindness during his miserable life that he wasn't perfectly certain what was happening.

She shook her head, appalled at such wanton cruelty. For all that Bart, and her grandfather, come to that, could be overbearing and downright obstinate on occasions, neither would treat a creature with such neglect. Which made her wonder who was responsible for the animal's poor condition. She was destined not to remain in ignorance for much longer.

The sound of a twig cracking behind her had her swinging round on her heels to discover not her groom, as expected, but the dullard whose position Josh had filled and the man for whom he now worked.

The look of unholy satisfaction she couldn't fail to see in the older man's pitiless dark eyes sent her heart-rate soaring, and prompted her to ask the question that even to her own ears sounded singularly foolish.

'What do you imagine you are doing here?'

'Happen you know the answer to that already,' Dodd's companion answered, peering in the cart at the contents that she had left uncovered.

He turned his attention back to her, his gaze insolently assessing as he looked her over from head to foot. 'Who would have thought when we set out this morning that such a fine piece of merchandise would fall into our hands, eh, Doddy, lad? Told you I felt lucky today, when you said as how we should wait for the soldiers to move on before doing owt else to Cavanagh.'

Fearing she would never reach her mare in order to effect an escape, Abbie swiftly suppressed the impulse to try. Instead, she focused her attention on Dodd, determined to brazen it out until Josh returned.

'Have you given any thought at all to what will happen when Mr Cavanagh discovers you've been on his land? You didn't leave his employ upon the best of terms,' she reminded him.

Dodd, betraying his unconcern at the prospect of possible repercussions, merely shrugged, and left it to his companion to give voice to their complete indifference at being discovered.

'Happen the Major'll have far too much to worry about to trouble 'imself over a few traps, pretty lady.'

She resented the over-familiar tone almost as much as the insolent way he continued to regard her, as though she were some tasty morsel on his plate. Most worrying of all, though, was that, although a relative stranger in these parts, he seemed to know a deal about the master of Cavanagh Court. His knowledge of the rank Bart had held in the army led one to suppose that he and Bart were not total strangers. Was this person responsible for the recent malicious acts? His uninvited presence on Bart's land suggested strongly that he could well be.

'Evidently you are acquainted with Mr Cavanagh?'

'Oh, aye, lassie,' he acknowledged, seemingly quite happy to satisfy her curiosity. 'The Major and me, we goes back a long way.' There was a faint rasping sound as he rubbed dirt-ingrained fingers back and forth across the stubble on his chin. 'Not that we've seen much of each other in recent years. But I never forgets me friends. Nor me enemies, come to that.'

Just for a second Abbie allowed her eyes to slide past the stranger's left shoulder to scan the woodland beyond. Where was Josh? Why hadn't he returned? She began to experience the most uneasy feeling, but maintained her self-control as she said, 'And I strongly suspect that Mr Cavanagh falls into the latter category.'

'Well, let's just say there be no love lost between us, lass.' Lips drew back to reveal an incomplete set of badly decayed teeth. 'I'm thinking, though, the Major's feelings for you be a mite warmer than they were for any of those Spanish beauties he had out in the Peninsula. But then he did always 'ave an eye for a pretty woman. Happen he'll pay reet 'andsome to 'ave you back safe and sound.'

His intent could not have been plainer, and Abbie instinctively took a step away, only to find her back pressed against the side of the cart. Escape seemed impossible without help of some sort. 'You forget that I didn't come here alone.' She knew she was grasping at straws, hoping that one of Bart's workmen, perhaps even his gamekeeper, would just happen along and offer aid.

Sadly Dodd's unexpected bark of laughter didn't precisely boost her flagging confidence. 'That dolt Arkwright won't be of no use to yer,' he told her bluntly. 'I 'it 'im 'ard. It'll be a long time afore he comes round...if ever he does.'

It would have afforded Abbie the utmost satisfaction to have been able to slap the self-satisfied smirk off Dodd's unpleasant face. Unfortunately the opportunity to make the attempt was denied her by his companion who, having edged closer, had her upper arms clasped in a firm grip, before she could make even a token attempt at escape.

Her valiant struggles were in vain. She was no match for the two of them. They swiftly had her wrists and ankles bound, and Dodd's neckerchief covering her mouth, effectively stifling her belated screams for help. She then found herself airborne, before being tossed unceremoniously into the cart, and covered with several layers of filthy sacking.

Abbie was now firmly convinced that it had been none other than Dodd himself who had been responsible for many of the malicious acts perpetrated against Bart. She was equally convinced that he had been carrying out the orders of his companion. Just why the stranger bore such a grudge against Bart remained a mystery. What had been made frighteningly clear, however, was that his thirst for revenge had yet to be satiated.

During the mercifully short journey, Abbie was too preoccupied trying to stop herself from coming into contact with the sharp metal edges of the traps to concern herself overmuch with her ultimate fate. Understandably, fears returned with a vengeance when the cart came to a halt in the yard behind the neglected tavern and she was carried into the ramshackle building that functioned as a stable.

The lascivious gleam in the men's eyes, after they had tossed her down on to the pile of filthy hay, which resulted in her skirts rising above the knee, only served to increase her apprehensions. Yet her fears proved groundless, at least for the present, for, apart from ogling his fill of her slender, shapely legs, Dodd's companion merely grasped her from behind and dragged her back towards one of the upright wooden roof supports.

'First things first, Doddy, lad,' he said, after securing Abbie to the beam with a length of rope, wrapping it several times about her waist. 'We'll have our fun, never you fear, but not afore we've got Cavanagh 'ere to see us enjoying his wench.'

The gleam of hatred in his dark eyes was unmistakable. 'I've waited a long time to get even. I want to hear 'im beg. He wouldn't for himself…' he looked briefly at Abbie before rising to his feet '…but he would for her. And afore I kill him he'll suffer. Oh, I'll make him pay with much more than just the golden guineas he'll give us to see the lass again. We'll get 'er to write a letter, so he's in no doubt that we 'ave 'er. But first we'll drink to our good fortune and to the man who'll make sure we can live comfortably for a while to come afore he meets his maker.'

The taunting sound of malicious laughter seemed to echo off the stone walls long after the sounds of rusty bolts being thrown across the wooden doors and heavy retreating footsteps had died away.

Tears born of frustration and anger blurred her vision, but Abbie managed to hold them in check, as she attempted to free herself from her bonds. The fact that she had only herself to blame for her present predicament didn't precisely improve her flagging spirits. Fully aware of recent happenings, she had blithely gone to investigate when she had stumbled upon something suspicious. Most disturbing of all was the knowledge that, if she couldn't manage to effect her own escape, she would be placing Bart in the gravest danger.

This very real possibility forced her to ignore the painful chafing of her wrists as she strained against the ropes, until finally she was forced to admit defeat, and acknowledge that she would never get free without help. The trouble was that no one, with the possible exception of Josh, would have an inkling of where she might be. And poor Josh, if Dodd was to be believed, might never be able to reveal what he knew. And then there was Bart. When he received that letter, he would be walking straight into a trap, unless...

For a few moments Abbie toyed with the idea of flatly refusing to do her captors' bidding, but then thought better of it. She didn't doubt that they would resort to force. Besides which, there was just a chance that she might be able to pen some cryptic warning in the missive. Dodd, she felt sure, was illiterate. Unfortunately there was no guarantee that his vengeful companion was. He could in all probability read sufficiently well to be able to decipher what had been written. There was just the chance, though, that he might overlook the occasional misspelled word wherein she might be able to offer a clue as to her whereabouts. Given that there was precious little else she could do, it was worth a try.

Abbie was quick to hear the sound of footsteps again. Evidently her captors were eager for her to pen the ransom note, and she was now very willing to oblige them. But it might be a mistake to appear so, she swiftly decided, as one rusty bolt was drawn back far more slowly than it had been thrown a short time before. The last thing in the world she wanted was to ruin what was likely to be her one and only chance of warning Bart of the danger awaiting him should he attempt a rescue.

Chapter Fourteen

Exerting immense will power, Bart successfully resisted the temptation to pay a visit to that certain poorly maintained wayside inn on the Evesham road on his way home. It wasn't that he felt in the least daunted at the possibility of coming face to face with the black-hearted wretch whom he had been unfortunate enough to have under his command for a few short months when fighting in Spain. He did, however, appreciate his own limitations, and very much feared that the desire to mete out the justice the Army had lamentably failed to do during the Peninsular Campaign might prove too strong.

Consequently he made directly for Cavanagh Court. Turning his mount off the main road, he took advantage of the highly convenient short cut through his wood, as he had every intention of arriving in good time to partake of the last luncheon he would enjoy in Abbie's company. The good Lord only knew how long it would be before he was in a position to commence his courtship in earnest. If, however, his instincts proved correct, and his nemesis did turn out to be none other than Septimus Searle, perhaps it wouldn't be too long before he was journeying to Bath again.

It was a highly pleasing prospect upon which he could happily have dwelt had it not been for a sudden movement off to his left capturing his attention. He turned his head, surprised to discover not the deer he had been expecting to see foraging in the undergrowth, but the mount Abbie had always favoured riding. Not too far away from the dapple mare, and equally happily engaged munching the sweet grass, was the gelding used by the stable lads when undertaking the duties of escort and groom.

Abbie had remarked that she enjoyed riding through this wooded area of land, and the fact that she had chosen to take full advantage of the shelter provided by the trees on this very warm day came as no real surprise. What he found a touch disquieting, though, was that both Abbie, and her protector, undoubtedly Josh, had left their mounts unattended, and free to wander. It was so unlike the stable lad to be so neglectful; Abbie, too, come to that.

Bart's unease increased when no response was forthcoming to his several calls, and after securely tethering the horses, including his own, he decided to take a look around. For several minutes all he could hear were snatches of bird song and the occasional sound of some frightened scurrying creature, then he detected that certain sound all too frequently heard in the aftermath of a battle, that guttural moan from a man in pain.

Bart wasted no time in locating Josh's whereabouts and managed to force some of the contents from his flask, which he habitually carried with him when out riding, between the young groom's bluish-tinged lips. The crust of blood now forming in the blond hair was proof that Josh had sustained a severe blow. Blessedly the brandy quickly revived him, and a glimmer of recognition was not slow in coming to his eyes.

He made to rise, but Bart, easily restraining him, coaxed him to sample more of the brandy before finally allowing him to sit unsupported. 'Just take your time, lad,' he urged gently, when Josh made to rise again, 'and tell me what happened to you?'

Bart experienced the uneasy feeling that Josh's injury might be severe indeed when he caught the hushed response to his question. 'Mantraps?' he echoed, totally at a loss to understand to what the groom was alluding.

'Aye, sir. Miss Abbie and I saw 'em in that there cart. She were certain sure you wouldn't 'ave ordered the laying of such 'eathen objects. Thought someone were up to mischief, so I took a look around. That's all I can rightly recall.'

As there was no sign of a cart now, Bart could only assume that Abbie had left the wood in that conveyance, and he very much feared that she hadn't done so willingly. She would never have callously abandoned Josh, unless she had been forced to do so.

Bart betrayed none of his rapidly mounting fears as he asked, 'And you've no idea who attacked you?'

Josh shook his head, wincing as he did so. 'Came at me from behind, sir, so I didn't get a look at 'im, 'cepting…' He took a moment to frown down at the ground between his boots. 'I could swear I 'eard 'im laugh before I blacked out, and it put me in mind of that stupid barking laugh o' Dodd's.'

Bart didn't wait to hear more. He rose at once to his feet, his mind working rapidly. Abbie's abduction, and he was in no doubt that she had been taken against her will, changed everything. He had to get to her without delay, for he was sickeningly aware of what would be her fate if she remained in Septimus Searle's hands for any length of time. There was no question now of waiting for Major Wetherby.

Offering his support, Bart assisted Josh to rise. Clearly the groom was in no fit state to go careering about the countryside on horseback. But what other choice was there? Time simply wasn't on his side, and he wasn't prepared to waste a precious second in returning to the Court to get help.

The walk back to the horses wasn't achieved speedily, for not only was Josh understandably unsteady on his feet, but both men were scanning the path immediately ahead for any sign of a lurking trap, which would effectively thwart any possible rescue attempt. Thankfully both successfully reached their goal unscathed, and Bart wasted no further time in asking the question at the forefront of his mind.

''Course I can ride over to Lord Warren's, sir. Have no fear. Once I'm in the saddle I'll stay there.'

Bart wasn't so sure, although by the time they had reached the fork in the road, where they were destined to part company, he was experiencing a degree more confidence in the injured groom's ability to reach Warren Hall, and apprise those present of what had occurred. He was certainly in no doubt at all that Wetherby would come to his assistance at once. No matter what he thought of him personally, he knew Wetherby to be a conscientious officer who never shirked his duties. Nevertheless he had no intention of delaying for the time it took for the Major to marshal his troops and come to his assistance, and set off along the Evesham road the instant Josh had turned his mount in the direction of the Hall.

By the time he had reached the wayside inn Bart had formulated a plan. He would begin his search for Abbie in the outbuildings. He couldn't imagine Searle being so foolish as to imprison her in the inn itself, where her whereabouts might just be stumbled upon by one of the patrons, even though it was highly unlikely that the ill-kept inn was ever well patronised.

Tethering his mount some distance away, Bart circled round to the back of the buildings, careful to take advantage of stone walls, hedges and trees in the hope of concealing his approach. As luck would have it he found the yard deserted except for an undernourished, work-weary horse harnessed to a cart, of which he didn't hesitate to make full use by crouching down below the high wooden side of the vehicle while he carefully threw back the bolts on the barn's rotting wooden door.

Bart masterfully suppressed a shout of pure joy at the variety of emotions he saw clearly mirrored in those gorgeous blue eyes after he had taken a step inside the barn. Truth to tell, he was experiencing a degree of astonishment himself, for he had never supposed for a moment that he would discover her whereabouts without encountering some opposition. Most rewarding of all was finding her, apart from dishevelled, appearing none the worst for her ordeal, a fact that she wasn't slow to confirm the instant he had knelt down beside her and had removed the hated gag.

'How on earth did you manage to find me?' Abbie asked, experiencing not the least degree of maidenly modesty as he blithely raised her skirts, and she felt the touch of those shapely hands brush against her ankles as he proceeded to release her from her bonds. 'Did someone witness my abduction? Was it Josh?'

'No, I found the poor lad just coming round, after the blow he'd received to the head.'

'Then how?' she persisted, determined to have her curiosity satisfied.

'Well, I suppose in a way it was you.' Bart couldn't forbear a smile at the mingled exasperation and disbelief clearly writ across her face. 'No, I'm not spinning you a yarn, my little love,' he assured her. 'It was you who urged me to think long and hard about the past and consider anyone who might well bear me a grudge.'

'And the owner of this inn does?'

'If it's the devil I think it is…then yes.'

'Well, he's certainly a most unpleasant fellow,' Abbie assured him, experiencing a tingling in her toes now that the bond had been removed. 'It was his intention to extort money from you for my safe return.' She had no difficulty either in interpreting the look on his face before he turned his attention to the rope securing her to the wooden support. 'No, I didn't suppose for a moment that he had any intention of releasing me once he had managed to lure you here.'

Abbie cast an anxious glance towards the door before returning her attention to the rugged features which, against all the odds, she had grown to love.

'They might return at any moment, Bart. You didn't come here alone, I trust?'

The note of concern in her voice was crystal clear. 'Don't worry. Josh has gone to the Hall, so help is on the way. Besides…' Delving into his pocket, Bart drew out a pistol, which he placed on the ground between them. 'I never ride out unarmed, a habit one swiftly acquires when in the army.'

And Abbie for one was glad of it. Yet she couldn't help but feel that it hadn't been wholly sensible to come alone… But then it wouldn't have crossed his mind for a moment to consider his own safety.

Lowering her head, she bit down hard on her lip to stop its trembling. Now was not the time to give way to foolish emotions, she told herself sternly. Unfortunately the silent reprimand did little to help, and she found herself plagued by a veritable barrage of self-recriminations. How she could ever have thought so ill of Bartholomew Cavanagh she would never know. He hadn't a cowardly bone in his body. Avarice and conceit were foreign to his nature. Nor was he in the least petty-minded. She wasn't now so blinkered by her regard that she could no longer see his faults. Yet she loved him as much for his imperfections as she did for his many wonderful qualities. He was quite simply a man, and a very fine one withal.

She felt the telltale pricking at the corners of her eyes, and closed them tightly, determined not to give way to those all too frequent recurring feelings of regret and self-pity.

She could hear Bart's occasional sharp intake of breath as he struggled with the occasional stubborn knot. Then she detected another sound close at hand, and opened her eyes. Unfortunately her stifled warning scream came just a fraction too late. Dodd wielding a heavy stick caught Bart a stunning blow across his temple as he half-turned, making to rise, sending him crashing to the dirt floor, clearly revealing the pistol he had only minutes before placed on the ground.

This time Abbie's reactions were far quicker. By moving her left leg slightly, she successfully concealed the weapon beneath the folds of her skirts before Dodd had noticed it was there. Still half-stunned by the blow, Bart was endeavouring to rise to his knees and was fortunately holding his attacker's full attention, a circumstance of which Abbie didn't hesitate to take full advantage. Blessedly Bart had succeeded in loosening the knots sufficiently for her to be able to move her wrists. Striving to ignore the pain, she strained against the bonds until her own attention was captured by the arrival of Dodd's accomplice, brandishing a pistol of his own.

His expression was ugly, and grew more menacing still when his gaze fell upon Bart's half-kneeling form. 'Why, if it ain't my old, gallant Major,' he sneered. 'How I've been looking forward to meeting up with 'ee again!'

For answer Bart seated himself beside Abbie and, easily interpreting the silent message in her eyes, placed his hand beside the skirt of her habit, before fixing his attention on the unkempt figure by the door.

Abbie, watching closely, was amazed at what she saw. She knew Bart didn't try unduly to conceal his feelings. He was far too candid by nature to dissemble. She had seen him betray annoyance and anger on numerous occasions since their reunion in Bath, but never before had she glimpsed such an expression of utter loathing on his face.

She couldn't help but feel that it wasn't entirely wise to betray antipathy at such a time. With any luck Josh might already have reached the Hall, and help would hopefully not be long in arriving. Surely it was better to attempt to stall for time by distracting the villains than risk an immediate attack by showing hostility? All she required was a minute or two more in order to prise her hands free. Then she might possibly be of help by putting up at least a token resistance.

'You have the advantage of me, Bart,' she said, having swiftly decided on pinning her hopes on delaying tactics. 'Aren't you going to introduce me to this gentleman?'

'Gentleman?' Bart snarled. 'Gentlemen do not

commit cold-blooded murder, Abbie.' If anything, his expression grew increasingly contemptuous. 'Oh, Septimus Searle had a splendid war, until I took command of the company. One of his more despicable exploits was to force the wives of the men to sleep with him in order to spare their husbands a flogging for some false charge, which in my book is tantamount to rape. It didn't take me very long to get his measure and put an end to his sickening pleasures.'

'Aye, you served me a reet bad turn there, Major. And I've never forgotten it neither. My life weren't worth living when you took away my stripes. It were a case of deserting or being killed sooner or later by the men in the ranks. I asks you, what choice did I 'ave?'

If he expected a show of sympathy, he was doomed to disappointment. Bart's expression remained a contemptuous mask, and Abbie experienced nothing but a surge of revulsion towards the being who clearly experienced no remorse for his misdeeds, though she had no intention of betraying the fact. Searle seemed locked in the past, content to reminisce, and Abbie was more than happy for him to continue doing so. The longer he was allowed to lament over what he evidently considered to be his ex-commanding officer's grave injustices, the more likely it was that help would arrive in time

''Course, when I escaped from the Preventives,' Searle continued uninterrupted, 'I swore I'd 'ave my revenge on you once the war were over, if the Frenchies didn't get you first. It took me some time to get back to dear old England and cost me most everything I'd—er—put aside while I were a soldier. Managed to do all right for myself since I've been back, mind,' he revealed with a noticeable degree of smug satisfaction. 'And as soon as I'd money enough I sets about finding you.'

'No need to ask how you acquired the means to do so,' Bart muttered loud enough for Searle to hear. Fortunately he seemed to find the disparaging remark amusing.

'Aye, you're a downy one and no mistake, Major. Pity, really, you decided to make me your enemy. Reckon you and me would 'ave got on reet well iffen we'd become friends.'

'There was never any likelihood of that,' Bart didn't hesitate to assure him. 'I select my friends with care.'

'Expect you do, Major.' Searle's gaze slid to Abbie. 'You always had your pick of the womenfolk, at any rate, not like us poor common soldiers. We 'ad to make do wiv any old trollopy camp follower. Always 'ad a mind to sample a bit of what you'd tasted.' The sinister leer returned to his eyes, betraying his intent. 'What do you say, Doddy, lad? Fancy a tumble with that there piece of flash goods? You'd best be quick, mind. There's no saying when they'll start searching for the Major, 'ere, and 'is ladylove. We'll need to get rid o' their bodies reet quick.'

Abbie didn't know what sickened her more— Searle's callous declaration of intent, or the sight of Dodd's grubby fingers fumbling with the buttons on his breeches. She had no intention of allowing herself to be violated without putting up at least a token struggle. And blessedly she could do so now! Quite unobserved, she had succeeded in freeing one of her wrists during the verbal exchanges between Bart and his sworn enemy. It was an easy matter to slip her right hand free from the ropes.

But before she had even attempted to rise, Bart's voice, icy cold and controlled, successfully checked Dodd's evil purpose. 'So much as lay a finger on her, and I'll kill you.'

'I've got 'im covered, lad,' Searle assured him. 'Have yer fun, but be quick about it.'

Had he glimpsed the pistol, he might not have given such poor advice, for Bart's skill with firearms had been common knowledge throughout the army. One moment Dodd had been dropping to his knees, eager once again to satisfy his lust; the next his lifeless body lay sprawled on the floor.

Hardly had the deafening report died away than Bart was rising and hurling the pistol across the barn. Unfortunately Searle recovered in an instant from the painful blow he had received to his arm, and had his own weapon steadily levelled before Bart could bridge the distance between them.

For a few brief seconds it was as much as Abbie could do to watch in horrified silence as Searle's finger curled round the trigger, and his unpleasant mouth twisted into a malicious, self-satisfied smirk. Bart had succeeded in placing himself directly in line of fire, his intention clear. He would take the bullet so that she just might survive.

But how could she let him? She didn't want to live… couldn't live without him…

Bart hardly knew what had happened. One moment he had been poised, about to make what would undoubtedly have been a final, and possibly fatal, attempt to disarm Searle; the next, Abbie had cannoned into him, sending him stumbling sideways, while a second deafening report was ringing in his ears.

Instinctively he reached out and caught Abbie before she slumped to the floor, his eyes quickly focusing on the unmistakable dark trickle of liquid steadily seeping through the charred portion of her gown.

As she lay there, motionless, like a lifeless rag doll in his arms, Bart would have given everything he owned to be able to reject the evidence of his own eyes, to have been able to believe that she had merely fainted, that those delicate lids would flicker open at any moment and he would find himself the recipient of that lovely teasing gaze. Sadly he wasn't the kind of man who couldn't accept cruel reality. Nor was he the type to succumb to the emptiness born of grief when his strength was needed to finalise an unpleasant task.

Tenderly placing Abbie on the ground, Bart could feel white-hot rage going some way to fill the chasm of despair that was growing ever wider within him, as he caught sight of his adversary attempting to slink unobtrusively away. Galvanised by an overwhelming desire for revenge, he was on his feet in an instant and easily caught up with Searle halfway across the yard.

A life of dissipation having taken its toll, Searle was no match for Bart, who overpowered him in a trice, effortlessly bringing him to the ground. For several moments mercy didn't enter into Bart's thinking. Wrapping one strong arm about Searle's neck, he was determined to mete out the punishment the army had failed to do years before. Then, unbidden, some inner voice reminded him that he had once been a courageous soldier, taking life only on the field of battle, not some cold-blooded killer, bent on revenge. He found the muscles in his arm automatically relaxing, as his ears detected the sound of approaching horses. Yet it wasn't until urgent fingers began to tug at his jacket and a more urgent voice succeeded in penetrating the layers of numbness that still clung to him that he at last released his hold and rose to his feet.

'You'll find your mistress in the barn,' he managed

finally to reveal in response to Josh's repeated enquiry.

'Are there any more of them?' Major Wetherby
asked, after ordering his men to take Searle in charge.

Bart gestured towards the barn. 'Yes, in there. He's
dead.'

The Major's intention to discover for himself
was checked by Josh who, dashing out of the barn,
almost cannoned into him. 'Sir...Mr Cavanagh, sir,
oughtn't you to be getting Miss Abbie to the doctor?'

Bart's initial reaction suggested that he hadn't
heard a single word. He just stood there, with the
hunched posture of a desolate, broken man, staring
dumbly at the ground. Then very slowly he raised his
head, and it seemed to the two men avidly watching
him that a bright lamp had suddenly been ignited behind his eyes.

Before either could move or utter anything further,
he had brushed past them. Not daring to hope or believe, he dropped to his knees beside Abbie and
stretched out decidedly unsteady fingers towards the
slender neck. It took several moments, but eventually
he was certain he had detected that pulsating throb—
faint, certainly, but blessedly there.

Early that evening, as he sat in his library, Bart appeared at first glance much the same as usual—dis-
passionate, a man in full control of his emotions.
Perhaps only those who knew him well would have

suspected that all was not as it should be; maybe only a few highly observant souls would have detected the evidence of tension along the line of the jaw, and the anguish, partly concealed, behind the half-hooded lids.

From the instant he had realised that life still throbbed in Abbie's veins, he had taken complete control, issuing instructions to Major Wetherby and his men as though he himself had been in command. That he had taken every precaution, done everything humanly possible to ensure Abbie's continued existence, now brought scant comfort.

Not daring to risk jolting her on horseback, he had travelled back with her in that tumble-down old cart, holding a pad over the wound in the hope of stemming the flow of blood. The journey had seemed interminable, and there had been times when he had thought the undernourished horse would fail to reach the Court. Thankfully, under Josh's skilful handling and gentle coaxing, it had.

The doctor, summoned by one of Major Wetherby's men, had been awaiting their arrival, and the servants, forewarned, had everything prepared. That Lady Penrose, ably assisted by her highly efficient maid, had taken immediate charge of the sick room had brought little solace either; and he hadn't needed the dour, though highly skilled, local practitioner to confirm his worst fears.

'Well, Cavanagh,' he had announced, on entering

the library an hour before, 'I have managed to extract the lead shot and clean the wound, and can confirm that it touched no vital spot. However, the young woman has lost a considerable amount of blood, and is very weak. If no infection sets in, there's a chance she'll survive.' Here he had paused, the inference only too painfully clear. 'I shall be able to tell you more in the morning.'

His venture into the sick room, shortly after the doctor's departure, had done nothing to improve Bart's state of mind. The sight of her lying there, motionless, the blue tinge about her lips the only vestige of colour in her beloved face, had added substantially to the heavy burden of guilt.

Why hadn't he checked for signs of life at the outset? Yet again that damning question passed through his tortured mind. Had he been so obsessed by a desire for revenge that he had been incapable of rational thought? Why had he not taken a moment to consider her dishevelled state? With what she had been forced to endure, her clothing had become crumpled. But when he had caught her in his arms the bodice of her habit had stretched across her breast, giving the impression that the wound had been fatal, when in fact the ball had entered her body several inches higher. Precious minutes had been wasted dealing with Searle—time he ought to have spent with Abbie, attempting to stem the flow of blood.

The sound of an arrival interrupted his distressing reflections. He had given strict instructions, after Major Wetherby had called to assure him that Searle was now safely behind bars, awaiting trial, that no more visitors were to be admitted to the house. Consequently he was surprised when the normally efficient Barryman entered to inform him that a gentleman insisted upon seeing him.

'Be assured, sir,' he went on apologetically, 'that in the normal course of events, I would not have hesitated in denying admittance, but—'

He got no further. The door behind him was thrown wide, and a tall, distinguished-looking gentleman with a decidedly military bearing came striding into the room, demanding without preamble, 'What the devil do you mean, sir, by sending me that damned impertinent letter?'

Chapter Fifteen

Abbie, supported by a mound of pillows, sat up in bed, dutifully awaiting the return of one or other of her self-appointed gaolers in order to gain permission to rise. It wasn't that she was incapable of dressing herself, far from it in fact. Unlike those early days of her convalescence, when she had been as helpless as a babe, unable to so much as feed herself, she was now sufficiently restored in health to do most everything for herself. Yet, sensible of how much she owed both her godmother and Felcham for nursing her so tirelessly during the past month, she had no intention of undoing all their good work by attempting to do too much too soon, even though she felt it was time to regain at least some of that treasured independence.

In truth she could recall little of those early days when, under the influence of laudanum, she had slept for much of the time. She had discovered from Lady

Penrose how Bart and Josh had brought her back to the house in a cart. From Dr Phelps she had eventually learned just how critical her condition had been and how her life had hung in the balance for several days. Her most vivid recollection had been waking to discover her grandfather, pale and drawn, a mere shadow of his former self, seated beside the bed.

Needless to say, in face of the touching concern he had displayed throughout her recovery, she had found it no difficult matter to forgive his past behaviour towards her. He wasn't a man given to displays of emotion, at least not the more tender ones. All the same, she was in no doubt now of just how much she really meant to him. How she wished she could be as sure of quite another gentleman's feelings towards her!

From her godmother's own lips she had learned how Bart had spent many hours watching over her during those first days. She vaguely recalled seeing a tall, shadowy figure seated beside the bed; vaguely remembered, too, the comforting clasp of a warm hand about hers. That, of course, might well have been her grandfather, for Bart hadn't made a habit of visiting her regularly since her strength had begun to return. When he had put in a brief appearance, it had always been when someone else had been present.

A sharp knock on the door forced her to abandon her melancholy reflections, and she looked up to find her grandfather striding purposefully into the room, his attire clearly revealing how he intended occupying his time that morning.

'So, you are going out riding, Grandpapa,' she said, after receiving the loving salute he had never failed to place upon her cheek each morning during these past weeks. 'How I wish I could accompany you!'

'It will not be too long before you're able to do so. Believe me, my darling child, you cannot possibly look forward to the occasion more than I.' For once he chose not to avail himself of the chair beside the bed. Instead he took up a stance at the window, before adding, 'Which prompts me to raise a matter we must discuss—namely, your future.'

Abbie clearly detected the note of reserve in his voice that she had grown increasingly accustomed to hearing in recent years. Only this time she knew that it wasn't because she had fallen from favour. She strongly suspected the reason for the slight constraint stemmed from discomposure and bitter regrets.

Colonel Graham wasn't slow to corroborate this presumption. 'I've been a crass fool these past years, child,' he burst out. 'And I can only ask…beg you to forgive me for the unhappiness I've caused you.'

Abbie would have given much to hear him say that before she had left Foxhunter Grange, but not now. He had been so right in his belief that she and Bart were well suited. It ought to be she begging forgiveness.

She was therefore able to respond with total sincerity, 'There's nothing to forgive, Grandpapa.'

'Oh, but there is, child,' he countered softly. 'I came here full of self-righteous indignation, and preconceived notions that were foolishly unjust. I was more than happy to point the finger of blame at you for persuading Bart to write what I considered a damned insulting letter. Needless to say, he wasn't slow to set me right on several points.'

'I imagine not. Bart isn't one to hide his teeth.' Abbie couldn't prevent a wry smile, even though she thought the confrontation should have been avoided. 'You and Bart are very similar in many ways, Grandpapa. Both of you have strong, determined natures, and are never afraid to speak your mind.'

'Very true,' he concurred, smiling briefly himself now. 'But at least we're not too proud to own when we have been at fault. And I have been most unjust in my dealings with you, Abbie, my dear,' he continued, as he came to stand beside the bed, so that not only could she hear the deep regret in his voice, but also see the sadness in his eyes. 'Bart forced me to acknowledge that on the night I arrived here. He freely admitted that your refusing to marry him six years ago was the right decision, that it would have been a grave mistake if you had formed a union.'

This wasn't precisely what Abbie wished to hear, even though deep down she had suspected it was true. 'Although Bart would never hurt my feelings by admitting as much, I do not believe my refusal caused him much heartache. In fact, I believe his offer of marriage came more from a desire to please you, Grandpapa, than himself.'

'You are possibly right, child,' he said, unaware of just how much it had hurt her to be so candid. 'I do recall that he appeared rather surprised when I broached the subject quite out of the blue that evening. With hindsight I now realise it would have been wiser to have waited a year or two. But, as I remember, Bart was due to leave us the following day, and I had no real idea how long it would be before he visited us again. As things turned out he never did, as he decided to join the army.'

Although Abbie had paid her grandfather the common courtesy of listening to everything he had to say, one salient point had remained in her mind—namely, the timing of the proposal. Unless she much mistook the matter, her grandfather hadn't touched on the subject of marriage until after Bart had returned from his assignation with Lady Fitzpatrick in the summerhouse.

She favoured her grandfather with a searching stare. 'When precisely did you first raise the subject of marriage with Bart?'

'Oh, good heavens, child! I cannot recall precisely. It was over six years ago.' The flicker of irritation swiftly faded from his eyes and was replaced by one of contrition, as though he regretted his mild show

of impatience. 'Well, let us see if I can remember…
I do believe he'd been out for much of the day. So it
must have been early evening, just prior to going in
to dinner.' He paused to watch an odd expression
flicker over her face. 'Is it important?'

It might have been at one time, Abbie mused, smiling to herself, but certainly not now. It didn't matter
a whit. 'No, Grandpapa, it isn't important.'

'In that case, may I now turn your thoughts to the
more urgent matter of your future?' All at once he
seemed ill at ease, and reluctant to meet her gaze.
'Will you grant me the dearest wish of my heart and
return to Foxhunter Grange? Of course I'm happy to
remain here until you feel able to undertake the journey. And—and I do not want you to think it will be—
be as before,' he continued, with less than his
customary aplomb. 'It shall not. You will, I'm sure,
wish to visit your godmother now that the two of you
have become reacquainted. And then, too, I should
like for us to visit the capital. Perhaps this autumn,
if you are agreeable?'

Once she would have given much to be offered the
opportunity of meeting a gentleman of her own class
with whom she might form an attachment. Much,
however, had changed in the space of a few short
weeks. The only man with whom she would ever
willingly share her life resided right here, in this very
house. So why waste her time and her grandfather's
money in the hope of one day meeting Bart's equal?

She never would, and in truth she felt not the least desire to try.

Feeling the need of their support, she fell back against the mound of pillows. 'I see no reason why we shouldn't leave at the end of the week.'

Evidently she had sounded far more enthusiastic at the prospect of leaving the Court than she truthfully was, for she instantly won a smile of approval.

'Capital! When I've returned from my ride, I shall begin to make arrangements. Even though Bart has shown excellent hospitality, I dare say the boy won't be at all sorry to have the house to himself again.'

Abbie was spared the necessity of responding by the arrival of Lady Penrose, which in turn prompted her grandfather's immediate departure. Although the two were unfailingly polite to each other, at least within her hearing, Abbie had gained the distinct impression that Colonel Graham had yet to win favour in her godmother's eyes.

'Felch will be along presently to help you dress, child,' Lady Penrose revealed the instant they were alone. Receiving no response, she cast a swift glance down at the bed and wasn't slow to note her goddaughter's wan expression. 'I sincerely trust your grandfather hasn't tired you. I sometimes think he forgets how gravely ill you've been.'

'No, he hasn't tired me in the least.' As though adding credence to the assertion, Abbie swung her feet to the floor, and reached for her robe. 'In fact, I think I shall take the opportunity of enjoying some late summer sunshine by sitting in the garden this morning. It's high time I entered the real world again. You see, I intend to accompany Grandpapa when he leaves the Court at the end of the week.'

Nothing in her demeanour betrayed the fact that Lady Penrose was not best pleased to learn this. The instant she left the bedchamber, however, it was a different story. Her expression changed and no one could have been in any doubt that something had occurred to vex her deeply.

It wasn't that she objected to Abbie leaving the confines of her room. In fact, she was very much in favour of it, and perhaps later would suggest that she eat with the rest of them in the dining-room from now on. On the other hand, this notion of leaving the Court at such a time could well prove a grave mistake, adversely affecting her goddaughter's future happiness.

So what on earth had prompted the girl to agree? True enough, Colonel Graham's attitude towards her had definitely changed. He was now all touching concern. But surely Abbie had overcome her former dislike of Bart? Yes, of course she had, Lady Penrose decided a moment later. The girl knew she belonged here at the Court with him. So what was persuading her to leave? And now that she came to consider the matter, why on earth had the master of the house shown no inclination to declare himself?

of satisfaction the look of concern that instantly sprang into dark eyes. 'She hasn't suffered a relapse. In point of fact, she's ventured out of doors for the first time today. She's at present sitting in the garden enjoying the fresh air.'

This did little to ease Bart's mind. 'Is that wise, ma'am? The doctor insisted that she does not exert herself unduly for some time yet.'

Lady Penrose dismissed this with a wave of her hand. 'The girl is all but fully recovered. Which is perhaps just as well,' she added, favouring the Colonel with a blatant look of disapproval herself now, 'since she will be forced to undergo the rigours of a long journey in a few days.' She transferred her gaze back to their host. 'If you permit her to leave, that is.'

Like an echoing taunt, Lady Penrose's last words seemed to hang in the air. Colonel Graham, whose colour had increased alarmingly, appeared to be battling to contain his wrath. Bart too was not altogether pleased, as his suddenly compressed lips revealed, before he swung round to stare resolutely out of the window.

'You forget yourself, ma'am,' he said, in a milder tone than he might otherwise have used had he not held the lady in such high regard. 'I have no say in the matter.'

'A feeble excuse!' Lady Penrose scoffed, clearly undaunted by the coolness of his reply. 'I would never have supposed a man of your stamp, Cavanagh, would calmly stand by and allow the woman he loved to walk out of his life.'

This brought his head round, as she knew it would, hope and uncertainty clearly mirrored in his eyes.

'Surely you don't imagine that your feelings are not reciprocated? Good God, man! Have your wits gone begging? The girl came perilously close to losing her life in order to save yours.'

'That is something I'm never likely to forget,' Bart responded softly. 'But it isn't as simple as you seem to suppose.' Tossing the wine down his throat, he set the glass aside. 'There are reasons, ma'am...obstacles that must be overcome before I—'

'Bah!' Lady Penrose interrupted crudely, before following his example by consuming her wine in one go. 'Tell me, Bart,' she added, rising to her feet so that she could face him squarely, 'have you ever viewed the portrait you commissioned Abbie to paint?'

The abrupt change of topic surprised him, and he didn't attempt to hide the fact before he shook his head.

'I thought not,' she said, appearing smugly satisfied. 'Well, if it is proof positive you require before taking action, then I suggest you follow me. You too, Colonel,' she added, favouring him with a look that dared him to refuse. 'Hopefully it might persuade you not to commit yet more folly.'

Like a galleon at full sail, Lady Penrose majestically glided out of the room and up the stairs, leading the men on their journey of discovery. She had taken the trouble earlier of removing the protective sheet and turning the easel so the painting could be viewed the instant one entered the chamber. Thus, Bart found himself for the second time that morning halting momentarily on the threshold of a room.

Colonel Graham too, betrayed a marked degree of surprise. 'Fine piece of brushwork,' he opined, after taking a few moments to study the portrait more closely. 'Takes after her grandmother,' he added with simple pride. 'She was a very gifted artist too.'

'For once we are in complete accord, Colonel,' Lady Penrose announced, while staring resolutely in Bart's direction. 'It is a fine piece of work. She has captured that certain look so very well, don't you agree? That certain tenderness of the gaze, that marked softening to the set of the mouth. But then she shouldn't have found it too difficult a task. After all, it is a look she has observed often. A look, I have noticed, reserved for her alone.'

Lady Penrose smiled when the Adam's apple in Bart's throat protruded further than usual as he swallowed hard. 'If I have one slight criticism, then it is that dear Abbie has had a tendency to flatter the subject by making him appear rather better looking than, in fact, he is. But then, one must make allowances, mustn't one…? She does, after all, view him through the eyes of love.'

For several disappointing moments Lady Penrose thought she had failed to remove those shackles of uncertainty. Then, quite without warning, she was imprisoned in a pair of strong arms and lifted quite off her feet to receive a smacking kiss on one plump cheek.

'You will forgive me if I leave you now,' Bart announced, already halfway to the door. 'There's a matter requiring my urgent attention.'

'Don't give us another thought, dear boy,' Lady Penrose urged him. 'I'm sure the Colonel and I can manage to rub along together reasonably well until your return.'

In truth, Bart wasn't unduly concerned whether they would succeed in doing so or not, for already that tiny voice advocating caution was making itself heard, regenerating those old doubts. Against all the odds, Abbie loved him—yes. There wasn't the least doubt in his mind about that any longer. But it did not automatically follow that she would be any more willing to marry him now than she had been six years ago.

Part of her endearing charm, and what set her quite apart from most other females of his acquaintance was her sense of proportion, her level-headedness. She wasn't a young woman prone to flights of fancy or given to foolish starts. She would consider long and hard before making a decision that would effectively alter the course of her life. Ergo, it was not inconceivable that she might retain grave misgivings, that she would reject his suit a second time. The alternative, though, was to watch her walk out of his life, and perhaps not for a short time either.

Coming upon her sitting in the garden in that peaceful way of hers succeeded in bridling his qualms, if failing to eradicate them completely. Abbie, catching sight of him a moment later, would never have supposed for a moment that the mere sight of her had instantly restored some of his spirits, for as he drew nearer she detected the crease between his dark brows, clearly revealing concern over something.

'I sincerely trust you haven't been sent out to scold me for remaining in the garden too long? The truth of the matter is I've been making the acquaintance of your latest acquisition.'

Refusing to be daunted by his lack of response, Abbie smiled as he lowered himself on the bench beside her. 'You don't fool me any longer, Bartholomew Cavanagh. I know well enough that beneath that stern exterior lurks a great soft-hearted fellow. Most gentlemen would have had no compunction in consigning that poor beast to the knacker's yard. Though I must confess he bears little resemblance to the undernourished creature I encountered a month ago. He's prancing round the paddock at this very moment like a playful colt.'

Although Bart didn't attempt to feign ignorance, he

wasn't prepared to accept credit for the gelding's vastly improved state either. The truth of the matter was he hadn't given the animal he had purloined on that eventful day a single thought, after he had carried Abbie back inside the house. It was almost a week later, when he was certain she was out of danger, that he had once again taken up the day-to-day running of his property and had paid a visit to the stables.

Thankfully Josh had not been so negligent, and had taken it upon himself to care for the late Septimus Searle's maltreated horse, and under his tender care the animal's general health had improved dramatically. Bart couldn't deny, however, that he simply hadn't the heart to dispose of the gelding after its heroic labours in returning them to the Court.

He smiled crookedly. 'Well, I dare say he'll earn his keep when he's eventually put to work.'

'Which means that you're content to let him remain idle for the most part.' Recalling an oversight on her part, Abbie was suddenly serious. 'I've never yet thanked you, Bart, for putting your life at risk by seeking my whereabouts that day. You possibly saved my life.'

His smile was crooked. 'Yes, I might possibly have done so,' he conceded. 'But you definitely saved mine, you foolish girl.'

It might have been intended as a criticism, but to Abbie's ears the stricture sounded more like an endearment, so softly had he spoken. 'Well, you'll not need to put up with my stupidity for much longer,' she said, desperately striving to keep her tone light, and ignore the painful ache that had suddenly attacked her throat. 'Has Grandpapa mentioned that we intend to leave on Friday?'

A long silence, then, 'Don't go!'

It wasn't so much the command itself that persuaded Abbie to remain seated beside him, when she had been about to rise, as the raw feeling she couldn't fail to hear in his voice. 'Why...? Is there something else you wish to say to me?'

'Don't go, Abbie,' he repeated, lowering his head to stare fixedly at a spot between his boots. 'Don't leave me here alone to dwindle into a lonely, irascible old man. I should, you know, without you. I need you to coax me out of my ill humours, reprimand me if I become overbearing, tease me if I grow too arrogant.'

No clearer declaration of love could have been given, and all Abbie could do as the silence between them lengthened was to watch through the mist of unshed tears when he rose abruptly to his feet, the response she so longed to utter suppressed by the painful obstruction that had lodged itself in her throat.

'Don't think me so insensitive that I cannot appreciate your misgivings,' he continued, staring straight ahead of him across his land. 'I can understand how disgusted…insulted you must have felt years ago when I—'

He got no further. Abbie was beside him, the fingers of her left hand pressed gently against his lips. 'Don't you dare apologise to me for being a man, Bartholomew Cavanagh,' she managed to force past that lingering constriction. 'I don't want a paragon…I only want you.'

Abbie watched dawning wonder replace disbelief in dark eyes before Bart lowered his head and kissed her, at first with infinite tenderness before suppressed passion demanded release.

'I shall never give you cause to regret it, my darling,' he vowed, keeping her a very willing prisoner in his arms.

She didn't pretend to misunderstand and smiled lovingly up at him. 'If I thought for a moment that it was your intention to stray, Bart, I shouldn't consider marrying you,' she admitted with total sincerity, but couldn't resist adding, 'However, I think it only fair to warn you that should you ever succumb to temptation, you'll rue the day you ever met—'

It was Bart's turn to silence her this time, and he did so very comprehensively, blissfully unaware that his peerless display of masculine passion was being witnessed by the two people who had once again taken refuge in his library.

'By gad! What is going on out there, do you suppose?'

Lady Penrose favoured her companion with a look of comical dismay. 'I should imagine, Colonel, that they have just become betrothed. And without any assistance from you this time.'

'By gad!' he said again. 'Well, this is a turn up for the books. Not that I didn't always consider they would suit admirably.'

'Yes, Colonel, and you may have the satisfaction of knowing that you have been proved right,' Lady Penrose responded, exerting admirable self-control. 'The mistake you made was imagining that you could decide the matter for them. All things considered, though, I believe you can be forgiven.'

Wisely she chose not to elaborate, especially as he appeared to be having a little difficulty in comprehending the very favourable turn of events. Instead she suggested that he might like to order a bottle of champagne brought up from the cellar in readiness for the perfectly matched couple's return to the house.

'Of course, I suppose I must not neglect my duties by leaving my goddaughter unchaperoned for too long,' she added, taking refuge in one of the comfortable chairs. 'In the meantime, I think you and I might enjoy a celebratory tipple while we await the arrival of the champagne, don't you, Colonel?'

'By Jove, I think we should too, ma'am!' he agreed heartily. 'Port, was it not?'

An expression akin to approval spread across her ladyship's plump features. 'Colonel Graham, I actually think I'm beginning to find you most agreeable!'

* * * * *

HISTORICAL ROMANCE™

LARGE PRINT

THE MARRIAGE DEBT
Louise Allen

Marrying a highwayman awaiting execution is
Miss Katherine Cunningham's only hope – for that way
her crippling debts will die with him. But Nicholas
Lydgate, her new husband, is innocent – and the son of a
duke! She won't hold him to a union made in such
circumstances – until he shows he cares for her…

THE RAKE AND THE REBEL
Mary Brendan

Miss Silver Meredith is just eighteen – and vulnerable to
the worst sort of scandal after an attempted elopement
goes wrong. Her reputation and her future depend on
one man – Adam, Marquess of Rockingham. And he's
still smarting from the rejection of the only woman to
whom he's ever proposed marriage – Silver Meredith…

THE ENGAGEMENT
Kate Bridges

Being jilted was a humiliation no woman should have to
bear – but Dr Virginia Waters had survived it. Now she
anxiously awaited her wedding to Zack Bullock – the
brother of her former fiancé! Zack had vowed to do the
honourable thing in marrying Virginia. But neither had
predicted the danger looming – a danger that threatened
to keep them apart…

MILLS & BOON®

Live the emotion

HIST0206 LP

HISTORICAL ROMANCE™

LARGE PRINT

A REPUTABLE RAKE

Diane Gaston

Cyprian Sloane's reputation is of the very worst. Gambler, smuggler, rake and spy, he faces the greatest challenge of all – respectability! But then he meets Morgana Hart, whose caring nature thrusts her into the company of ladies of the night and risks a scandal that will destroy them both. Is there a way for the rake to save them?

CONQUEST BRIDE

Meriel Fuller

Baron Varin de Montaigu is a soldier for King William. By royal decree he must uncover a plot to overthrow the King – and he is suspicious of everyone. Lady Eadita of Thunorslege hates the Normans with all her heart, and wants them out of her country. Varin is certain she is plotting, and is intent on keeping her close…

PRINCESS OF FORTUNE

Miranda Jarrett

When an exiled princess becomes too much for her hosts to handle, Captain Lord Thomas Greaves is called in. Playing nursemaid to a pampered beauty isn't exactly how he wants to serve his country, and he counts the days until he can return to sea. The homesick Isabella is imperious and difficult – but she can't deny her attraction to her handsome bodyguard…

MILLS & BOON®

Live the emotion

HIST0306 LP

HISTORICAL ROMANCE™

LARGE PRINT

THE OUTRAGEOUS DEBUTANTE
Anne O'Brien

Theodora Wooton-Devereux and Lord Nicholas Faringdon are not enthusiastic participants in the game of love – until a chance meeting sets them on a different course. Soon the handsome gentleman and the beautiful – though unconventional – débutante are the talk of the town, but fate is not on their side. A shocking scandal rears its head and forbids that they be united...

THE CAPTAIN'S LADY
Margaret McPhee

When Lord Nathaniel Hawke rescues a girl from drowning the last thing he expects is for the same girl to turn up on board his ship – disguised as a boy! Ship's boy George – alias Miss Georgiana Raithwaite – is running away from a cruel impending marriage and Nathaniel must conceal her identity from his men...

WINTER WOMAN
Jenna Kernan

Cordelia Channing – preacher's wife, preacher's widow – is left to survive the deadliest season in the mountains alone. Praying for someone to save her, she finds her hopes answered by Thomas Nash. He has come to the mountains to rail against the fates that seem out to destroy him – but now he has Delia to care for – a woman who begins to transform his life...

MILLS & BOON®

Live the emotion

HIST0406 LP

THE VENETIAN'S MISTRESS
Ann Elizabeth Cree

An English widow in Italy, Cecily Renato has heard murmurings about a past tragedy which has caused a bitter rift in a neighbouring family. Suddenly the Duke of Severin returns, and there's danger in the air. Cecily, too, is in danger – most especially from her feelings for the darkly alluring Duke…

BACHELOR DUKE
Mary Nichols

Orphaned and destitute, Sophie Langford had no choice but to throw herself on the mercy of the Duke of Belfont. But instead of the elderly gentleman she had envisaged, she was confronted by the fifth Duke, James, a most eligible bachelor. James took Sophie into his household, although he little guessed what he had let himself in for…

THE KNAVE AND THE MAIDEN
Blythe Gifford

Sir Garren owes much to the Earl of Readington, even his very knighthood. So when his lord falls ill Garren knows he must save him – even if it means embarking on a pilgrimage and deflowering an innocent woman. Domenica is steadfast in her determination to take the veil – but every step of her journey seems to lead her straight into Garren's arms…

MILLS & BOON®

Live the emotion

HIST0506 L